D0192274

END OF DAYS

ALSO BY ERIC WALTERS

Bi-Focal

House Party

Boot Camp

Camp X—Fool's Gold

Tiger Trap

Sketches

We All Fall Down

Shattered

Laggan Lard Butts

Stuffed

Elixir

Triple Threat

Camp 30

Grind

The True Story of Santa Claus

Juice

Run

Overdrive

I've Got an Idea

Underdog

Death by Exposure

Royal Ransom

Off Season

Camp X

Road Trip

Tiger Town

The Bully Boys

Long Shot

Ricky

Tiger in Trouble

Hoop Crazy

Rebound

The Hydrofoil Mystery

Full Court Press

Caged Eagles

The Money Pit Mystery

Three on Three

Visions

Tiger by the Tail

Northern Exposures

War of the Eagles

Stranded

Trapped in Ice

Diamonds in the Rough

Stars

Stand Your Ground

Splat!

The Falls

In a Flash

The Pole

When Elephants Fight

Voyageur

Safe as Houses

Alexandria of Africa

Tiger Trap

Black and White

Wounded

Special Edward

Tell Me Why

Shell Shocked

United We Stand

Wave

Home Team

Branded

Trouble in Paradise

Beverly Hills Maasai

Shaken

ENDOF DAYS

ERIC WALTERS

DOUBLEDAY CANADA

Doubleday Canada and colophon are registered trademarks.

Library and Archives Canada Cataloguing in Publication

Library and Archives Canada Cataloguing in Publication

Walters, Eric, 1957-
End of days / Eric Walters.

Issued also in an electronic format.
ISBN 978-0-385-67006-7

I. Title.

PS8595.A598E64 2011   JC813'.54   C2011-900107-1

Cover and text design: Jennifer Lum
Printed and bound in the USA

Published in Canada by Doubleday Canada,
a division of Random House of Canada Limited

Visit Random House of Canada Limited's website: www.randomhouse.ca

10 9 8 7 6 5 4 3 2 1

PART 1

CHAPTER ONE

T MINUS 28 YEARS

It looked like a giant butterfly fluttering through space, the wings of its solar panels extended to gather in the power from the sun's rays. Different instruments attached at strange angles gave it an awkward and fragile look. But it was strong—strong enough to survive as it sailed silently across the frigid, bleak, black expanse of open space.

With each second it left Earth farther and farther behind. But attached to the satellite was a small part of its planet of origin, a gold disc showing a diagram of our solar system and an illustration of a man and a woman with their hands open in a gesture of friendship. No one could hope to predict, but maybe, just maybe, this wanderer might someday meet somebody in its travels.

First it travelled toward the giant of the solar system, the planet Jupiter. The journey of 759 million kilometres took nearly three years. Arcing into a perfect elliptical orbit above the poisonous atmosphere, it began its task. The lifeless satellite bristled with activity as it observed, recorded, analyzed, and transmitted information. Never before had man observed this mysterious planet at such close range.

With this job completed the satellite was ordered out of orbit. Using its booster rockets and the gravity of the planet, it was slingshot farther out toward the more distant planets at the very edge of the solar system.

It was connected to Earth by a continuous trickle of information, like the string on a kite. Travelling at 300,000 kilometres per second, the signals raced back to Earth as the satellite continued on its relentless journey. With each passing hour it moved a further 17,000 kilometres away from Earth, and to places never before visited by man or his instruments.

Six years after leaving Jupiter, having made close passes of five different planets, it passed beyond the outermost orbit of the outermost planet. In breaking this imaginary line, it left behind the solar system of its birth, but it refused to die. It kept travelling, kept recording, kept transmitting.

No one could have believed that despite the passing of eleven years and more than 24 billion kilometres, the satellite still had the will to live. As it rocketed farther and farther it continued to send back its messages: a faint, feeble voice coming from somewhere out there. Like a little lost child in the dark night sky, it called out, "I'm here. I'm still here."

The scientists who had dreamed and conceived and then watched the life of the satellite would have marvelled at its continued existence. But the country that had sent this satellite skyward, the Soviet Union, no longer existed. It had been broken into smaller pieces, none of which now had the will or the resources to track the ongoing journey away from our solar system. The satellite called out, "Look at this!" but nobody was there to hear.

Thirty-three years after its launch, twenty-two years after it left our solar system, the satellite cruised toward a small planetary body. With the gentle pull of gravity it settled into a perfect orbit. This new home was a lifeless chunk of rock with a diameter of 500 kilometres, roughly one-sixth the diameter of Earth's moon. This became the centre of the satellite's universe as it sailed around and around and around, once every fourteen hours. And like the good machine that it was, it started to observe, record, analyze, and transmit its findings.

Just by chance, somebody *was* listening. The satellite transmitted its messages in its only true language, the language of mathematics. Its faint signals were accidentally heard and translated.

At first nobody thought it could be possible that the traveller still existed. This was cause for great celebration. With each orbit, at fourteen-hour intervals, as it faced toward Earth, it sent back information. But the messages didn't seem to make sense. Somehow the satellite appeared to be moving *closer*. Somehow the world that it was attached to was moving closer. And the one message that the satellite wasn't transmitting was the most important—perhaps the most important message in the history of mankind.

"I'm coming back, I'm coming home . . . and I'm not coming alone."

PART 2

CHAPTER TWO

The car turned onto a tree-lined street. The houses, almost identical, were neat and orderly and set well back from the road. This place had the feel of a rich university town.

It was the middle of the night and there were no signs of activity. The street lamps cast isolated pools of light onto the road, but the houses were dark, the residents quietly asleep in their beds. The car slowed to a crawl. The window on the passenger side glided down to allow the passenger with infrared goggles to see more clearly, to pick out the addresses of the houses.

"64 . . . 72 . . . there it is, 82."

The vehicle pulled over to the curb and stopped. All four doors of the luxury automobile opened and four men emerged, closing the doors behind them with hardly a sound. All four men were clean-shaven with short hair, dressed in almost identical suits and wearing leather shoes that made no sound as they walked up the front path of the house.

Without exchanging a word, two of the men walked to the front door while the other two split off, one on either side of the house, disappearing into the darkness. One man jiggled the door handle, then fished into his suit jacket pocket and pulled out a small metal device. He knelt down while his partner drew out a small penlight and shone it on the lock. Within seconds there was a click and the door swung open. They entered and closed the door behind them, still without making a sound.

Silently they moved across the room, following the thin beam from the flashlight. From another room came a second beam of light and the other two men appeared, having picked the lock on the back door. Two stood at the base of the staircase while two checked the rooms on the main floor. The telephone line had been cut from the outside and the entire house had been electronically rendered a dead zone for cellphones. The men moved as though they knew the house, because they *did* know the house. They'd seen blueprints, and they had walked through a simulation more than a dozen times, until they could find their way blindfolded.

They started up the stairs. There was a creak on the third step that registered four times as the four men climbed. Each moved noiselessly in a different direction, checking out the rooms on the second floor. One man, the one who had been leading to this point, motioned the other three to the bedroom he had just left. In the bed was a solitary figure sleeping peacefully, a low, whistling sound coming from his mouth. Three of the men entered the room. The fourth positioned himself at the door. From inside his jacket he produced a gun. He held it firmly in both hands and took aim at the sleeping form.

The leader took the bedcovers and slowly peeled them away. He then gave a signal and the men sprang into action. The sleeping figure was grabbed by the arms and his legs pinned as the overhead light was flicked on. A look of shock, panic, and then fear flashed across his face as his brain tried to make sense of the situation.

"Who are you? What do you want?" he screeched.

A gloved hand was placed over his mouth and he felt the pressure on his limbs increase. He was completely powerless.

"We want you to be quiet," answered the leader in a flat, emotionless voice as he removed the gloved hand.

"I don't have much money, but whatever I have you can take," the man pleaded quietly.

"We don't want your money—we want you."

"There must be a mistake! You . . . you've got the wrong person!" he stammered.

"I don't think so, Professor Sheppard."

The man's look of panic grew.

"Don't offer us any resistance. We have orders to bring you with us. We'll only hurt you if you make it difficult. Do not make it difficult."

The professor was hauled out of his bed by two of the men, gripping him under his arms. His captors were large and muscular and pulled him up as if he were a rag doll.

"Put it away," the leader said, and the man at the door quickly holstered his gun.

Professor Sheppard was small and thin, his hair long and scattered wildly. He wore faded old pyjama pants, a ripped T-shirt, white socks, and for some unknown reason, a pair of tennis shoes. He was in his mid-forties and had the look of somebody who was neither fit nor active.

"Clothes, we need clothes. Grab some things from the closet. He already has shoes on," the leader noted.

The man who had been at the door followed the orders while the other two kept their iron grip on the professor's arms.

"He'll change later. Let's go," the leader said. He started to walk toward the door and then stopped. "And, Professor, if you make any attempt to escape or make a scene as we leave the house, you will leave me with no alternative. Don't make this difficult."

Down the stairs they marched—one in front, the two men pinning the professor on both sides, and the fourth directly behind carrying his clothes.

"Please . . . please . . . my glasses, on the night table beside my bed. Without them I'm practically blind," the professor pleaded.

They stopped. The leader nodded his head and the last man retreated to the bedroom. He returned with the glasses and was about to hand them to the professor.

"No, hang on to them for now. Let's keep him blind for as long as possible," the leader ordered.

Sheppard's feet barely touched the ground as they walked him to the car. He was placed in the back seat with a muscular guard on each side and his clothes on his lap. The engine started and the car slowly pulled away from the curb with its headlights off. The whole neighbourhood was still asleep, unaware of what had just happened or the reasons behind it.

Finally the vehicle came to a halt. Professor Sheppard looked at his wrist—where his watch should have been but wasn't. He thought they had driven for about thirty minutes but realized that he couldn't be sure of anything.

One of the back doors was opened from the outside and a wave of sound rushed inward. The man next to him exited, and Sheppard was pulled and pushed out of the vehicle. He looked wildly around, but in the darkness, without his glasses, he could see little. His attention was riveted by the roar of an engine. He quickly became aware that he was being walked toward a small executive jet that was revving for takeoff only a few metres away. The only visible light came from the dim glimmer of the thousands of stars that filled the night.

The grip on his arms remained tight as he was led to the waiting plane. He stumbled up the steps, and his head was pushed down to pass under the door frame.

"Take a seat, Professor, and enjoy the flight," offered the man who had been leading.

"Where are you taking me?" he pleaded with quiet desperation.

"We're taking you to your seat. Now sit down and be silent."

He did as he was told, and moments later the plane was moving down the runway, picking up speed until it became airborne.

Looking to his left, he tried to peer out the window but a dark screen obscured his view. He contemplated pulling up the shade but thought better of it. He felt utterly confused, alone, and scared. Who were these people? What did they want with him? He was just a scientist in an obscure field who had devoted his life to research. He didn't have much money, certainly had no enemies, and he'd never had so much as an overdue library book in his life. They knew his name, but perhaps it was another Professor Sheppard they were looking for—it had to be a mistake. Unanswered thoughts crowded his mind, and he closed his eyes to escape the nightmare. If only he could go to sleep he might be able to wake up in his room, in his bed, all of this just an illusion. With nowhere to turn, no escape, exhausted, he felt himself drifting off.

Sleep did not come easily, and it did not last. Over the next seven hours of the flight he was repeatedly shaken awake by his captors. Each time he managed to close his eyes, he was again roughly shoved and startled back to consciousness. The line between reality and fantasy became increasingly blurred.

CHAPTER THREE

SWITZERLAND

Professor Sheppard was jolted awake by the jarring bounce of the wheels as the plane hit the runway. His eyes opened wide, and in a rush he remembered the unreality of his situation. One of his captors sat directly across the aisle, staring at him with a slight smile on his face.

"We've landed, Professor. Here are your glasses and clothes."

Sheppard slipped on his spectacles. The world was no longer blurry, but nothing that was happening was even remotely clear. He struggled to his feet against the motion of the still-moving plane. He began to pull off his shirt but stopped short under the gaze of his captors. The thought of stripping in front of these four armed men was not appealing. Instead, he pulled his shirt on overtop of his pyjamas and buttoned it up all the way to the neck. Next he pulled his pants on, but they got stuck passing over his shoes. He tugged harder and his right foot popped through. When he pushed through with his left foot, there was a ripping sound as the cuff tore. He tucked in his shirt and zipped up the fly. In the process, part of his shirt got jammed in the zipper, and now it stuck out through the opening in his pants. Finally he stood before his guards, wearing white tennis shoes, no socks, ripped pants, and a checkered shirt. While Sheppard would never have been mistaken for a fashion model, his present attire suggested a homeless person clothed by the Salvation Army.

The plane came to a stop and the door hatch popped open. Sheppard was quickly escorted off the craft and was immediately blinded by the brilliant light. Almost in unison, all four of his captors put on dark-tinted sunglasses, the type that made it impossible to see their eyes.

He looked around, cupping his hand above his eyes to partially block the glare of the sun, which was either rising or setting behind magnificent mountains. Were they the Rockies? No, somehow he didn't think so. He struggled, his mind spinning, trying to at least determine what continent he was on. It was daylight, he decided—morning—but if they had flown east it could be morning in Europe. Were those the Alps?

Off to the side of the tarmac were two small jets that appeared to be identical to the one he had flown in on. He was being led now toward a small, nondescript building, with no windows and only one door. The door was guarded by two men dressed almost identically to his guards, including the sunglasses. Both men cradled machine guns in their arms. As the professor and his captors approached, the men nodded a silent hello and one opened the door.

They proceeded inside. Sheppard was propelled down a long corridor. It seemed very dim compared to the bright sunlight, but none of his escorts took off their glasses. They came to an abrupt stop at a set of double metal doors.

"Last stop," the leader announced.

"What . . . what does that mean?" the professor stammered. Was this the end for him?

"Last stop. Our orders are to deliver you to this point. You're on your own from here" was the answer.

"But . . . but . . . what happens now . . . to me?" He was finding it hard to force words out of his throat.

"You are to go through these doors without us. We are not authorized to proceed further."

"Not authorized . . . I don't understand," Sheppard said.

"Neither do we. But this is goodbye." The leader extended his hand, and Sheppard, dumbfounded, reached out to shake it. He watched as they retreated down the hall, leaving him alone in front of the doors.

He stood there, motionless, trying to decide what to do next. He thought about turning around and going back, but he knew that would never be allowed. He contemplated just standing there, going nowhere, but for how long? And ultimately, what good would it do?

He pushed against the doors and they opened. Ahead was more corridor, ending at another set of double doors. He walked forward and then jumped as the first doors slammed behind him with a crashing thud.

"Don't be such an idiot—it's just a door," he muttered to himself. But when he turned to look back, he noticed that his side of the door had no handles. No chance now of going back the way he had come. That was no longer an option.

He walked forward slowly, focusing on his breathing. He felt a little light-headed. The combination of limited sleep, no food, motion sickness, and anxiety bordering on a full-fledged panic attack left him feeling almost sick to his stomach. He stopped in front of the second set of doors. There was a small sign affixed to it, with gold lettering:

INTERNATIONAL AEROSPACE RESEARCH INSTITUTE
(AUTHORIZED PERSONNEL ONLY)

Not only was Professor Sheppard not "authorized personnel," but he had never even heard of this institute. This was almost as troubling to him as his abduction. There was nothing about space agencies, or for that matter space, that was not known to Sheppard—after all, this was his area of expertise.

His curiosity was now even greater than his fatigue or fear. He pushed open the door boldly and found himself face to face with a very familiar presence.

"Oh, my God . . . but . . . you're *dead*!" Sheppard gasped.

CHAPTER FOUR

"You look like you've seen a ghost!"

"I have . . . I *am* seeing a ghost," Sheppard stammered. "Andrew . . . I was at your *funeral.*" He was now standing in what looked like a boardroom, with a table and chairs, a whiteboard, even a small kitchen area.

"As you can see, the reports of my death were greatly exaggerated," Dr. Markell said.

Andrew Markell and Daniel Sheppard had been colleagues, researchers, and friends. His "death" had been a tremendous blow to Sheppard personally, as well as a loss to the scientific community. Sheppard had few true peers, and Markell was one of them.

"But . . . but . . . I *saw* you . . . I saw you in the coffin," Sheppard sputtered.

"The corpse was certainly supposed to look like me. Was it lifelike?" Dr. Markell asked.

"Yes . . . no . . . I don't understand."

"Well, as you can see, I *am* alive. I did *not* die in a traffic accident. Matter of fact, I wasn't even in my car that day."

"But . . . why . . . why . . . why were you killed? I mean, why did you pretend to be dead?"

"Like you, I was picked up in the night and brought here. It certainly wasn't my idea. Any more than it was *your* idea to die."

Sheppard gasped. Had they brought him here to kill him, or—?

"Not that you'll really be any deader than me, but apparently you suffered an acute cardiopulmonary episode—a heart attack."

The professor didn't know what to say, what to think, how to feel. None of this made any sense.

"I'm guessing you have a history of heart disease in your family?" Markell said.

"My father died of a heart attack when he was forty-seven."

"And you are now forty-five, if I am not mistaken."

"I'll be forty-six in March."

"Obviously you should have taken better care of yourself. Daniel, how many times did I tell you to get more exercise and eat healthier?" Markell laughed. "Sorry if I find your death humorous. Once you've been dead for a while yourself you'll see the comedy in the tragedy. My own death was dictated by my rather poor driving record."

In spite of himself Sheppard smiled. He thought

back to comments made at Andrew's funeral about his numerous accidents and near-misses, and how he'd made excuses himself so that he wouldn't have to be in a car with Andrew at the wheel. This had, at times, presented a problem, since Sheppard himself had never learned to drive.

"You'd think that as a world-renowned space theorist, I'd have a better grasp of the time-space continuum between moving vehicles," Markell joked. "I guess I'm better at understanding distances travelled at the speed of light than at fifty kilometres per hour."

"Could you please help me understand? Why am I here? Why are *we* here?" Sheppard pleaded.

"I think you will quickly deduce the answer. Especially once you meet the others."

"What others?" the professor asked.

"Dr. McMullin, Professor Harris, Dr. Sanjay, and Sir Edward Fuller."

"They're all *alive*?" Sheppard gasped.

"They certainly wouldn't be here if they weren't alive. Didn't you start to think that it was a little strange when almost all of the world's most renowned astrophysicists, astronomers, and theoretical mathematicians died within an eight-month period?"

"I thought it was unfortunate and unusual but within the very outer limits of probability, when the ages and physical condition of the people were factored into the equation."

"Spoken like a true mathematician."

"But why . . . why are we here?"

"Isn't that obvious? Think about what all of us were working on, either independently or in unison."

"I was doing background analysis of data from Sky Search, as were you," Sheppard said.

"We're here because of what Sky Search has discovered . . . what you have proposed in your latest thesis."

"I'm here because of a *theory*?"

"You're here because that theory is more than just a theory—it is *fact*."

Those calculations, the numbers, all seemed so cold and clinical. It was nothing more than a theory proposed in his laboratory, not something that had application in the real world.

"But, Andrew, I still don't understand how my calculations about a long-forgotten space vehicle reappearing in our solar system could cause *this*. For me to be kidnapped at gunpoint and flown halfway around the world . . . Where are we, by the way?"

"Switzerland. You really don't understand the implications of your theory, do you?"

Sheppard blankly shook his head.

"Each person working in isolation holds a small piece of the puzzle. Have you heard the story of the three blind men who were asked to describe an elephant? One held its leg and said the elephant was like a tree. The second held the tail and said it was like a snake. And the one who was touching its side said it was like a rock wall. If they had been able to see, or if they'd bothered to speak to one another, they would have come up with a better answer."

"Obviously you are saying that I don't see the whole picture," Sheppard said.

"You will soon understand the full implications of that spacecraft getting closer to Earth, and it is not only—"

"I'm still going over my figures," the professor said. "I have to make sure that there was no mistake."

"There was no mistake. Your figures are correct. But what is more significant than the spacecraft itself is what will accompany it when it arrives in slightly less than twenty-four years."

"How do you know about my most recent calculations?" Sheppard demanded, suddenly feeling protective of his research. "You were dead . . . I mean, gone long before I came to that conclusion, and I have kept my figures completely secret. I didn't want to release any findings until I was absolutely certain."

Markell laughed. "Your computer has been linked to our computers. Your phone calls have been monitored, your laboratory bugged. And where do you think the financing for all your work came from?"

"From here . . . from this Aerospace Institute?"

"You were working for the institute long before you were invited to come here. We were all working together without even realizing it."

"But that still doesn't explain why I was taken, why all of your deaths were faked—"

"Why *your* death was faked."

"My death . . . my God, that's right . . . everybody will think I'm dead."

"One of the advantages is getting the opportunity to read your own obituaries. I think you'll fare well. You have numerous scientific awards and an excellent research background, and you're the author of three books—not to mention that nomination for that Nobel Prize. You will be remembered for your outstanding contributions to science."

"But my family . . . my mother and sister . . . her children . . . my friends . . . they'll think I'm *dead*." He felt a sudden wave of anger. "Who's behind this? They can't just kidnap people and pretend they're dead."

"I hate to be the one to tell you this, but actually they *can*. Can and have, on numerous occasions. You'll soon learn that there is practically nothing they can't do, either *for* you or *to* you."

The professor felt a renewed surge of fear that drove away his stunted anger.

"Cup of tea?" Markell filled the kettle in the room's small kitchen. "Don't worry, Daniel, you will be treated kindly. And even better, you will be provided with every resource your research could possibly require. Tell me, what has been the purpose of your life?"

Sheppard was at a loss and struggled to provide an answer. "That is certainly a much deeper question than I can answer at a moment's notice."

"Doesn't your life revolve around your research?" Markell asked. "Isn't it the focal point of your thoughts, your actions, and your hopes? Isn't it why you never married or had children or pursued even the faintest semblance of a hobby?"

"Well, of course I live for my work and—"

"Here you will be free to pursue your research. You will not have to cook or clean house, be driven to work, contend with traffic jams or telemarketers. If you need something for your research, *anything*, you'll simply have to ask and it will appear, almost like magic."

He thought about that. In some ways it did seem so desirable, so positive, so good . . . but still . . .

"I don't understand. Why did they kill us . . . I mean, stage our deaths? Why did they come for me in the middle of the night and drag me from my bed?"

"They felt they had no choice. They couldn't risk leaving you out there in the world to report what you suspect, what you *know*, and they couldn't risk the chance of you refusing their offer to join the program."

"Is that what you call it, an offer?"

"Consider it an offer you couldn't refuse." Markell laughed again. "It makes them sound like gangsters, which they're not."

"But who are they?"

"I think it's best that I allow them to answer. Daniel, you do still take five sugars in your tea, don't you?" he asked as he walked back to the professor carrying two steaming mugs.

Sheppard nodded as he accepted the tea. "Andrew, I just don't know you can be so matter-of-fact about all of this. You're acting as if we simply bumped into each other at the corner market or you invited me over for a drink. Doesn't this all seem absurd to you?"

"Absurd, yes, but you have to remember that I've been here for over six months, so the uniqueness has worn off a bit. At this point my daily routine is not dissimilar to my workday at the university. Besides, like you, I left practically nobody behind. It's been harder for people like Dr. McMullin."

Sheppard thought back to McMullin's funeral and remembered his wife at the grave, two small children crying for their father.

"His family doesn't know he's alive?"

"It is difficult, but he has learned that it is far less dangerous for his children to believe that he is dead."

"You don't mean that they would . . . these people would kill his children?"

"No, I don't believe they would do that."

"You don't *believe?*" the professor exclaimed.

Andrew shrugged his shoulders.

"I can't fathom how you can be so calm, Markell. These people stole me from my bed in the middle of the night, and now, according to you, they have told the world, told all the people I know and care for, all those who care for me, that I am dead. They have brought me to who knows where to do who knows what. And it is almost as if you have been brainwashed into somehow believing that all of this is right."

Andrew didn't answer at once.

"Daniel, I know what you're feeling. And you have every right to feel, think, and say it. The difference is that I *understand* why we are here. You really do need to see the whole elephant." He paused. "But it's not my place to explain."

"Then whose place is it?"

Markell gestured to a large mirror next to the door at the end of the room—a mirror Sheppard hadn't noticed.

CHAPTER FIVE

Seconds later, the door opened and a woman and a man entered the room, followed close behind by four men—the men who had kidnapped Sheppard. No, these were *different* men, albeit dressed identically, right down to the dark sunglasses hiding their eyes.

The professor felt his blood chill. He had to assume that the mirror was two-way, used for observation. These people had obviously heard everything he'd said.

The man and woman took seats at the table at the end of the room, and the four men stood silently, two at each end. There were two seats left empty.

"You're about to get your answers," Markell said.

Sheppard was reassured and frightened at the same time. He was no longer sure he wanted those answers.

Andrew guided him by the arm and the two men slipped into the seats.

"We'll start with introductions. My name is Dr. Hay," the woman began.

"And I am Donahue," the man said.

"We would like to apologize for the manner in which you were brought here," Hay said. "We realize it was somewhat disconcerting."

Sheppard, against his own will, laughed. "*Disconcerting* is not the word you would have chosen if you'd ever had the experience of being hauled out of your bed by armed men, thrown in a car, and then flown halfway across the world!"

Both smiled. Not the reaction he'd been expecting.

"Professor Sheppard, how do you think *we* arrived?" Hay asked.

"And because we experienced exactly what you experienced, we understand your distress, and we offer a sincere apology," Donahue added.

"An apology does not change the fact that I have been kidnapped and am being held here against my will."

"*Kidnapped* is such a strong term," Hay replied. "We would like you to consider yourself a very honoured guest."

"A guest?" Sheppard couldn't believe his ears. "Does that mean I'm free to leave?"

He started to get to his feet, but Andrew reached out and took his arm.

"Let them talk, Daniel . . . please."

He slowly eased back into his chair.

"I can appreciate your need for an explanation, and we wish only to provide that, so please let me continue," Hay requested calmly. "We sit in the boardroom of the

International Aerospace Research Institute. This agency was created only four years ago, and its existence has been kept completely secret. So secret, in fact, that even those being funded to conduct research are unaware of their funding source. Each person in this project—including you—has been conducting research that has been directed and funded by this agency. You and all the others have been unknowing associates of this agency and have been working toward its goals."

"Whether you funded my research or not, you have no right to do what you have done," protested Sheppard.

"That's where you're wrong. We have every right to do exactly what we have done. We have full authorization."

"No one has the authority to do that!" he protested.

"No one *had* such authority until our inception. Now this agency has the power to . . . shall we say, *enlist* staff, as well as many additional powers," Hay noted with a firm but friendly tone.

"You're saying that you have the right to kidnap a person?"

"Yes."

"Next thing you'll be telling me you have the right to take the life of anybody you please," Sheppard said.

Neither answered, and that silence was chilling.

"Let me ask you a question, Professor Sheppard," Donahue said. "Do you think that all human life is sacred?"

"Of course I do."

"And is each life equally important?" he asked.

"Theoretically, of course."

"So your life is no more valuable than that of any other person. Correct?"

"That would be the logical position."

"And if there was an opportunity to save either the life of one man or the lives of ten, which would be the logical choice to make?" Donahue asked.

"Ten lives, of course."

"How about one life or the lives of a million?"

"The million," Sheppard answered.

"So there's no doubt in your mind that your individual life would not be as important as the lives of a billion or two billion or eight billion other human beings?"

"Now you're just being facetious," Sheppard said.

"He's *not*," Hay replied. "You are here because there are billions of lives at stake, and you are one of those who holds the key to their very survival."

"That's ridiculous. I can't see how—"

"Daniel, let him explain," Markell said, putting a hand on the professor's shoulder. "Just *listen*."

Sheppard silently nodded.

"You and many others have been working independently, and in isolation. This was by design. As long as you moved forward with your research, and there was no risk of you revealing the results, you were allowed to continue in this way."

"So I am here because I was going to publish."

"You're here because of *what* you were going to publish, and the potential reaction to that knowledge becoming public," Hay explained.

"I still can't see how the return of a long-lost space explorer is of such consequence."

"Can you please tell me, in a few words, your findings?" Donahue asked.

"According to what I've been told, you are already well aware of my results, but regardless, in brief, the space explorer, which was launched over thirty years ago and left our solar system over fifteen years ago, has miraculously reappeared, sending radio signals back to Earth."

"Miraculous indeed," Hay agreed.

"Having plotted those signals over the past two years I have been able to project, with a fairly high degree of mathematical probability, that the explorer is returning home. It will, on some day twenty-four years hence, make a close pass by the planet of its origin, Earth."

"And to what factor or causal event do you attribute the return of the explorer?" Hay asked. "What caused it to reverse its course and plot its way back to our solar system?"

"That is well beyond my area of expertise," Sheppard admitted. "There might be numerous factors, though, certainly."

"Perhaps if you had more information, you could reduce numerous possible events to one probable event," Donahue suggested. "Are you aware that the explorer is programmed to maintain a positional lock on Earth?"

"That would only make sense. How else would it be able to send back signals, either during its initial stage of exploration or subsequently upon its re-emergence? That would be the only reason we are even aware that it's returning."

"What you are *not* aware of, however, is the fact that we receive those signals on a regular basis—approximately every seventeen hours."

"Seventeen hours . . . but that makes no sense. Any interference from another planetary body would be sporadic. It wouldn't be at any regular interval. The only thing that could possibly explain such a phenomenon would be that the explorer is somehow in an—" He stopped. He felt as if the blood had all rushed from his body, leaving him light-headed.

"Yes," Hay confirmed, "there is only one possible answer: the space probe, the one on course to approach Earth, is in orbit around a large planetary object."

"But . . . how large an object?"

"There are too many unknown variables, including orbital speed and height, making precise calculations almost impossible. But obviously this object has to be of sufficient mass to have captured the ship in its gravitational pull."

"To do that, it would have to be at least two hundred kilometres in diameter," Sheppard said, answering his own question. "But that would mean . . . " He couldn't bring himself to finish the sentence.

His mind spun feverishly, trying to come to grips with the panic that filled his body. He was so much better with thoughts than he was with emotions. Maybe he had to force those emotions down and focus on the numbers, on the mathematics, on the logic.

"But if all this is true, then—"

"It is true," Markell said. "An object, an asteroid of

at least two hundred kilometres in diameter, is travelling toward Earth."

"But if that was to strike Earth, or even have a near miss, then the impact on Earth, on all life forms, would be catastrophic!"

"It would most probably mean the end of life on the planet," Hay said. She uttered the words so casually, with such a lack of emotion, that for Sheppard they were almost unreal.

"It's so hard to believe," Sheppard said, his voice barely a whisper.

"You have to believe," Markell said. "You have to believe because it is true."

Sheppard nodded his head. He knew Andrew, and more important, he trusted him, not only as a scientist but as his friend.

"Then shouldn't the world know what is happening?" Sheppard asked. "Don't we have a moral obligation to make others aware of the danger to humanity?"

"In fact, I believe we have a moral obligation *not* to let them know," Hay replied.

"I don't understand."

"There is no benefit in letting them know their possible fate before we have had the opportunity to at least present them with an alternative, an answer, a solution," Hay explained.

"In fact," Donahue continued, "their knowledge, and possible reaction, could produce consequences that would make it impossible to execute a solution."

"I don't follow you," Sheppard said.

"What if people started to act like there was no tomorrow?" he asked. "What would happen to society, to civilization, and to those hundreds of thousands of individuals whose help we need in our efforts?"

"Wouldn't they have an even greater incentive to be part of the solution?" Sheppard asked.

"Possibly, but that knowledge might have the opposite effect. We have decided that the people of the world will be happier, and our success more likely, if they are left unaware."

"For how long?"

"If we can find the solution, it is possible that they will never even become aware of the danger. That would be the ultimate success of our efforts."

The professor thought through what he had just heard. His understanding of human nature was restricted to casual observation and limited experience. Perhaps they were right.

"But you didn't bring me here only to silence me," he said. "That could have been done much more simply and with less possible risk of complications. So why am I here?"

"Professor Sheppard, the skills that allowed you to confirm our greatest fears are the same skills that might lead to our salvation. You are more than simply a scientist. You are one of the greatest minds of your generation, and your knowledge and expertise are among the keys to finding the solution—to saving humanity."

He felt complimented, flustered, and scared all at once.

"You were brought here to be an important member of our team, a team dedicated to finding that solution."

"Daniel," Andrew said, "they have assembled the greatest minds on the planet, brought them together as one body, given them near-infinite resources in order that they might discover, create, and implement a solution. The end of life is probable, but not definite."

"And that is why you are here," Hay said. "We need you—humanity needs you." She stood up and extended her hand. "Do you accept our invitation?"

This was all so incredible, so improbable, so unbelievable. How could he even begin to understand, begin to allow himself to consider that this was true? But it was . . . he was certain. He was also certain of only one other fact.

He took her hand. "I accept."

PART 3

CHAPTER SIX

A line of cars and vans waited at the big metal gate. The house, an enormous white mansion, sat in the distance, separated from the waiting vehicles by both a high stone wall and a long driveway that meandered through the immaculately kept grounds.

At precisely 9:00 a.m., two men left the gatehouse and waved to the first vehicle. It responded instantly.

Leaning into the car the guard spoke. "Could we please see your press accreditation?" he asked very formally.

"Sure, no problem," the man replied as he pulled his wallet from his jacket pocket. But he was accustomed to being recognized and he was slightly annoyed at being asked. "Don't you watch TV?" he asked the guard.

Unsmiling and without answering, the guard handed him back his papers.

"Do you know what this is all about?" he asked the guard.

"No, sir."

"It's not like Joshua Fitchett to call a press conference."

"Yes, sir. Please continue to the main house."

"Before I go, what is Joshua Fitchett really like?" the reporter asked.

"I don't know, sir. I've never met him."

"Never met him? How long have you worked here?"

"Twenty-one years. Now please continue to the main house as directed or clear the lane so that others may be processed."

"Okay, don't worry." The car rolled forward and the procedure was repeated with the next vehicle in line.

Once inside the mansion each reporter passed through a security corridor similar to those used at airports: a metal detector, X-rays, examination of cameras and recording devices, and finally, a body search.

A select group of twenty television people, newspaper reporters, and Internet bloggers had received an invitation, a phone call waking them early in the morning, to attend this event. Most figured it was some kind of practical joke. Who could believe that the elusive Joshua Fitchett was holding a press conference? He was not only the world's richest man, but perhaps its most mysterious. Still doubting, but unwilling to miss the opportunity of a lifetime, not to mention running the risk of being scooped by other media, they scrambled at the chance to meet with the legendary Fitchett.

Joshua Fitchett's inventions, the fruit of his genius, had changed the world. Yet the man was a virtual unknown. His enormous wealth gave him the means to keep the world away. It had been years since anyone in the outside world had even cast eyes upon him, though not for lack of trying.

Five years before, a newspaper had offered a million-dollar reward to anybody who could produce a recent picture of Fitchett. That offer was rescinded the next day, when the newspaper was purchased and all its senior editors and publishers dismissed. One more company added to an empire that spanned the globe. Only Joshua Fitchett would spend millions to guarantee his peace and privacy. Only Joshua Fitchett *could* do that.

Word came from Fitchett only when one of his companies announced its newest discovery, breakthrough, innovation, or invention. From computer software to metal alloys, from medical breakthroughs to theoretical analyses of human nature and aerospace technology, his work knew no bounds. He was quite simply the greatest mind of his time, even, some argued, the greatest mind of all time. Others simply said he was what da Vinci would have become if he'd had the modern materials and resources at his disposal.

The reporters gathered together in a small private theatre The lights dimmed and a hush fell over the room. A man, tall, with a thicket of flaming red hair and a full beard, walked onto the stage. He was thin and no longer young, but there was a spring in his step. He moved with authority. He stopped dead centre and faced the audience.

"Ladies and gentlemen, thank you for coming on such short notice. I am Joshua Fitchett."

There was a burst of flashes as cameras captured the image that had so long eluded them. Those same images were being taped by the television cameras set in the corners, as well as those streaming live to the Internet. In that one split second, the most sought image in the world became the most seen across the globe. Within thirty minutes of being placed online this would become the most downloaded footage in the history of the Internet—with even more hits than the dancing cats and celebrity gossip.

"I have a statement to read." He cleared his throat as he produced papers from his pocket and unfolded them. "Last night, at approximately 3:30 a.m., a team of ten men came onto the grounds of my estate. Their intent was, I believe, to either abduct or execute me. They, in turn, were stopped by my security forces."

The kidnapping attempt was shocking, but the fact that it had failed came as no surprise to anyone in the audience who knew about Fitchett. The men assembled to keep Fitchett's world safe and secret were nearly as legendary as Fitchett himself. They were gathered from some of the most famous, and infamous, security forces known to the world and were reputedly paid a small fortune. By virtue of their training, they were capable not only of defending his life but of eliminating any who dared attempt to violate it.

"Six of the operatives were killed in the initial skirmish. Four others were apprehended, two unharmed and two suffering significant and life-threatening wounds. The wounded were immediately admitted to my private medical facility within the grounds for treatment, while the others were placed in secure custody, also on my property.

"It was my hope that we could learn more about their intentions and the people behind this plot. Unfortunately, while in my custody all four men died by self-inflicted means, ingesting cyanide.

"Though I grudgingly admire their determination to die without yielding information, their deaths were unnecessary as we had already gathered sufficient evidence—we only wanted confirmation." He paused. "These men were part of the security force of an agency called the International Aerospace Research Institute. Before this moment, that name was known only to international government officials in the highest echelons.

"My attempted abduction was part of a program by that agency that has seen dozens of renowned scientists kidnapped and their deaths staged to cover up their abductions. They are alive and have been taken to a secure setting, located in Switzerland. The names of these abductees and their exact location will be provided by my assistant at the conclusion of my statement.

"Rumour is part of the human condition. Man is an animal whose evolution has been driven by curiosity as much as by need. Rumour expresses our need for understanding, explanation; it's a way to face our fears or shed light on the unknown. One persistent rumour over the past half dozen years has involved the belief that we are facing danger from an object from space, that a large asteroid has been targeted to make a close pass by Earth. The authorities have worked, with the co-operation of the media, to make this seem like nothing more than a legend, a false fear, a myth, a story of Chicken Little and the sky falling. But the only falsehood in this rumour is its denial.

"Every man born must someday die. It is a small blessing that we know neither the date nor the means of that death. At this time I am sorry to report that this blessing has been removed.

"Earth is on course to be intercepted by a large planetary body, a lifeless asteroid. There are three possible scenarios for this interception. The asteroid might collide directly with Earth, with obvious disastrous consequences. The second scenario would involve a near miss that would nevertheless destroy Earth's atmosphere. Even the third scenario, a more distant miss, would likely result in a significant alteration of our orbit around the sun. In all cases the outcome is identical: all life on this planet will cease to exist. This interception will take place in seventeen years, four months, plus or minus three days."

He paused. There was an eerie silence, complete but for the shuffling of feet and papers and the soft whirr of the cameras. Fitchett looked out at the stunned faces of his audience. Did they not understand, not believe, or were they simply not allowing themselves to accept the truth of what he was saying?

"Doubt is understandable," he said, "but I have extensive evidence to support my statements. This evidence, however, is of such complexity that it can be understood by no more than a handful of people on the planet, all of whom are now securely in the grasp of the International Aerospace Research Institute and not available for comment. Other so-called experts will no doubt be put forward by the authorities to deny, ridicule, and counter my statements.

"The leaders of the agency that sent those men to kidnap me are neither malicious nor evil. They believe in their mission, which is to somehow alter the course of this asteroid and thereby save the planet. They have chosen to operate in secrecy to save humanity from the anguish and chaos associated with this news. Today, by means of this press conference, I have chosen to spread this news to the world instead. I believe that humanity has the right to know its fate.

"I am not in a position to state definitively whether any efforts they undertake will succeed in altering the course of this asteroid, and in so doing alter the fate of mankind. In my opinion, however, they are on a fool's mission. The technology available now is not adequate to the task, and short of a technological breakthrough, we will not possess it within the brief window of time before the asteroid strikes. People have the right to know what is at stake, but more than that, should a breakthrough, our only chance of salvation, be possible, it will come about through the combined efforts of all humanity.

"Efforts will be launched to silence any further attempts I might make to alert the world. If I am taken or killed, let my death serve as notice of the truth of my statements this morning.

"I am not, by any common definition, a religious man, but I am aware that in most religions there is a time of judgment. This is, in essence, our day of reckoning. Perhaps we will come together as a species to save the planet. Perhaps not. If we are unsuccessful, perhaps we do not *deserve* to survive.

"That concludes my statement. I am not prepared to answer any questions. Good day."

The reporters sat in stunned silence and watched as the figure left the stage.

"Is he kidding, or what?" asked one cameraman.

"I don't know, but it sure as heck makes one great story," answered his soundman.

En masse, the reporters left to file their reports, the newspapers trying desperately to catch up to the coverage that was already spreading across the Internet like wildfire.

The story, even coming from a genius like Joshua Fitchett, seemed too impossible to believe, and as he had predicted, immediately the airwaves were flooded with "expert" denials.

Who knew what to believe? It sounded like a crazy statement made by a crazy man. The world ending in seventeen years, who knew? Anyway, at least the people finally got a good look at Joshua Fitchett . . . if that was even him.

The world ending? Never!

CHAPTER SEVEN

Less than twenty-four hours passed between the end of the Fitchett press conference and the first fire trucks appearing at the front gates of his mansion. Even before they'd made it through the security gates, it was obvious to the firefighters that the blaze was completely out of control. The entire mansion, from one end to the other, was engulfed in flames. Thick pillars of smoke rose from each of the dozens of windows and joined together in a black cloud, hanging low in the dawn light above the dwelling.

The trucks quickly took up positions around the perimeter of the building and began pumping water onto the raging fire. There was no thought of trying to enter the mansion. Fire blocked all entrances. If anybody was inside they were now incinerated. No point in risking the lives of firefighters just to bring the corpses out sooner.

The whereabouts of Joshua Fitchett were unaccounted for.

The order was given by the fire chief to contain the inferno and prevent nearby structures from being ignited. This was a simple task. Surrounded by extensive gardens and lawns, the mansion was well away from any outlying buildings, and the fire certainly presented no danger to the neighbouring homes in the distance. The mansion itself was beyond salvation.

Given the circumstances, a call had been put in to the arson squad right away. It was obvious, even to the first reporters on the scene, that this was a suspicious blaze. The members of the arson squad stood and observed the fire until it was finally subdued. Then they waited for the wreckage to cool sufficiently to allow them to begin their work.

Quickly, these "fire detectives" uncovered frightening evidence from the charred ruins. They discovered that the security and fire-control room had not been burned up but had been blown up by explosives. There were twenty-four separate places, spread throughout the mansion, where fire had been started with highly flammable chemicals— accelerants. At all entrances they found that furniture had been piled high to stop anyone from leaving. And in the master bedroom, they found the charred remains of a human being. It was incinerated not only beyond identification but almost beyond recognition as a human being. Tissue samples were scraped and stored to allow DNA testing. The dental pattern was charted for comparison with known records.

Before long, however, they discovered that no records existed of Mr. Fitchett to compare with these samples. As far as they could tell he had never been to a dentist or a doctor—at least outside the confines of his private clinic, and there were no records there. They knew that a human had died in Fitchett's room, but they had no idea if it was, in fact, Fitchett.

The press coverage of the fire was overwhelming. There were many more reporters on the scene than fire personnel. Had Fitchett been killed, as he had predicted, to silence him?

Rumours swirled around. In the absence of definite truths the press speculated about the cause of the fire and the number of corpses recovered.

Finally, three days after the fire had started, an official announcement was made.

"The only possible conclusion is that the fire at the Fitchett mansion was set in a skilled and deliberate manner. This was not an accidental blaze but one planned to burn the dwelling to the ground.

"One body has been recovered from the ruins. The body was too damaged to support positive identification, and attempts to use dental and tissue matches have been unsuccessful. However, the body was discovered in the master bedroom, and Mr. Fitchett's whereabouts are unknown. Therefore, we believe that the body is that of Joshua Fitchett.

"We have no leads as to the person or persons responsible. The investigation is ongoing. That concludes the statement. Thank you."

The world press, and the population that they reported to, needed no further proof to reach their conclusions. The charred remains *did* belong to Joshua Fitchett. He had either been murdered or killed himself in some final act of insanity. Was this proof of the claims that Fitchett had made concerning the world ending, or simply proof that he was insane? Who knew, and today, who cared? They already had one fantastic story, the death of Fitchett, complete with fiery film footage of the mansion.

CHAPTER EIGHT

SWITZERLAND

Sheppard and Markell came into the boardroom and looked around earnestly. They had heard about Fitchett's "death." They had more reason than most to question it.

"Do you see him?" Markell asked.

"No, Andrew. Maybe they want to talk to us all first before they bring him in."

Both men took their seats around the table, eager to start the meeting. They settled in to their usual spots, at the end, side by side. After meeting weekly for seven years, everyone had settled in to a pattern, and when one of the scientists absent-mindedly took the wrong chair it seemed to unnerve the whole proceeding.

Most often, the content of the meetings made it seem as though they were discussing a purely theoretical assignment, as if none of it were real. Sheppard suspected that after Fitchett's announcement—letting the entire world know of the threat and the existence of their organization—and then the inferno at Fitchett's mansion, things were about to change, and that change would be reflected in today's meeting.

They had sat together for seven years—seven years of intense theoretical work, separated from the world, locked inside their own little bubble, a small band of scientists working together. As promised, they had been provided with all the resources they needed. They had been freed from all extraneous activities, thoughts, worries, and needs, to allow them to pursue their research.

"Everybody, please take your seats," Dr. Hay said. "We have a great deal of information to share and discuss."

Sheppard couldn't help but notice how much she had aged during these past years. The weight of the world on her shoulders seemed to have worn her down. She actually looked smaller, her complexion sallow, and he wondered if she slept at all.

The rest of the people stopped talking or milling around and sat down.

"Obviously," Dr. Hay began, "the major issue on the table today concerns the events of the past two days involving Joshua Fitchett."

Sheppard was pleased that they were cutting to the chase. The technical issues could wait.

"As you are all aware, many rumours have surfaced over the past years that have risked exposure of our project," she continued.

"Subsequent to these rumours surfacing, we have always

been able to use our resources to discredit, deny, or create counter-rumours to cause these reports to be discounted," Donahue added. "Although, quite frankly, we're not sure how successful our counter-efforts have been."

Hay continued, "While some questions have remained at an academic and scientific level, we have been largely successful in protecting the general population from discovering the true nature of both our organization and the problems facing our planet . . . until now."

"We had some forewarning that Fitchett was planning to make an announcement," Donahue said. "And that led to our attempt to invite him to participate in the project."

"Do you mean the botched kidnap attempt he mentioned in his press conference?" Markell asked.

Donahue shot him a dirty look. Seven years together had not caused the two of them to like each other any better. Andrew was Sheppard's closest friend, his confidant, and the man he worked with most closely, but even he had to admit that Markell was a bit of a hothead who almost seemed to enjoy poking those in charge—people like Donahue. If it hadn't been for his genius, his off-putting behaviour might have been less tolerated.

"Yes, those were our operatives," Donahue admitted.

Hay picked up the story. "Unfortunately, we were not successful in preventing his announcement. Subsequently, through the use of the Internet, traditional news outlets, and the personal participation of some of the most distinguished and reputable journalists, Fitchett released his information to instant international exposure. Since then, we have been monitoring world reaction to determine if our best option is to ignore, deflect, or provide disinformation that would discredit both the message and the messenger."

Sheppard knew that the organization had always reacted with lightning speed when some scientist or researcher threatened to make the world aware of the truth. The person's professional or personal life was brutally attacked, or he or she was simply "killed" and brought to work within the organization.

Both Sheppard and Markell had fully expected to see Fitchett sitting at the table the morning after his "death"; the fire and the report of human remains would have been nothing but a cover story to disguise the abduction.

"Fitchett's dual reputation as the richest man in the world and one of the greatest minds of his generation allowed him not only the credibility but the means, and the platform, to launch his announcement successfully," Hay explained.

"Not to mention that he had enough security in place to stop you from kidnapping him to begin with," Markell said under his breath, but loudly enough for all to hear. He never stopped. His annoyance with all forms of authority was too strongly embedded, even when he was a vital part of the authority he was bucking.

"His announcement also included specifics, some of them verifiable. He divulged the names of the people involved in the project, including all of those sitting at this table, our location, and most important, the specific nature of the problem, including the projected date of impact," Donahue added.

"In fact, the amount of detail he was able to provide leads us to believe that he had access to our organization, and an investigation is under way to determine if there is a spy in our midst."

Sheppard looked around the table. Nobody there looked anything like James Bond, as far as he was concerned.

"Up to this point, world reaction has been mixed," Donahue said.

The far wall came to life and revealed itself to be a viewing screen. It showed a large crowd and police in full riot gear dispersing tear gas and charging the protesters.

"Demonstrations and riots have been reported in over twenty countries, with the worst taking place in France, Germany, and Pakistan. The protests in the Middle East have taken a decidedly anti-American flavour, with demonstrators blaming the U.S. for the asteroid and believing that somehow it will be used against them to promote American interests."

Sheppard could hardly believe his ears. The world was on the brink of destruction by cosmic catastrophe, but somehow the U.S. was behind it.

The screen changed. It now showed a heated discussion in what looked like the British Parliament, and then the more familiar scene of the U.S. Congress and its representatives discussing the report.

Sheppard suspected that the institute's operations were known at the highest level of the government, but he doubted that hundreds of congressmen were part of that equation.

"World money and stock markets have reacted to the announcement," Hay noted. "The Dow Jones Industrial

Average reported its largest three-day decline in history, by far dwarfing both the Great Depression and the economic upheaval in 2008–09 that shook the world."

"The exception has been around high-tech, those firms dealing with bio-tech, weapons, and aerospace-related industries. The world might be ending, but in the meantime some people believe there is money to be made from investing in those industries that might offer solutions," Donahue said.

"It appears that there is little to no probability that we will be able to fully counter the announcement. The genie is out of the bottle and we cannot put it back in. It has been decided that within the next week, we will be holding a press conference to confirm not only the existence of the asteroid and the danger to Earth, but our existence and our complete confidence that our work will save the planet."

"Complete confidence?" Markell asked. "So . . . we're going to lie to them?"

"We're going to tell them what they *need* to know," Hay replied.

Sheppard wasn't sure what to think or feel or believe. Finally the world would know what they were doing, and that they were still alive. Did this mean he could contact his family? His mother had passed on three years earlier, but he still had his sister and her children. Really, though, the bigger issue was that Andrew was right—were any of them that confident they would be successful?

"We are asking that each department head produce a short report that might be incorporated into our press conference," Dr. Hay said. "We ask that you try to be brief, avoid scientific jargon, and provide a positive spin."

"Even if that is a false spin?" Markell asked.

"The world will be given formal confirmation that we are on a collision course with an asteroid that might well destroy all life forms on the planet. I think a little positive news might be warranted," Donahue said sarcastically.

Markell was about to respond when Sheppard put a hand on his friend's shoulder, silencing him.

"Will we have an opportunity to meet with Joshua Fitchett?" Sheppard asked.

Both Hay and Donahue looked confused by his question.

"I'm sorry, Professor, I thought you were aware that he was reported to have perished in the fire," Hay replied.

"Yes, of course, I know about the news reports, but I was assuming that was simply a cover to explain his disappearance."

"No," Donahue said. "We had nothing to do with that."

"You didn't?" Markell exclaimed.

"Then who did?" Sheppard asked.

"We believe those events were facilitated by Mr. Fitchett himself. That he took his own life to punctuate his message to the world."

"And do you *really* expect us to believe that?" Markell asked.

Hay looked confused. "We're telling the truth."

"Like you've told the world the truth for the last seven years?" he demanded.

Donahue let out a big sigh. "Think about it—prior to his death, we still had the ability to deflect his claims. It is his very death that has given him credibility. Do you think we wanted that to happen?"

"So you're saying he *is* dead?" another one of the scientists asked. Apparently Markell and Sheppard weren't the only ones to have the same thought.

"Not by our hands, although, quite frankly, we can't absolutely state that he is dead. That is simply our assumption based on the available information."

"Yes," Donahue replied. "We had nothing directly to do with his death."

"And indirectly?"

"It could be argued that our failed attempt to capture him triggered the announcement that subsequently led to his death," Hay said. "We were not responsible beyond that. We did not set the fire."

"And you think that Fitchett set the fire himself, that he took his own life?" Sheppard asked.

"That is the most plausible explanation, although not the only one," Hay admitted.

"And will you share that other explanation?" Sheppard asked.

Hay and Donahue leaned together and spoke quietly so that they couldn't be overheard. Finally they broke their huddle.

"As you are all well aware, we have provided you with the best possible environment to allow you to proceed with your work. As part of this environment we have tried to keep distractions to a minimum," Hay noted. "Included in this is information about certain individuals or groups operating in the larger community."

"So you've been keeping us in the dark about some things," Markell said.

"Some things," she admitted. "It is time, for your safety, that we reveal one of these issues. We want to show you a broadcast that was shown after Fitchett made his announcement but prior to the fire."

The screen on the wall came back to life. It was filled with a choir singing an uptempo song. The cameras panned around a modern-looking church, or more accurately, a cathedral. It was huge and ornate and every seat was filled. The scene shifted to centre stage, and dry ice was released as strobe lights pulsated.

A lone figure walked onto the stage as the audience's excitement reached a fevered pitch. And then . . . nothing. The noise, the lights, the choir all stopped. All eyes were focused on the man in the white suit, his head bowed in silence.

"Brothers and sisters, the world is in turmoil. All around people have stopped and have turned their eyes skyward. Are they looking for Heaven? Are they looking for the Lord? Are they looking for salvation? No!" he screamed. And then he paused before beginning again in a soft, almost whispering tone. "They do not look for these things because they do not believe, because they have no faith, because they do not trust in the Lord.

"Today we were told about the end of the world. A man spoke to tell us the time of the end, in seventeen years. But more importantly, he spoke to provoke fear in us.

"I fear nothing. Why? you may ask. Why does he not fear? Why is the Reverend Abraham Honey so brave?

Because I have been told of the coming of this end. The end of the world was prophesized over 2,500 years ago. God has spoken. He predicted, in the Book of Revelation, that the stars shall fall down to the Earth and every mountain and island shall be moved from its place. He spoke. Judgment Day is coming. The end of this world is coming, as God predicted. He is ending this world so that a new Heaven and a new Earth may rise in its place. This is not a thing of fear. This is a thing of celebration. I want you all to put your hands together and cheer!"

The cameras panned around the cathedral and showed the people on their feet, wildly clapping and cheering. Sheppard was stunned. Were these people really cheering for their own deaths?

Reverend Honey raised his hands and the audience fell into silence. "I do not fear this end, for it is being done according to the word of our Lord," he began, his voice sweet and smooth and filled with confidence. "And as was prophesied, all people, living and dead, shall be judged. He will find the people who have followed His word, who have not lied or cheated, who have not taken God's name in vain, and these people shall be saved. God in His wisdom will save the righteous. God has told us that He will save 144,000 people. These people have their names written in the Book of Life and they shall be saved. Looking around, I know— I *know*, that I can see people who will be coming with me. People who will be going with me. People who will enter into the Kingdom of Heaven. How do I know? Because God has spoken to me. He has whispered their names in my ear. Look around. Look at your neighbours. Look at those sitting beside you and behind you and in front of you. Look at yourself in the mirror when you go home tonight. You will have seen many faces whose names are written in the Book of Life."

A murmur rose throughout the cathedral. Again the cameras panned around the audience, focusing on specific people, their faces filling the entire screen for a few seconds. Were they the faces of the saved?

"What of the others? They shall run and they shall hide. They will hide themselves in the darkest and deepest of caves, but this will not save them. They will be thrown into the lake of fire. They will be no more!" he screamed.

There were beads of sweat pouring down Abraham Honey's face. His cheeks were red and he was straining for oxygen. As he was talking he had been moving energetically across the stage, back and forth. Now, spent, he staggered and took a seat at the very edge of the platform. There was total silence as he gathered his breath and then again began to talk.

"I want to tell you all a little story," he started in a soft, gentle voice. "A long time ago, man began to see himself as so good and so wonderful that he thought that he was God's equal. He set about to build a tower. A tower whose top might reach unto Heaven. Those men believed that they could enter into the Kingdom of Heaven by means of their knowledge and skill rather than by virtue of their faith and good deeds. These people believed that they could reach up and touch God! Can you believe that? Can you *believe* that?" His voice rose in a crescendo. "Can you *believe that?* Touch God!"

He shook his head, and his expression, which filled the entire screen, was one of disbelief. The camera panned to the crowd, shaking their heads, their faces filled with disgust that mirrored the expression of Reverend Honey.

"But it failed. They failed. God scattered these people and He separated them by giving them different languages so that they could no longer understand one another. They failed! Imagine, people being so misguided as to believe that they could interfere with God or His plans. Imagine. Could we stop God? Well, could we?"

A chorus of "No . . . no . . . no!" swelled up in a deafening roar from the audience.

"Today we have heard about so-called scientists. These scientists, from all countries across the globe, speak but one language. They all speak the language of science. We have been told that the very high priests of science, the leaders of this religion of science, this false god of science, have been gathered to explain how they would reach into space and change God's master plan. These puny mortals believe that they can stop Judgment Day.

"Imagine. Man still has the gall to believe that he can control God. God shudders and the world shakes and quakes and buildings fall to the ground. God sighs and storm winds engulf the world. Now God has chosen to send a small puff of space dust toward his people and we are powerless. God's will shall be done, in Heaven and on Earth. *God's will shall be done!*" he screamed to thunderous applause.

The screen was filled with bursts of dry ice, and powerful strobe lights pulsated. In the clouds of fog the Reverend Honey disappeared from view, and then he reappeared atop the altar at the very centre of the stage.

"We have been told that scientists will try to avert God's plan. They will embrace *their* god, the *false* god of science that they worship, so that we can all be saved. God will strike these people dead, like a bolt of lightning, an avenging fire. They will not be safe even in their very own beds."

Obviously he was talking about Fitchett . . . but hadn't this been broadcast *before* the fire?

"In the days to come we will witness a parade of scientists offering false hope and false information about the plan to save our lives."

Sheppard looked at Markell. How had this guy known there was going to be an official response? Sheppard had the strangest thought—had God whispered all this in his ear?

"Although these scientists will speak in big words and with brave voices, I can hear what they will really be saying. They will be saying, 'I am afraid. I am afraid.'

"We are here today, and I have said to you that I have no fear. Fear of death? Fear of Judgment Day? No!" he screamed. "It is not I who will be flung into the lake of fire."

His image filled the screen again, as though he were looking straight at the scientists in the boardroom. "It is those scientists who need to fear!"

Sheppard felt a shiver go up his spine.

"You may ask yourselves why God has chosen to end His world. You may ask why He sent down the rains from which Noah was saved. The answer to both questions is the same: purification. Purification by either fire or water. Purification. Look around at the world. Are we not in need of purification?"

The dry ice haze had all but gone. The house lights were turned up, and the reverend walked slowly across the stage. On a podium sat a glass filled with clear liquid. He moved forward and drank from the glass. He took a towel and wiped the sweat from his face and hands.

"All of you who know me know that I am a fan of the grand game of football. Many are the locker rooms in which I've led athletes in prayer. In the game of football there is a signal, the two-minute warning, signalling that the game is almost over. It is the last chance to change things, to play better, to do what is necessary to win.

"The game of life is now almost over. God has given us seventeen years. This is his two-minute warning. He is saying, 'Change your ways and follow My word before it is too late.' God, in His kind, gentle, loving, forgiving manner, has given us a warning. Are you listening? Are you willing to change? It is not too late. Time is running out but there is still time for you to win at the game of life. To win and find your eternal reward. It is not too late!"

The audience broke into a wild and spontaneous roar of approval. The cheering rolled on and on and on, getting louder and louder. Finally the reverend raised his hands and the audience obediently fell silent.

"Many are the times and many are the ways that God has told us how to enter into the Kingdom of Heaven.

Remember, it has been written that it is easier for a camel to pass through the eye of a needle than for a rich man to enter Heaven. Do not love your money or your possessions. These are false idols too! Love your Lord. Shed your earthly possessions. Pass them forward into God's hands. Help God, through my ministry, through *our* ministry, to reach out and spread the word. Remember, it is not too late for salvation. God is watching and God is listening and, most important, God is coming. Are you ready to be saved? Are you ready for Judgment Day? Praise the Lord!" he screamed, and then the choir, the lights, and the dry ice filled the screen.

"That's enough," Dr. Hay said, and the screen went black.

"Do you really think we should believe that man arranged for Fitchett to be killed?" Markell asked.

"Our intelligence sources indicate that he is part of an organization that has over one hundred thousand members around the world," Donahue said. "They have been aware of our actions for the past five years, and we suspect that they have been responsible for the deaths of at least thirty-five scientists and the sabotage of at least sixty-five facilities, including two of ours."

"But these people . . . they're just religious nuts. They can't present any real threat or danger," Markell said.

"They do present a vital threat. They have been responsible for deaths and destruction."

"If that's the case, why don't you just have this guy arrested or kidnapped or killed?" Markell asked. "It's certainly not like you people don't know how to do that."

"There was discussion about some form of intervention," Hay admitted. "But in the end, we realized it would probably not be effective."

"He is simply the mouth, not the mind or the muscle," Donahue added.

"What does that mean?" Sheppard asked.

"Essentially, he is not able to act on his own," Donahue explained.

"We felt it was best to observe, listen, and learn," Hay said. "No point in making him into a martyr for others to rally around. It's better to simply let him be. Our intelligence gathering has started to construct a profile that would lead us to believe that he is not a true believer, simply somebody taking advantage of the limelight."

"But remember that there are true believers who are prepared to sacrifice their lives, or yours, to make sure that we do not interfere with God's plan," Donahue said.

"If this is truly God's plan, do they really think that we would have the *power* to interfere with it?" Markell asked. "These people are lunatics."

"This is just crazy," Sheppard added.

"Crazy or not, we have to react. You have now all been publicly identified as the leading members of this organization. Within five hours of that announcement by Fitchett of our location there was an armed assault on our complex by these so-called lunatics."

Everybody looked around in shock, confusion, and fear.

"That assault was easily repelled—so easily, in fact,

that I know that none of you were even aware of it," Donahue said. "And subsequent to that, a bounty was placed on all of your lives."

"But why would they want to kill us?" somebody asked. "We're just scientists."

"As far as they're concerned, you are disciples of the Devil, and they are doing God's work in trying to kill you," Hay answered.

"But nobody could possibly believe that we're working for the Devil," Sheppard said.

"Never underestimate what people will believe, or the lengths they'll go to in order to follow those beliefs, especially when motivated by a distorted religion and the promise of Heaven," Hay said. "Most religious people simply follow their faith, but there are always others, the extremists, who will use religion as a justification for almost anything . . . up to and including your assassination."

"From this point on," Donahue said, "everything has changed. We will be working under the assumption that attempts will be made on the lives of the people in this room and on the facilities in which we work. You will all be given a full-time security officer who will be responsible for coordinating all aspects of your personal safety and leading that team."

Sheppard didn't like the sound of this. He wanted to be safe, but the institute's security people made him anxious, and their sudden and silent appearance was often startling— not to mention that they still brought back memories of his abduction.

"Maybe Fitchett has even done us all a favour," Dr. Hay said.

"Having people trying to kill us is a favour?" Markell asked.

"No, but now that the forthcoming event has been brought to the attention of the world, we can draw on the full resources of the planet to help us achieve our goal. Rather than wasting time and energy in doing things secretly, we can now devote ourselves completely to the task at hand. Perhaps we should mark this as the beginning of the beginning, rather than the announcement of the end."

PART 4

CHAPTER NINE

The police car moved slowly along the street, trying to avoid the potholes, piles of garbage, and abandoned vehicles, mostly metal skeletons stripped of tires, seats, and engines and undoubtedly drained of any precious fuel that might have been in the tank.

The only other movement in the street was the occasional skittering of a rat among the garbage or a cat leaping on a rat small enough to kill. The cats always looked emaciated and the rats large and plump. Neither cat nor rat registered as a concern for Officer Gordon, but his eyes and ears were always searching for the presence of dogs. Abandoned pets formed feral packs roaming the streets. The largest packs with the largest dogs were a danger to anyone careless or desperate enough to be out on the streets unarmed or unaccompanied.

Before bullets had become so scarce the police had been under orders to shoot dogs on sight. That order had never sat right with Gordon, an animal lover, until he'd seen the grisly results—human remains being consumed by a pack of dogs. Not only were they biting the hand that fed them, but they were devouring it. Gordon had thought how a poet or a writer might have captured that moment. He was neither. He shot a couple of the dogs and the others ran away.

In the beginning, the packs had been a cross-section of dogs of different breeds and sizes. It had struck him as almost cute—like a Disney movie about abandoned pets finding a new family. That wasn't the case anymore. The smaller dogs had all been eaten by the bigger breeds. Even the dogs had descended into cannibalism. In a dog-eat-dog world it was better to be a pit bull than a tiny poodle. The only remaining qualification for pack membership was size.

"I don't even know why we're out here," Gordon said.

"We're here because we're following orders," his partner, Sergeant Ramsey, replied. Ramsey was older—much older—and one of the officers who still tried to do the job "by the book," even though the book was being rewritten every day. "At least it's still light."

"Night would be crazy. It wasn't even that safe here years ago. You know . . . before."

"Before" was the term most people used to describe the time prior to the world knowing about the asteroid. For most people this was shorthand for a romantic memory, almost a fantasy, of how perfect things had been. Ramsey was old enough to remember that it was far from perfect, but . . . relative to today, it *was* perfect.

"I feel like we're being watched," Gordon said. He

gestured up to the thousands of open windows and doors in the abandoned buildings that hemmed them in on both sides.

"It's not just a feeling," Ramsey replied. "We *are* being watched."

"I never thought I'd say it, but I liked it a lot better when all the windows were boarded up."

"That was when there was wood to spare, and before people started using it for firewood. Can you pick out any addresses?" Ramsey asked.

"These places have addresses?" Gordon laughed. "Let's just go by the GPS coordinates."

"I would if that still worked . . . or the radio, or the siren. By the way, how many bullets do you have?"

"Five. At least I think I have five."

"You *think*?" Ramsey asked. "You think maybe four instead of five might make the difference between you getting back to the station alive, or more important, *me* getting back alive?"

"I'll check."

"You better."

Gordon un-holstered his revolver and removed the clip. "Yeah, five rounds. You?"

"Full clip in the revolver and shells for the shotgun."

"Pretty impressive," Gordon said.

"Being a sergeant comes with some privileges."

What Ramsey knew but Gordon didn't was that there was still enough ammunition that every officer on duty could have gone out with a full clip and a spare. What they'd found, though, was that the more bullets they gave them, the more targets they found to shoot—and not just dogs.

Ramsey missed the old days, when police officers made arrests and sometimes handed out a little "street justice"—a slap to the face, a punch to the gut, or an occasional beat-down on some deserving punk. Now things had evolved—devolved, maybe—to the point where they were acting as judge, jury, and executioner. For some of the officers it was harder to kill a dog than it was a person. After all, the dogs didn't know about the future. For the people, death would just be happening twelve months earlier than scheduled.

"Suicide by cop" had become an easy and quick way out for some. So far, Ramsey hadn't had to use his weapon that way. He was one of the lucky ones.

"You got your backups?" Ramsey asked.

"I don't leave home without them." Instinctively Gordon put one hand on the big baton on his belt; the other tapped the knife strapped to his leg.

"Looks like this is the place," Ramsey said.

Gordon looked out the windshield and saw there were six police cars already ringing the building. A shiver went up his spine. It should have been reassuring to see so many officers, but it wasn't. What had they gotten themselves into that would require this much firepower? He had to figure this was most of the cars and officers available across the whole precinct.

Ramsey, on the other hand, was pleased to see so many officers. There was never a guarantee that enough men or units would respond to any call. His precinct, like all the others, was operating on less than 30 percent of its regular complement of officers. Some officers had just quit, formally or informally. Others came and went as they wanted, preferring to spend time with family or friends, spouses or kids, girlfriends or mistresses.

In some ways he couldn't blame them. Why should police work be different from any other job that people had abandoned? What was the point? Maybe if he'd had a wife or kids he was connected to he wouldn't have been here either. But he'd failed as a father and a husband—three times. He didn't care where his ex-wives were but he still thought about his two kids, long lost to him years before any of this was even imagined.

The only thing he'd ever been good at was what he was doing. He was a cop. He figured his last moment would be sitting on the roof at the station, his gun in one hand, a good bottle of scotch—already half empty—in the other. He wasn't planning on running or hiding. He knew there was no point. He'd die the way he'd lived: in uniform, on duty, looking the end right in the eye.

They pulled up, and Ramsey quickly got out and took charge. Gordon and all the other officers climbed out of their cars.

"What's the deal, Sarge?" one of the officers asked.

"We're looking for somebody," Ramsey replied. "I have a picture, although it's a year or two out of date." He pulled out the picture and held it up.

"More like ten years out of date," one of the men remarked.

"No, two years, maybe three, like I said," Ramsey insisted.

"You're joking, right?" Gordon asked.

"Do you think I came out here for a joke?"

"But he's just a kid," Gordon said. "He can't be any older than thirteen or fourteen in that picture."

"He was around fourteen and now he's sixteen," Ramsey replied. "Any of you think a kid can't be dangerous, even a killer?"

There was a murmur of agreement. They knew. The gangs of kids who roamed the streets like the dogs were notoriously vicious. Deprived of food, bereft of caring, subjected to all manner of abuse, not knowing anything better but knowing that there was no future, they could be merciless.

"Does he have a name?" Gordon asked.

"William Phillips. He goes by the street name Billy the Kid."

"Like the Old West outlaw," Gordon said. "Cute."

"Who'd he kill?" one of the officers asked.

"Must have been somebody pretty important," another noted.

"Do we have to try to bring him in or just shoot him?" a third asked.

"We're to *capture* him," Ramsey said. "Uninjured, if possible. We're being promised a bounty, a big bounty, if we can bring him in alive and unharmed. Dead or badly wounded and there's no payoff."

Everybody thought of what the bounty might be. They all knew it had to be something that was scarce or completely unavailable. In these last days money meant little, but scarce merchandise meant everything.

"Any ideas what we might get out of this?" another officer asked.

"This is a high-priority operation, so expect the best," Ramsey replied. "Okay, two go in through the side doors to the left, two others through the right. Five come with me through the lobby, and four stay out with the cars."

Even a police car couldn't be left unattended for more than a few minutes before it became a carcass stripped down to the metal bone.

"We're going to do a floor-by-floor sweep. Any adults, or kids with adults, we let them through. All other kids who definitely don't fit the picture, let 'em go too. Others get pushed up to the top of the building."

"Is he part of a street gang?"

"That's my guess. I can't see how he or anybody else could live out here without being part of a gang."

"Any ideas about the size of the gang, how many there could be?" Gordon asked. There was anxiety in his voice that he was trying unsuccessfully to hide.

"Not many," Ramsey said reassuringly.

Ramsey was lying. He'd been briefed and knew there could be two hundred of them. Thank goodness he was a good liar, because if they all had known the truth he might have lost a few officers—easy enough to double back and drive off as soon as they were out of his sight. Even though the police had guns they were still badly outnumbered, and there was no telling what manner of makeshift weapons they'd be faced with.

"We can shoot other kids if we need to, right?" one of the officers asked.

"You can shoot anybody who threatens you," Ramsey replied. "Standard procedure. Just remember how many bullets you have."

"Good point," Gordon said.

"Let's move out."

CHAPTER TEN

The young boy ran into the room. "They're here, the police are here!" he screamed. "The cops are—"

He was knocked to the ground, and two sets of boots crushed his chest and legs. He looked shocked and terrified.

"Let him up," a voice called out.

There was no reaction from the two older boys pinning him to the ground.

"Now!" the voice yelled, and the feet were moved and the boy was pulled up, although he was now held so firmly by two sets of strong arms that his feet barely touched the ground. He still looked afraid. He was so much smaller and younger than the other two. He couldn't have been any older than ten or eleven to their seventeen or eighteen. Of course it was hard to tell. Lack of food had stunted the growth of so many of the children that a lot of them seemed younger than they were.

A man—no, it was a boy as well, the boy from the photo—came out of the shadows. He was obviously older but still recognizable; there would be no escaping the resemblance.

"Let him go," Billy said.

"We're just doing our job," one of the other two replied. "We're just protecting you."

Billy laughed. "Do you think I need protection from *him*?"

"He could have been carrying a gun," the larger of the two protested.

"He could still be carrying a gun. Frisk him and then let him go."

They did as they were told. "He's clean," one of them said. "Well, maybe not clean, but at least he's not carrying a weapon."

They both laughed at the joke. Billy didn't. Of course the boy wasn't "clean." His face was smudged and his hands were filthy. Water was too scarce and precious to use for anything except drinking.

"You're okay, son," Billy said.

"Son"—he couldn't have been more than six or seven years older than the boy. He just felt so much older. Regardless, it seemed to calm the boy down.

"You were saying something about police," Billy prompted him.

"Yes, yes, they're downstairs, in front of the building!" the boy exclaimed.

"Do you know how many there are?"

"A bunch! Maybe thirty or forty, even!"

Billy nodded his head thoughtfully. He knew there weren't that many—there were fourteen. He'd been aware of them since the first car had appeared two blocks away; their movement and numbers had been constantly monitored and relayed to Billy. There wasn't anything that happened around these buildings that Billy wasn't fully aware of. Being aware kept you alive.

"Thank you for telling us that," Billy said. "We appreciate what you did. We'll take care of things. I want you to go back to where you normally hide and—"

"But what do they want?" the boy asked.

"I'm not sure," Billy said, "but I'm sure it will be okay." He turned and looked into the shadows. "Can somebody get him something to eat—an apple or a piece of bread— and help him get back down below?"

At the mention of food the boy's face lit up. "Thank you so much, thank you!"

"No, no, thank *you* for coming here. That was very brave of you," Billy said.

The boy was led away. Almost instantly more than a dozen others materialized out of the shadows, male and female, all in their late teens.

"I don't understand why you gave him anything!" one of the two guards—the bigger of the two—snapped. "It's not like he told us anything we didn't know!"

"Sometimes it's just wise to be kind," Billy said.

"And sometimes it isn't!" the boy exclaimed.

A hush fell over the room. This wasn't just a statement—this was a challenge, to Billy and his position.

Slowly, silently, Billy walked across the room until he was standing directly in front of the guard. He didn't look angry and he certainly didn't look afraid. There was a slight smile on his face, as if he were amused. That look sent a chill up the spine of the boy he was approaching.

"Sometimes you *do* have to be *brutal*," Billy said, his voice barely audible. "Do you think this is one of those times?"

"Umm . . . no . . . no . . . I didn't mean anything . . . I was just—"

"Just being concerned for all of us, right?" Billy asked.

"Yes, of course, just being concerned!"

"Like a good guard should be," Billy said. "And I appreciate your concern. Well done!" He smiled and slapped him on the back, and the tension in the room vanished. Another challenge averted, and another person who could have become an opponent remained an ally.

"Good, now I want you to go down that stairwell with your partner. We don't want any more guests right now. I'm counting on you," Billy said.

"Yes, sir. Thank you, sir!" he said as the two of them hurried out.

What had just happened came as no surprise to anybody in the room. They were those closest to Billy, his most loyal "troops," and they'd often seen him commit similar acts of kindness—and equal acts of violence. Keeping hundreds of people in line, controlling this thin slice of the city, had required both. Right up until that last second nobody could have predicted how he was going to react. Was he going to slap that guard on the back and thank him, or plunge a knife in? Either way, they would have supported him.

Billy wasn't somebody you wanted to cross, and the balance of fear and respect, violence and kindness, had brought some order to their lives—an order that had somehow translated into more food and drinking water and more safety than they had known for years. The outside world was still vicious and life was violent. But here, it was a little less so. And so he was their leader . . . at least until somebody else stepped forward.

"So what are we going to do about the cops down there?" a girl asked.

"Nothing . . . at least not yet," Billy said. "Let's see what they want. No point in provoking a fight we don't need. It might be nothing."

He knew that many police didn't appear in one place for nothing, but he wanted to keep things calm, and his people were afraid of the police. Not as much as they were afraid of the rival gangs, but in some ways the cops were just as unpredictable and dangerous. And with the police, brutality came with a thin veneer of respectability. Death was death. Murder was murder, no matter whose hand was holding the gun.

"They're entering the building!" a female voice called out. "They're covering all the exits and moving in!"

All eyes turned to Billy. His word was as close to law as any of them knew.

"Get everything prepared, but take no action . . . yet."

People scrambled away to get the "reception" ready. They all knew what they had to do.

CHAPTER ELEVEN

Room by room, floor by floor, the police swept through the building. Their progress was neither fast nor safe. The absence of doors on the apartments made entry easier, and the open windows allowed daylight to penetrate, but it was still difficult work. Each time they entered an apartment, each time they entered a room in that apartment, they risked running into something unexpected, something dangerous. It could have been a person with a brick or a knife or a crude zip-gun. All three could injure or even kill. And with the shortage of medicines, with doctors and hospitals falling to ruin, even a simple injury could result in death.

But so far there had been nothing except the sound of rats scurrying away. That was good and bad. Good because they were clearing floors. Bad because after clearing each unoccupied apartment the officers would relax a bit more. Ramsey didn't want that to happen. Being relaxed led to people being hurt.

He motioned for Gordon to provide cover as he got ready to go into the next apartment. The door was gone but there were a couple of boards nailed across the entrance, partially blocking it—a sign that somebody was, or had been, in there and wanted to restrict others from entering. Ramsey took off his hat, holding it in one hand and his revolver in the other. He had ducked down, ready to go under the boards, when he heard a sound . . . a human sound. He froze in place and listened, waiting. Silence. Whatever it was, it wasn't there anymore. Still, better to announce his entry.

"Police," he called out into the opening. "We're coming in."

"Who are you talking to?" Gordon asked.

"I'm talking to whoever might be in there."

He eased forward ever so slowly, stepping through an opening between two of the boards, head up, eyes forward, scanning the room. It was strewn with garbage but there wasn't anybody visible. He put his back against the wall and his hat back on top of his head. Gordon followed behind him, and then a second officer. They were working in teams of three as two more sealed off the stairwells on either side.

Room by room they searched the apartment. It was empty. Whatever sounds they'd heard hadn't come from here.

"Another one down," Gordon said. "Looks like we're not going to find anything, including a bounty."

"Let's keep looking and—" Ramsey was silenced by a sound coming from one of the other rooms. "Did you check the closet in there?" he whispered.

Gordon looked guilty.

"No point in searching if you're not going to search everything," he said. *Lazy idiot* is what he thought.

All three men returned to what had been a bedroom. The window was smashed out and it was completely empty. Unlike the rest of the apartment, the floor here was free of garbage. Ramsey walked across the room and the two other officers split off, coming at the closet from opposite sides. Ramsey dropped to one knee, his revolver in front of him, and motioned to Gordon.

In one swift motion Gordon pulled open the door. There was somebody in the closet. Ramsey brought his gun up and froze in place. A woman and two small children were huddled on the floor. The children were wrapped in her arms.

"Please don't hurt us!" the woman cried out. "Please!"

"Jeeze . . ." Ramsey lowered his gun and tried to hide the fact that he was shaking. "I could have killed you."

"Please don't hurt my children," she pleaded desperately.

"Nobody is going to harm anybody," Ramsey said. "Just get up, get out of the closet."

He reached out to offer her a hand and she instinctively recoiled. He grabbed her hand and helped her, still holding the two children in her arms, to her feet.

"Why didn't you answer when I called in?" Ramsey asked.

"I was afraid. How was I to know that you really were the police?"

Of course she had a point. "Why were you in the closet?"

"I heard you coming, so we hid."

Ramsey pulled out two chocolate bars from his pocket. "For the kids."

"Thank you . . . thank you so much."

She put her children down and quickly unwrapped the two bars for them. The older child was a boy who couldn't have been more than four, and the little girl was maybe a year younger. They started to eat greedily.

"How long has it been since you last ate?" he asked.

"Not that long. We had something yesterday."

Her response made him cringe. Things had certainly changed when eating nothing for a day meant "not long."

"My partner, the children's father, went out looking for something for us to eat. When I first heard you coming along the hallway I thought it might be him."

"I'm sure he'll be back soon," Ramsey offered. "Maybe you can help us. We're looking for somebody."

"There are lots of people in this building I think the police should arrest."

"We have a picture of him."

Ramsey showed her the picture.

"No, I don't know him," she replied instantly.

It was obvious that she was lying—he could tell by her expression, the slight widening of her eyes.

"The picture is a couple of years out of date, so he'd look older. Maybe his hair is different," Ramsey said.

"No, I haven't seen him."

"There's nothing to be afraid of," Ramsey said reassuringly. "Nobody will know that you told us anything."

He looked at her harder. She didn't look afraid. In fact, she seemed calmer, as though looking at the picture of this boy reassured her. She did know him—probably well—but wasn't willing to talk about it. What could that mean?

Ramsey reached deeper into his pocket. He pulled out two more chocolate bars and a package of beef jerky.

"We'd be really grateful for any information you might have that could assist us," he said, trying to be charming.

"It's just that I don't have anything I can say."

"*Can* say or *will* say?" Ramsey asked. "Come on, I know you know him." He smiled. "We just want to talk to him. Don't worry," he lied.

She shook her head. "I don't know—"

Just then Gordon rushed forward and pushed her, pinning her against the wall, his hand around her neck. "I don't know if you're protecting this punk or you're afraid he might hurt you. But you have to know that it's a certainty I *will* hurt you if you don't give us what we want to know!"

"I don't know anything," she hissed.

"Brave words. How about if I hurt somebody else?" he said, looking at her children sitting on the floor, licking the wrappers of the chocolate bars.

Ramsey stood there, silent and without expression. He knew that he wasn't going to let this go too much further. It was important that the woman didn't know that, though. Nothing like this would have happened in the olden days, in the *before* days, but now . . . what choice did he have? They both understood the roles they were playing. It was time for him to play *good cop* to Gordon's *bad cop*.

Ramsey grabbed Gordon and spun him around with such force that he released his grip. "That's not the way we do things."

"That's the way *I* do things!" Gordon snapped. "You want to find this kid or what?"

Ramsey stared him down. "Not on my watch. Wait in the hall."

"I'll wait in the hall, at least until she doesn't give you what you want. Then I'm coming back, and I won't be coming back happy!" Gordon stomped into the hall.

Ramsey was impressed. Even though he knew it was all play-acting, it was frighteningly believable.

"You go too," Ramsey said to the second officer. He turned back to the woman. "Sorry about that. Are you all right?"

"I'm okay," she said. She was rubbing her throat where he'd been holding her.

"Look, just between me and you, you do know this boy, right?"

She nodded her head ever so slightly. "I've seen him," she said, her words so soft he could barely hear her.

"That's what I thought. Come on, we just want to talk to him. We have information for him about his parents."

"But his parents are—" She stopped herself, but not before she'd revealed more than she meant to.

"You've more than just seen him around," Ramsey said. "You know that I'm trying to do right for you here, but you're not doing right by me. Any more lying and I can't be responsible for what might happen."

He took a quick glance toward the hall, where they both knew Gordon was waiting.

"Just tell me what you know . . . between you and me. Nobody else will have to ever know anything. Okay?"

She hesitated, but then she said, "He's a good kid."

"That's what I heard," he said. *Yeah, right, such a good kid that they sent half the police station to capture him.* "We just want to talk. Where can I find him?"

"Top floor . . . that's where they all live."

"All? How many of them are there?" Ramsey asked.

She shook her head. "I don't know. A lot. Maybe a hundred or two hundred or more. They don't bother us . . . none of them . . . he makes sure everybody is okay."

"That's what we want to talk to him about," Ramsey said.

He cleaned out his pocket, pulling out the last package of jerky he had. That was supposed to be his supper. "You take this, and make sure that you eat some of it too. Your kids need you to keep your strength up."

"Thank you. And thanks for not letting him hurt me."

As he got up to leave she gathered the children, and all of them retreated back into the safety of the closet.

Ramsey ducked out into the hall to the waiting officers.

"Forget the next eleven floors. We go straight up to the top and seal it off. He's up there."

CHAPTER TWELVE

The officers filed up both stairwells, their big boots on the concrete steps foiling their attempt to move silently. They'd have to rely more on speed than stealth.

Ramsey and Gordon led the group of seven. Three other officers, asked to seal off the other stairwell but not assault the floor, rushed up the opposite end of the building. With each floor the noise level increased and the officers' speed decreased in direct proportion.

"Two more floors," Ramsey puffed, "and then—"

His words were cut off by a hail of rocks that rained down on them from above, bouncing off walls, steps, and shins. A shot rang out with a deafening crack and the bullet ricocheted as it hit concrete. Ramsey had felt the bullet whiz by his ear! It had just missed him. He smelled the gunpowder and looked around to see the smoking gun of one of the officers who was right behind him. He had to fight the urge to turn around and slug the guy. Instead, he realized that the shower of rocks had stopped. The shot had had the desired effect.

"Come on, and be careful that we don't shoot each other!" he hissed.

They crept up to the next landing, Ramsey leading, all of them with their guns drawn as if they could hide behind them. There were rocks and hunks of brick littering the stairs and landings. Judging by the quantity of rocks that had been hurled, there were a whole lot of people waiting at the top.

Ramsey approached the apex of the final flight of stairs. Carefully he peeked over the last step, bobbing his head up and down until he had a complete picture. Where there should have been a door there were boards nailed in place with only a small opening—almost like a doggy door—at the bottom, and that was blocked by a piece of heavy cloth. There was no way to see, or know, what was on the other side of the passage.

"You, to the left," he said to one of the officers. "You, to the right," he told another.

Reluctantly, the two officers scaled the stairs to the landing and took up positions on opposite sides of the boarded-up doorway.

In the olden days this would have been easy, Ramsey thought. In the olden days, he would have had the use of tear gas, bullhorns, SWAT teams with tactical equipment, trained negotiators, radios, and even a helicopter. He doubted there was now any tear gas left anywhere. There had been so many riots, so many out-of-control crowds over the past few years. Police had tried to subdue the outbursts . . . then they'd given up even trying to do that. Things had calmed down only when the crowds had begun to thin out. People had abandoned the cities in droves, and those who had remained . . . well, so many had died.

"What now, Sarge?" Gordon asked. "Should we put a few rounds through the wood?"

"Let's try talk first," he said. He edged slightly toward the opening. "Hello in there!" he yelled.

There was no response. No surprise.

"This is the police!" he called out. "We don't want to hurt anybody, but I need to talk to somebody in charge!"

Still no answer.

"If there is no response, if you don't want to start talking, then we'll start shooting, and I'm not guaranteeing the safety of the people inside. Actually, I can guarantee there *will* be casualties."

This was not so much a promise or a threat as an inevitability. People were going to get hurt—people on both sides. Ramsey had no desire to harm kids, but he wasn't going to let anybody harm any of his officers. His blood was blue.

"We have weapons too!" called out a voice from behind the boards. It was a boy, trying to sound older. Was that the boy they were looking for?

"That only means that we'll have to use ours," Ramsey said, "and ours are a lot more deadly than stones and rocks."

The reply came back instantly. "So are ours."

Ramsey had spent a lifetime assessing people. There was no threat, no bluff in that voice, just a calm statement of fact. It made him think—what did they have? Probably not guns, although that couldn't be ruled out entirely. More likely something that was explosive or flammable. Molotov cocktails wouldn't have surprised him. They were easy to make, requiring no real technique or expertise, and the ingredients were common and easy to get. A number of street gangs had been using them.

The best way to fight fire was with more fire—let them know that the police had more firepower. It was shock-and-awe time.

"You should all move away from the doorway," Ramsey said. "I don't want to hurt anybody, so step away and take shelter!"

He turned back to his men. "On my signal I want two shots each."

The officers all dropped down or kneeled, putting themselves in a firing position. Ramsey pulled up the double-barrelled shotgun and pumped it, finger on the trigger.

"Now," he said.

There was a deafening hail of gunfire, punctuated by the blast of the shotgun, and the centre section of the boards splintered and disappeared. The smell of gunfire filled the stairwell.

Ramsey waited for the echo to die down. "That was our warning shot," he said.

"That was probably half the ammunition you brought with you," the voice called back.

"You'll soon find out. If we have to come in there's going to be a lot of people getting hurt." He paused. He thought he'd take a chance. "Is that what you want, Billy?"

There was no immediate response—no "Who is Billy?" He'd probably guessed right.

"Come on, Billy. I hear you take care of everybody. Do you really want some of them—a *lot* of them—to be hurt because of you? I am talking to Billy Phillips, aren't I?"

"Who am *I* talking to?"

"Ramsey, Sergeant Ramsey. I just want to talk. Why don't you come out?"

"Why don't you come in?"

"That won't be happening, Billy. You need to come out so we can talk. I'll give you thirty seconds to make up your mind."

"And if I don't come out?"

"Then we come in . . . all of us . . . and the lives that will be lost, the kids we'll have to shoot, will be on your head." He paused. "Aren't you at least interested in how I know who you are and what I want to talk to you about?"

There was no response. What Ramsey didn't know—couldn't know—was that a heated but quiet discussion was taking place on the other side of the shattered divide.

Billy knew that he and his "troops" could inflict damage on any intruders. He also knew that there was nothing they could do to stop a squadron of armed officers. They could fight back, harm, even kill some of the officers, but in the end there'd be many, many more dead on his side. And ultimately, they'd either kill or capture him anyway. There was no advantage to anybody in fighting. If only his top lieutenants felt the same way. They were trying desperately to convince him not to go out, not to give himself up. They lost.

"I'm coming out!" Billy yelled.

"Put your hands in the air," Ramsey said. "Make sure we can see that you have no weapons!"

Billy turned to his closest friends. "Whatever happens, make sure things run the way they're supposed to run . . . okay?"

The three boys, all around his age, nodded silently. They weren't happy, and they didn't agree, but they'd learned to listen to Billy even when they thought he was wrong.

"Before I come out you have to give me your word that you're not going to harm anybody, that we're just going to talk!" Billy shouted.

"You have my word."

Billy took a deep breath and stood up. He wanted to appear confident and hoped the shaking in his legs wouldn't betray him. And Ramsey was right, he *was* curious—what did they want to talk to him about?

Slowly, with hands raised high above his head, he moved to the opening. He stopped, peering through the hole in the boards that had been created by the gunfire. He looked out and saw half a dozen guns pointed at him. The officers looked scared as well.

"I have to lower my hands to climb out through the passage at the bottom," Billy announced. "I have no weapons."

"Slowly, hands first," Ramsey said.

Billy dropped to his knees. He started to crawl, pushing through the blanket that covered the opening and then poking his head free. He continued to crawl until he was free and then got to his feet.

"Lift up your shirt!" Ramsey said.

"My shirt?"

"I want to make sure you have no weapons. Lift up your shirt and turn around. I want you to walk backwards toward us."

Cautiously he edged toward them, careful not to trip for fear that the sudden movement would be met with gunfire. Suddenly two pairs of hands grabbed him from behind, a pair of handcuffs was snapped onto his wrists, and he was pulled down.

"Just take it easy," Ramsey said.

"I thought we were going to talk," Billy snarled.

"I lied about that part," Ramsey said. "But I did tell the truth about you being the only one we wanted."

Billy was dragged backwards by two officers, one on each side, his legs banging against the stairs as they hauled him down. Behind him were another two officers and Ramsey, still holding the double-barrelled shotgun in front of him, aiming back up the stairs. They moved quickly, hitting landings and flights of stairs in rapid succession until they reached the ground floor, where they headed through the foyer and out the front door, toward the waiting police cars.

As they approached the vehicles there was an explosion just outside the building. A Molotov cocktail had been thrown from one of the upper windows and it burst into flames on the pavement.

"Quick, everybody run!" Ramsey yelled.

The officers, two still dragging Billy between them, raced across the open space as another, and another, and another gas-filled bottle smashed down and burst into flames! A direct hit would have incinerated anybody in its path.

The officers at the cars fired up and at the building, and as the other officers reached them they too joined in and started shooting. The Molotov shower stopped.

"Cease fire!" Ramsey yelled. "Everybody in your cars and let's get out of here!"

He opened the back door to his car. "Put him in here!"

Billy was swung and then thrown into the back, so that his head hit the far side. The door was slammed behind him. Within seconds Ramsey and Gordon had jumped in and they raced away.

Awkwardly, Billy pushed himself up to a sitting position. He was sealed in the back, separated from the two officers by a metal screen.

Ramsey turned around. "You did the right thing, kid. No point in anybody getting hurt back there."

Billy couldn't help thinking that maybe nobody back there had got hurt, but what was in store for him now?

CHAPTER THIRTEEN

Ramsey sat sideways in his seat so he could see both the road and Billy in the back seat. He didn't know what this kid had done, but it had to have been something important to have set all this in motion, and he didn't want to underestimate him. Maybe he was a kid, but there had to be something about him that merited this special attention.

"You must be wondering what this is all about," Ramsey said. He was fishing for answers himself.

Billy stayed silent, staring at him through the metal grating.

"I'd tell you if I knew," Ramsey said. He turned to Gordon. "Take the next left."

"The station isn't that way."

"We're not going to the station. Just do what you're told."

Gordon wasn't about to argue. He slowed down and took the curve.

"What if I told you that you have the wrong person?" Billy asked.

"I'd tell you that you can't bluff your way out of this."

Ramsey held out the photo and pushed it against the screen so Billy could see it. Billy tried not to react—it was him—but why, and how had this cop got a picture of him?

"That's not me," Billy said.

"Don't you know it's not nice to lie?" Ramsey asked.

"Look who's talking about lying."

"Sorry about that, kid."

"Yeah, right. Real sorry," Billy snarled.

"Sorry I had to lie to you. I'm *not* sorry that nobody got hurt on either side. But I've got a question, kid. What exactly did you do, and who did you do it to?" Ramsey asked.

Billy didn't answer. He didn't know, but even if he had he wouldn't have said anything.

It was impossible to live on the streets as he had without doing lots of things that were all kinds of wrong, but there was nothing he could think of that would have brought all of this down on him.

What he did know was that he was scared, and that he had reason to be. What he needed to do was calm his nerves and think . . . think of a way out of this. Right now he was handcuffed, hands behind him, in the back seat of a moving police car, and two men with guns were in the front seat. All he could do was bide his time, look around, listen, try to figure out what was happening, and wait for the right moment to make his move.

"Do you know what's going to happen to me?" Billy

asked. He was trying to sound innocent, young, and scared. He *was* the last two, but he couldn't let the fear mar his judgment.

"Don't know much, kid. Just know we're meeting somebody and handing you over to them."

"Do you know what they want with me?"

"I don't even know *who* they are," Ramsey replied. "I'm just following orders."

"You can't think that's right," Billy said.

"I didn't say it was right, just told you what it is. Besides, it's important that somebody follows orders."

Ramsey tried not to think about it. He *was* just following orders—for which he was going to be handsomely rewarded.

They drove along in silence, leaving behind the worst parts of the city first, and then the city itself. As the apartments turned to houses, and then the houses got farther and farther apart until they were replaced by forest and fields, Ramsey began to feel more relaxed.

It was all having the opposite effect on Billy. He kept his eyes open, trying to memorize the route, figuring out how he was going to get back after he'd made his escape.

"How much farther?" Gordon asked.

"Not much. Take the next left . . . a small road. There should be a car waiting."

Billy's ears perked up. Soon would come his best chance. He didn't know how it was going to happen, but it would happen between this vehicle and the next. He'd make a run for it. He just had to break free. He knew they had guns, but he was willing to bet that they hadn't gone to all this trouble just to shoot him in the back as he ran away. Although that still didn't answer the question of why anybody had gone to so much trouble to begin with.

The car slowed down and turned onto another road, not much more than a narrow dirt path. There, just along the path, was a car . . . a big black car. Gordon brought the squad car to a stop directly in front of the other vehicle, the two cars nose to nose.

"Stay here," Ramsey said to Gordon.

"Why?"

"Just do as you're told. Cover me."

"Are you expecting trouble?" Gordon asked.

"I don't know what to expect, and that's the trouble."

Ramsey undid the flap on his holster, which prompted Gordon to remove his weapon completely and cradle it in his lap. The shotgun sat in the holder between the two men. Ramsey pulled out two shotgun shells from his jacket and handed them to Gordon. "Load it when I get out. Have it ready."

The doors of the black car opened, and three people— two large men in dark clothing and darker glasses and a young woman—got out. Ramsey thought they looked like military men, or secret service, or somebody's private security. As society broke down and crime became more common, those people with money and power had started to hire their own security. Some people even had their own little armies—militia.

Ramsey looked anxiously at the two men. If anything was going to be dangerous to him, it was them. They were big and solid, and there was a precision about the way they moved, even about the way they stood. They were standing still but he knew that their eyes, hidden behind those glasses, were looking all around, scanning, assessing, watching. He knew their type. He *was* their type.

The woman was young, with blonde hair, and she looked very proper, like an elementary school teacher. He knew *she* wasn't here to protect them, so they were the muscle for her. She was in charge of whatever was going to happen.

"That's my cue. Be ready."

Ramsey got out of the car and slammed the door closed behind him.

"Hello," he called out.

"Do you have him?" the woman asked. "Is that him in the back seat?"

"Could be. Who are you?" Ramsey asked.

"It doesn't matter who I am, Sergeant Ramsey," she replied.

In that statement she'd at least identified that she was who he was looking for.

"It's him. Have a look."

Ramsey walked to the back door of the car. She followed, and one of the bodyguards came along with her. The second drifted out to the right, to be in a position to watch them and to keep an eye on Gordon in the squad car.

The woman looked in through the window, and Billy quickly turned away so she couldn't see his face. He wasn't going to make this easy. The door popped open.

"Don't you know it's not nice to turn your back on a lady?" Ramsey asked.

Billy turned partway around.

"Are you William Phillips?" she asked.

"Who?" Billy asked.

"It's him," Ramsey said. "Look at the picture."

Ramsey offered his photo, but Billy noticed that she was already holding one. Where was everybody getting these pictures?

"It looks like him," she said.

"Get out of the car, kid." Ramsey reached in and grabbed Billy by the arm, pulling him out of the vehicle.

Billy looked around. This was the moment that he'd been waiting for. He was out of the car and had to assume that any second he would be shoved in the back of the other car. The only problem was that he now had five people to evade, and his hands were still cuffed behind his back.

"This is for you," the woman said, handing Ramsey an envelope.

"What's in it?"

"Directions to where you will find what has been promised for successfully completing your assignment," she said.

"How do I know it's really there?"

"It is. Besides, how do we know this is the person we want?" she asked.

"He is the—"

"I've never even heard of this Phillips guy," Billy snapped, cutting Ramsey off.

"Shut up, kid," Ramsey said. "They wanted you alive, but they didn't say anything about being unhurt."

"Nobody is going to hurt you," the woman said.

She sounded sincere, but that didn't mean anything.

"I guess we'll just have to trust each other," the woman said, turning her attention back to Ramsey.

"Is that why you brought those two?" Ramsey asked, gesturing to her two escorts. "Because you trust us?"

"Would you come out here unarmed?" she asked.

Ramsey shrugged. "You've got a point."

"We'll take him from here," she said.

One of the big guards took Billy by the arm and started to lead him away.

"Nice and easy," he said to Billy, "and don't even think about doing anything stupid." His fingers dug into Billy like Vice-Grips, and his jacket fell open to reveal the butt of a gun. That should have been a threat, but now Billy simply knew what he was dealing with—something this guy didn't. If he could get a hand free he'd soon show them.

The second man opened one of the back doors but didn't even look at them. Instead he was watching Ramsey and Gordon. So much for trusting each other. Billy's head was eased down to get him into the car. He was then pushed to the far side, so that he sat behind the driver's seat. Billy noted that there was no screen separating the back from the front. His escort came in beside him, closing the door.

Billy watched through the windshield. The woman and Ramsey shook hands, and then Ramsey looked at him, gave a little wave, and climbed into his vehicle. The police car turned and sped off, leaving behind a small cloud of dust.

The woman climbed into the passenger side and the other man got behind the wheel. That was good. It meant that his attention would be on the road and not on the prisoner.

Billy started to look around. His best window of opportunity had closed, but he still needed to find a way out.

He was in a large, expensive luxury car. The seats were plush and the windows were all tinted so darkly that he doubted anybody on the outside could even see that he was in there. He noticed that the back door had handles, unlike the police car. Even if they were moving, he could open the door and drop out—if only his hands were free. That had to be the first step.

"How about taking these cuffs off?" Billy asked.

"No can do," the man beside him replied.

"I wasn't talking to *you*. I was talking to her," Billy said.

"Not yet," she answered quietly.

"Come on, what are you afraid of? You have two gorillas carrying pieces to stop me from doing anything. I promise I won't overpower them. Please, these things are digging and hurting me," he pleaded. "Didn't you tell me that nobody was going to hurt me, that we had to learn to trust each other?"

She turned around to look at him. She looked sympathetic. Billy tried to look innocent and pathetic.

"Well, what harm could it do?" Billy asked.

"I advise against it" was the reaction from his seatmate.

"I already told you I wasn't talking to you. Why don't you leave the thinking to people who are paid to have brains?"

"I think we can safely—"

"We were told not to take any unnecessary chances," the man snapped, cutting her off. She didn't look pleased to be interrupted.

"And you think that's taking an unnecessary chance? Even when you've got two men with guns guarding one kid?" Billy asked. "You really think you and your guns can't guard me unless my hands are cuffed behind my back? That probably says more about you and your partner than it does about me." He paused and turned to the woman. "Or it says that you're really not in charge."

"I'm in charge," she said.

"Yeah, I can see that." He snorted, then took a different tone. "Sorry . . . I'm sure you are in charge, and I'm sure they're really good at what they do. You just have to understand . . . I'm scared, and these do hurt. They're really digging into me . . . badly."

"Take off the cuffs," she said.

"He won't be happy if we mess up," the escort said.

"It's my decision and I'll deal with any consequences," she said. "Here are the keys." She handed them to the guard in the back seat. She had gotten them from Ramsey when Billy was being placed in the back of the car.

"Turn around," the guard said to Billy. He fiddled with the keys and the first cuff popped off, quickly followed by the second. He dropped the cuffs to the floor.

Billy brought his hands forward and examined them. There were red marks on both wrists. The cuffs *had* been cutting into him. He rubbed his wrists and flexed his fingers. It was important to get the blood flowing into them again.

"There, does that feel better?" she asked.

"Yeah, better, thanks."

"I suppose introductions are in order. I'm Dr. Miller, but you can call me Amanda."

This was where he was supposed to announce that he was William—Billy—Phillips, but he didn't. He didn't say anything.

"I know you must be scared, but believe me, there is nothing to be afraid of. You'll see. It will all be explained to you in time. I'm sorry we have to worry you needlessly until then."

"Right now I'm more worried about going to the washroom. I haven't gone to the can since I got up this morning. Can we pull over so I can go?" he asked pleadingly.

"He'll have to wait until we've arrived at a secure location," the driver said. "ETA is less than thirty minutes."

"If that means I can't go for thirty minutes that's too long. I have to go badly. If we don't stop I'll end up messing my pants."

"They're your pants, do what you want," his seatmate said.

"Do you think this is a joke?" Billy demanded. "Come on, just pull over and let me go on the side of the road. How can I run away? You have guns! Do you think I can outrun a bullet?"

"It's not *our* bullets we're worried about," the driver said. "This area isn't secure, and we don't have any backup. We keep driving."

"I'm sorry," Dr. Miller noted. "You'll be able to go once we reach the plane."

"Plane!"

"Yes, we have a jet waiting," she replied.

The vehicle slowed down as it rounded a corner. Suddenly Billy sprang forward, and in a flash he had an arm around the guard's neck. In his right hand, almost as if by magic, there was a thin blade, light glinting off the sharp edge.

"Stop the car!" Billy screamed. "Let me out or I cut him open like a fish!"

Silence. The car rolled on.

"I'm not bluffing!" he yelled. "Stop the car or he's dead!" He tightened his grip around the guard's neck.

"Please be careful," Dr. Miller said calmly. "If he hits a bump you'll kill him."

"If you stop the car there won't be any bumps!"

"Slow down," Dr. Miller said to the driver.

"I said stop the car, not slow it down!" Billy threatened.

"Billy, let's talk this through before you do anything rash. This could cost more than just his life."

"I'm as good as dead already. Stop the car, now!" Billy said. There was no bluff in what he was saying. That was how he felt.

"Sorry, we can't do that." Her voice, her whole demeanour, was calm—too calm. It made Billy feel even more anxious.

Suddenly the guard spoke, his voice strained by the pressure of Billy's arm against his neck. "If you're going to cut my throat, just do it. You're not getting away whether I'm dead or alive."

"He's right," Amanda said.

It was then that Billy saw she was holding a gun.

"If you shoot me, he's dead."

"I'm dead anyway," the guard said. "Now or in twelve months . . . what does it matter?"

"I can do it, you know," Billy said, a slight flutter in his voice. "Don't think that I won't."

"We know you could do it if you wanted, Billy. We hope you won't. But either way, nothing will change. You have to come with us. You need us, and ultimately, we need you. You're very valuable," she reassured him quietly.

Billy felt the blade in his right hand, felt a trickle of sweat running down his side, and felt his forearm against the man's windpipe. He could kill this man in an instant. Maybe he could even go for his gun, and knock away her gun before she shot. He knew he could kill, but could *she*?

"Billy, you're going to have to trust somebody, sometime. I'm that person, and this is the time."

Being able to read people, figure them out, was what had kept Billy alive for so long. But this, these people . . . he couldn't figure any of it out.

"Just give me the blade," Miller said again. Her voice was so calm, her expression so friendly—except, of course, she was still holding a gun.

Billy released his grip. The guard sputtered and coughed as he tried to catch his breath. Billy took the razor, grabbing it gently by the blade, and passed it to her handle first.

"Thank you," she replied.

"I just want to know what this is all about," Billy gasped. "Please tell me."

"You'll be told everything, but first you have to rest."

"Rest? There's no way I can—" Billy jumped as he felt a sharp jab in his arm. He looked down. The guard, freed just seconds before, had plunged a needle into his shoulder.

"You said to trust you and . . . and . . . " He slumped down in the seat, unconscious.

"Sorry about that, Billy," Miller said, talking to herself. Then she asked the guard, "How long will he be out?"

"Four or five hours. He'll come to just about the same time the plane touches down."

"I guess this is the best thing," she said. "Do you think he would have killed you?"

"Yes," the guard said. "He would have if you hadn't talked him down. You saved my life."

"If I'd listened to you in the first place and kept those cuffs on none of this would have happened," she said.

"I should have searched him when he got in the car, and there's no way he should have been able to get the jump on me. I'm getting lazy, or maybe it's just spending time around the other kids in the project."

"They're certainly *nothing* like him," she agreed. "Nothing at all."

"The only thing those kids might pull on you is a calculator," he said. "*This* kid I like."

She couldn't help but laugh. "He just tried to kill you!"

"No," he said. "He didn't *try* to kill me. He *threatened* to kill me . . . and he didn't. He could have, but he didn't. Besides, at least *him* I understand."

CHAPTER FOURTEEN

SOMEWHERE OVER IDAHO

He sat quietly, watching Billy. Billy was still in a sleep-like state, or at least that's how it looked. The guard wasn't going to underestimate him again. Besides, he wanted to make sure he was still all right. Those drugs he'd shot into him were pretty powerful, and while they were harmless to most people they could have side effects for others. Side effects like not breathing. He'd been checking on Billy every fifteen minutes throughout the flight.

It had been almost five hours since they'd taken off, and they'd land in less than thirty minutes. The flight wouldn't have taken that long if they'd flown directly but that wasn't the way things worked. They'd flown south for close to an hour before turning west—best way to throw off anybody tracking their original route.

"How's he doing?" Dr. Miller asked.

"I just checked on him. Sleeping like a baby. I still can't

believe he was able to get the jump on me. After all my training, after all I've been through . . . to have been killed by a kid would have been just too ridiculous an ending."

"He's not just any kid."

"That's for sure. Kid moved like a panther. But that wasn't the impressive part."

"What was?" Miller asked.

"Think about it. Despite everything that was going on around him he was still cool as a cucumber. He came up with a pretty good plan *and* he was able to execute it. At his age, I would have been crying and wetting myself."

She laughed. "It sounds as though you're more impressed than angry."

"Why wouldn't I be? Besides, like I said, at least this is a kid I can understand. Not like those others."

"They are . . . different," Miller agreed.

Over the past month their "special guests," children and young people from around the world, had been transported to the centre. There were now almost a hundred of them, with more arriving daily. They were coming from the four corners of the planet. Specially selected and trained, they seemed more like small, serious adults than the children or teenagers they really were. They were unfailingly polite, quiet, and spent more time talking and reading than playing. Actually, had anyone ever seen any of them play?

The pilot made an announcement instructing everybody to prepare for landing.

Dr. Miller checked Billy's seatbelt—it was snuggly on— before quickly taking her seat and clipping on her belt. The aircraft banked suddenly and began a fast descent. It felt as though the plane was coming straight down. That was the way it always was. Coming in through the narrow passage between the mountains left little choice, but it was also part of the strategy—along with false flight plans, flying in the wrong direction from any city, flying too low to be seen by radar—to confuse any attempts that might be made to track the plane.

The plane banked sharply and then levelled out. Miller looked out the window. There was nothing to see but wilderness up close and the tips of snow-capped mountains closing out the distance. The wheels touched down and the plane bounced slightly before settling back to the pavement. The engines roared loudly as the pilot initiated back thrust to slow them down. The runway was short and surrounded on all sides by dense brush. There was little room for error, and it took a skilled pilot to stick a landing on this strip. The plane quickly slowed down and then came to a stop, the engines dying almost immediately.

"It's time to wake him up," Miller said.

She got up from her seat and knelt down beside Billy. She pulled out a small kit and from it produced a hypodermic needle and a small vial of liquid. She pushed the tip of the needle through the top of the bottle and drew in the clear liquid. She then injected it into Billy's arm.

"That should do it," she said. She gently shook Billy by the shoulders. "Time to get up, Billy."

Billy heard a voice, but in his sleepy, drugged state he couldn't figure out who it was or why it was calling to him. He forced his eyes open. A woman was looking back at him, but he couldn't make out her face clearly. Who was it?

"It's okay, Billy, it's Amanda Miller . . . we're here."

Here? Where was *here*?

"Time to get up."

He didn't want to get up. He just wanted to stay in bed and . . . suddenly his mind started to come back to life. He remembered the things that had happened: the police, being captured, the fight in the car, and finally the needle sticking into his arm. Was that why he was feeling so light-headed, because of what was in that needle?

"We're going to help you get to your feet," the guard said.

Billy felt his seatbelt snap open and then two sets of strong hands—the two guards—helped him up. His feet felt heavy and his legs rubbery.

"Best thing to do is walk it off," the guard said. "That stuff is pretty powerful."

"What . . . what did you give me?" he stammered.

"A sedative."

"But . . . but . . . I *gave* you the blade."

"We couldn't take the chance that you might try something else, especially on the plane ride."

That was right, they'd mentioned a plane. He looked around, and through the fog in his eyes he could see that he was on an airplane. He was still having trouble focusing but everything was becoming clearer. Billy slid his hand down his left leg to the place where he always kept his second knife secured in a sheath in his sock—it was gone. They had thoroughly searched him after he'd been knocked out. They weren't going to be surprised again.

"I was sorry we had to do that," the guard said.

"Everybody keeps telling me they're sorry, but they keep doing things to me. Let go of me," he demanded.

To his surprise they listened and released him. His knees buckled and he would have collapsed to the ground if they hadn't grabbed him again. So much for any thought of running. So much for any thought of even standing on his own, without their help.

They walked him toward the open hatch. The light was bright and he held up a hand to shield his eyes. He looked all around. He was surrounded by trees and rocks as far as he could see in all directions. Somehow they had landed in the middle of a forest.

The two guards helped him down the stairs. He was still so unsure on his feet that if they hadn't been holding him he would have tumbled down the stairs to the ground . . . wait, there was no ground at the end of the steps. It was a river! They'd landed in a river!

"That's water—we can't go down there!" Billy protested.

"It just looks like water," one of the guards said.

They stepped off the stairs and onto the "river." It was solid, smooth asphalt. He strained to look along the length of this strange runway. It was then that he realized it was painted to look like a stream instead of a landing strip.

"Why . . . why is it like this?"

"From the air, or from a satellite, it looks like an off-shoot of a river that runs right by here. We prefer that nobody know there's a runway here," Dr. Miller explained.

"Where are we?" Billy asked.

"You'll be told everything. Just not by me," Dr. Miller said.

A Jeep was waiting off at the side, along with a third guard.

Billy sensed that he was quickly coming back to normal. His vision was clearing, he could feel the life returning to his legs, and his thoughts seemed to be more connected. Instantly he began to think again about getting away, but his newly returning faculties allowed him to realize that this wasn't the moment. Whatever they'd given him was still impairing his system. If he couldn't get away from two guards, he wasn't going to be able to evade three. Besides, where was he going to run to? There was nothing but rocks and trees, and how far was he from home? He'd been on a plane—a *plane*—for who knew how long!

Billy was placed in the back of the Jeep, with guards pinning him in on both sides. Dr. Miller sat next to the driver in the front.

The Jeep followed a narrow road, not much more than twice its width. Billy tried to see where they were going but his view was restricted by the trees that hemmed in the road on all sides. He suddenly realized that this road was painted to match the runway. From the air, it too would appear to be a branch of the river. That explained why it was so winding and narrow.

"There it is, home sweet home," Dr. Miller said.

Billy leaned forward to glance through the front windshield. "Where?"

"Right there. Don't you see it?" Amanda said, pointing straight ahead.

Straight ahead was a high rock face, the side of a mountain. "All I can see are rocks and trees," Billy replied.

"Hold on to your hat," the driver said as the Jeep started to accelerate.

They were driving directly at the rocks! They were going to crash! Billy braced himself for impact and— They drove *through* the rocks and were in a tunnel! Billy's mouth dropped open. Was he hallucinating? Were the drugs they'd given him affecting his mind, or—

"Holographic imagery," Dr. Miller explained, "to camouflage the entrance. I guess we should have mentioned that."

They whizzed through the tunnel—all white walls and bright lights—and when they came to a stop and climbed out of the vehicle they were standing in a large chamber, three or four storeys high, as big as a concert hall.

"This is . . . this is . . . I've never seen anything like this," Billy stammered. The walls were shiny and oddly curved, and while the room was well lit, the source of the illumination was unseen.

"It is hard to describe," one of the guards said.

"A little more impressive from the inside," Dr. Miller noted. "From the air the whole place looks like nothing more than an abandoned factory and mineshaft sitting in the middle of forest, rocks, rivers, and lakes. You'll see that the next time you're in a plane and awake."

"The next time?" Billy asked.

"I'm sure there will be one," she noted. "But first things first. You have an appointment."

"Who am I meeting?"

"The person who will answer all of the questions you must have. We'd better hurry. He doesn't like to be kept waiting."

They walked across the room and through a metal door into a long corridor. Here, too, the walls were curved, so it was more like a tube than a hallway. Again, unseen lighting gave off a warm, soft glow. The corridor was long and narrow, just wide enough for the two of them to walk side by side. The three guards walked in single file behind them. Billy ran his hand along the wall as they walked. It was metal but so incredibly smooth that it felt like glass. He banged his knuckles and a clear, round tone answered back.

They entered another, larger room. Sitting at the far side, behind a desk, was a woman working at a computer. She looked up at their approach.

"He's expecting you. Please go in," she said.

They started for a door at the far end of the room.

"No," the woman said. "Not all of you. Just the boy."

CHAPTER FIFTEEN

Hesitantly, opening the door only slightly, Billy peered in. His focus fell first on the only person in the room. There was a man—an old man—sitting behind a desk at the far end. Billy stepped in and closed the door behind him.

Instinctively he began to size up the situation—his survival depended on being able to see where danger lay, determining what he could use in his defence, or failing that, finding a way to escape.

The old man seemed so focused on his work that he might have been unaware of Billy's presence. There was no weapon on the desk that Billy could see, and the man himself— who was thin and old—didn't seem to present a threat. He could snap the old man's neck in two if he needed to.

On one wall were paintings. On the other was a gigantic mirror. On the third, behind the desk, were a large window and a door, obviously leading outside. Through the window he could see an open space and then a small fence, something he could easily scale, and beyond that a forest. Getting past the old man wouldn't be a problem. Then, if the door was unlocked, he could bolt across the clearing, hurdle the fence, and be lost in the forest in a matter of seconds.

"If you're wondering," the old man said, his head down, still working, "the door is unlocked. And while the fence that you see isn't high, it is electrified." He looked up. "It's to keep out the bears and cougars, but I've seen deer jump over it. They like to nibble on the grass in the compound. You appear to be in good shape. I would hazard a guess that you could probably clear it if you had a running start."

Billy didn't even need to guess. He'd get over.

"And once you get over the fence, you could be in the trees in seconds. It would be very hard to find you in there," the old man said, his eyes once again focused on the work on his desk.

Billy took a half step toward the door and then stopped. Why was he telling him all of this?

"Travelling *beyond* those trees would present the difficulty. There are over two hundred kilometres of trees, rocks, swamps, rivers, and total wilderness. Have you ever been in the wilderness before?"

Billy thought about that for a second. He had survived wilderness all right, but all of it inside the New York city limits.

"That's what I thought," the old man said, assuming the answer was no. "Even if you were an experienced woodsman it would take you close to a week to travel the distance to the nearest town—assuming you knew which direction to travel. I've heard that following a river downstream is an excellent strategy for finding civilization. But if you did find that town, you would still be close to four thousand kilometres away from New York. I would be shocked if you could reach it before the end, and even if you did, what then? You'd die in the midst of squalor and garbage. Is that how you want to face your death?"

The man started to write again, his head down, dismissing Billy as if he were no longer there.

Billy edged toward the door. Just because this old man told him these things didn't mean they were true. Maybe there was just a thin layer of trees, and once he'd penetrated that there would be a road right there, and maybe New York wasn't that far away . . . although he *had* been brought here on an airplane. They wouldn't have used that just to drive him across the street.

Billy pulled the handle and the door opened.

"Are you going for a walk?" the old man asked.

Billy didn't answer.

"You don't have to be afraid of me."

"You should be afraid of *me*," Billy said quietly.

The old man chuckled. "Good to hear that you can talk."

"Do you think that your guards could get in here fast enough to stop me from snapping your neck?" Billy asked.

"There is no one watching and no one listening."

Billy glided across the room until there was now nothing separating them but the desk—a distance he could easily hurdle.

"I've killed before," Billy hissed.

"Many times," the old man said calmly. "But never without reason or cause. Why would you kill me? What would you have to gain?"

His calm demeanour surprised and even troubled Billy. Why wasn't he afraid? What had Billy missed? Was there a danger here that he hadn't spotted? Was the old guy holding a gun underneath the desk? No, his hands were visible, folded on top of his papers.

"I'd want to kill whoever is responsible for me being brought here," Billy said.

"Kill? I should think you would want to *thank* the person who arranged that," the old man said. "And that person is me."

"You had me brought here?" Billy edged closer, leaning over the desk.

"Would you like to know why you were brought here and why you're not going to kill me?" the old man asked. There was a hint of a smile on his face.

"What makes you so sure I'm not going to kill you?" Billy said, his voice equally calm.

"First, because you really do want to know why you're here. Your curiosity is greater than your anger. Second, because you realize that if I am the person who brought you here, I am also the person who can arrange for your return. And finally, because I know you would not simply take a life that was not a threat to your own."

Billy laughed. "You really think you know me after being in the room with me for two minutes?"

"Not really, but I have read everything that has ever been written—and survived—about you." The old man held up a thick folder filled with papers. "Would you like to hear about yourself?"

"I know who I am," Billy snapped. He took a small step backwards to show his lack of interest, although he desperately wanted to see those papers.

"Then allow me a small indulgence . . . perhaps to confirm that we have orchestrated the capture of the correct individual." He put the folder down and opened it.

"William Robert Phillips," he began. "You were born on April 23, so you will be sixteen in two weeks. I think we should have a party to mark the occasion."

"Assuming I'm here."

"Yes, assuming that. Your parents are Robert, a computer expert and successful businessman, and Thelma, a nurse who was also a very proficient athlete . . . both golf and tennis."

It felt so strange to hear their names, to hear about his parents. They only came to him in his dreams these days.

"You are the first-born. Your younger brother, Jeremy, was born two years later. If he were alive he would have just turned fourteen."

Billy could picture his brother better than he could his parents. He often saw his face in the kids in his gang—his family. Sometimes when he was alone he would sit and stare at a photograph of his family, the only picture he had—and now it was thousands of kilometres away, hidden behind a loose brick in one of the apartments in the building where they'd captured him.

It wasn't just the only picture he had; it was the only *thing* he had of his family, the only thing to remind him of what his past used to be, of who he was. And now it was gone. He felt a surge of anger.

"A very attractive family," the old man said. He was holding a photograph.

"Is . . . is that . . . them . . . us?" Billy asked, his voice barely above a whisper.

"Yes, of course. Take it, please," he said, handing it to Billy.

Billy recognized the photo immediately. It showed the four of them sitting on a rock by a lake where they used to spend their summers. They were all smiles and happy, but why wouldn't they be? It was from a time when people still believed Earth could be saved, before things degenerated so badly. Hardly anybody could believe how quickly it had all happened, how everything had fallen into ruins and chaos and violence.

The man handed Billy an envelope. He looked inside. It was filled with photos. There was one of his mother, and one of him and his brother, his parents in their wedding clothes, a picture of a baby. He felt a rush of emotions—emotions he couldn't afford to feel. He stuffed the photos back into the envelope.

"How did you get these?" Billy demanded.

"A team was dispatched to your family home."

"You're lying. Our house was destroyed," Billy snapped. "Robbed and looted and burned to the ground!"

"Not much remained," the old man confirmed. "The team sifted through the debris, through the remains, and found a metal security box buried underneath. It contained these pictures, family records, some jewellery, and a diary . . . your mother's."

"I want to have them. They're mine!" Billy said defiantly.

"Of course they are. They will all be brought to your quarters."

"My quarters?"

"Where you'll be staying. Your room."

"You mean my *cell*," Billy snapped. He still wasn't sure why he was here or what they wanted—what this old man wanted—but he wasn't going to be lulled into a false sense of security by a few trinkets. Besides, why had they gone to so much trouble?

"I can understand your fears," the man said.

"I'm not afraid."

That was almost true. Billy had lived through so much that he didn't fear much anymore. Certainly not death.

"There is no lock on the door. You are free to go."

"Free except for an electric fence and two hundred kilometres of trees to lock me in."

"You were an exceptional student," the man went on. He appeared to be holding one of Billy's report cards. "As well as an exceptional athlete, like your mother. And always a leader, both on and off the playing field."

He shuffled some more papers.

"Ten is such a young age to lose your family," he said.

Billy laughed—his response surprised them both. He hadn't "lost" his family; they'd been stolen from him. Billy had spent hours thinking of what he would do if he were ever able to find the man who had killed his family. And almost as many hours thinking about the chance element that had caused him, at the last minute, to choose not to go with them—an assignment for school he'd wanted to finish. He knew it was luck. He could never decide, though, if it was good luck or bad luck that had spared him from their fate. He had stayed home with a sitter. Sometimes he thought how much easier it would all have been if he'd been killed too.

"Those first few months in foster care were difficult for you."

Billy didn't answer. He didn't want to think about it, didn't want to think about those horrible people who had pretended to be parents. He hated them almost as much as he hated the person who had killed his parents and his brother—at least that had been sudden.

"I survived" was all Billy could say. He couldn't let anybody see the hurt, see the vulnerability.

"You did far more than survive," the old man said. "And you got out." He paused. "Would you like to know what happened to those people who fostered you?"

"How would you know that?"

"There's not much I don't know or can't find out. In searching your history we found them, or more precisely, what has become of them."

"Are they dead?" Billy asked. He tried to hold his emotions in check, careful not to let on that he *hoped* they were dead.

"He is. She found God." He smiled. "Or at least what passes for God these days. Those Judgment Day people have certainly chosen which commandments to follow and which to ignore. Apparently, 'Though shalt not kill' is not big on their list."

Billy had heard the stories about religious death squads killing people who didn't agree with them, as well as destroying high-tech facilities that they felt could be used by scientists to destroy the asteroid. They were just nuts, but dangerous nuts.

"She apparently spends her time at one of those church compounds, praying for redemption for her sins," the old man said.

"There isn't enough time left in the world for that," Billy said. "If there is a Hell she'll rot in it."

"That would seem fair. Yet despite what happened to you, you somehow managed to not only survive them but thrive. Through your strength, cunning, ruthlessness, and most remarkably, your kindness, you were able to put together a group of children who were in the same situation as you . . . living on the street."

"They're my family now."

"A rather large family, numbering over two hundred."

"Two hundred and eighteen," Billy said. He knew that because the children weren't just numbers. They were all individuals, all valued. He knew each one of them.

"And you were able to lead them, provide protection and food and shelter. Create a system of internal justice for it all to function. How exactly did you do that?"

"We all worked together."

"But under your leadership. In a world of chaos,

violence, despair, and depravity, somehow you created a little bubble of caring and compassion for all of those children. They were willing to kill, or die, for you."

"And so would I for them," Billy said.

"My final report, the one on your capture, indicates that you surrendered only to stop a bloodbath in which members of your . . . your . . . *family* would have been hurt or killed."

"And that's why I have to get back. They need me," Billy said.

"They did need you, but no worries. Because of what you have taught them they will survive . . . for now."

The old man paused as those words sank in. Nobody was going to survive for much longer.

"I want you to provide me with a list of supplies, food and other items that would make their lives safer and more comfortable. I will arrange for them to be delivered. It's important that they live out their remaining days in better circumstances."

Billy looked at him in disbelief.

"You doubt me?"

Billy shook his head. "No . . . I don't. I think you'll do what you said. I just don't know why. Why would you do that?"

"I took something of great value from them—*you*. The least I can do is make the remaining days of their lives more bearable. There is still room for kindness in this world."

The old man rose from the desk. Billy was surprised by his height. He was thin but tall, almost a head taller than Billy.

"I think it's time for a formal introduction," he said. "My name is Joshua Fitchett."

He offered his hand and they shook.

"Have you heard of me?" he asked.

"Um . . . no."

Fitchett laughed. "How fleeting is fame?" he said, and laughed again. "At one time I was perhaps the most famous person in the world."

"I've never heard of you," Billy said. That gave him some satisfaction.

"I shouldn't be surprised. It's not simply the lack of schools and education but a whole attitude. For most people, desperate to survive today and aware that there will probably not be a future, it is too painful to look back. But believe me, I was famous . . . well, at least before my *death*."

"What?"

The old man smiled. "My *arranged* death. It was necessary to fabricate my own demise—"

"Wait . . . you faked your own death?" Billy asked. "Why would you do that?"

"I had no choice. I was being pursued by members of the International Aerospace Research Institute. You've heard of them at least, haven't you?"

"Of course I know *them*."

"You know *of* them, but you definitely don't really know them. They are very dangerous, ruthless people who will stop at nothing. There is hardly anything more dangerous than somebody who feels he has the moral right to do whatever he wants. Multiply that by a hundred thousand people and place them within an organizational structure that allows them to pursue those goals and there is no end to the havoc they can create. There was no choice but for me to pretend to be dead. It was the only way for me to accomplish all of this," he said, gesturing around him. "Of course you must be wondering what all of this is. So far I've done all the talking. You must have questions."

Billy had hundreds of questions, most of which were too scrambled, stunted, or stillborn to be put into words. But there were some he could articulate, and one, the most important, he'd leave for last.

"Where am I? Where is this?"

"We are located in the American West, in Idaho. We are sheltered on one side by the mountains and on the other by wilderness. This location was used for research and as a launch site for satellites and—"

"Satellites? This place was used to launch satellites?" Billy asked.

"Telecommunications satellites. Telecommunications and aerospace technology were two of the major industries within my network of companies."

"You had a whole network of companies?"

"So many it was hard to keep track of them. My fame was based on my wealth. I was the richest man in the world. But that's not what you asked me about. This place—I selected this location as the centre of my ongoing work because of its remoteness from civilization and its distance from oceans. Oceans are going to be problematic."

This made sense to Billy. He'd heard all sorts of rumours about groups making plans to survive the impact. They figured they'd need to be away from oceans so they would not be swept away by the tsunamis—gigantic waves hundreds of metres high that would race hundreds of kilometres inland following the impact.

When he'd first heard about that, he'd thought about trying to relocate everybody away from New York to higher ground, but he'd soon realized that two hundred kids, exposed, without shelter or food or familiar territory, would simply perish on the journey—a journey that would probably prove to be pointless anyway.

"The other factor in favour of this location is, of course, the mine itself. It has been extended to a depth of over six hundred metres, and it is set in extremely hard rock that will minimize the possibility of cave-ins or collapses."

This only confirmed what Billy was thinking. He'd heard that around the world, old mineshafts were being used to build homes below the surface. That's what they were doing here. Somehow they thought they could survive the impact by burrowing beneath the surface. Maybe they could.

"Your next question?" Fitchett asked.

"Are you the government?"

He burst into laughter. "Governments scarcely exist anymore, with the possible exception of the International Aerospace Research Institute—and as I have made clear, I am *certainly* not them. I don't think my aims could be any further away from theirs," he said. "They actually believe they can stop the asteroid."

"And you don't?"

"Would I be doing all of this if I felt they could?" Fitchett asked. "We are operating here on the assumption that they will fail, and that the only hope for mankind's salvation is to prepare for that eventuality." He paused. "You still have your biggest question to ask. You want to know why you are here . . . correct?"

Billy nodded his head ever so slightly.

"You have been *chosen*."

"Chosen for what?" Billy asked.

"Chosen to *live*. For you, there is not just a *before* . . . there will be an *after*."

CHAPTER SIXTEEN

Billy got to his feet. The bed was soft and he was tired, and he knew that if he lay down any longer he'd fall asleep. That was the last thing he wanted to do. The only thing keeping him awake were all the thoughts spinning around his head. Then again, maybe he *was* asleep and dreaming, because none of this could be real.

Slowly he walked around the room. The walls were shiny, curved, and metallic—they pinged when he tapped them with his knuckles. The light, as in the corridors, was bright, and although he knew it had to be artificial it seemed like natural daylight. The room itself was furnished with a desk, chair, dresser, and that very comfortable bed. Other than that there were no decorations, no pictures, nothing to mark it as belonging to anybody or any place in particular.

He had been given a card—his identification—and was told he should carry it at all times. In an act of defiance and mistrust, he'd taken it out of his pocket the instant he'd entered the room and placed it on the dresser. This was, they said, his "room," but he knew it was more like a jail cell. He looked over at the door—was it locked?

He went to check, but just before he got there it opened, sliding to one side. He was so startled that he stepped back, and the door slid shut again. He regained his composure and moved toward the door, and again it opened. Noted—automatic door. No question, he was free to leave the room, for now.

Billy stood in the open doorway and peered around the corner, first in one direction and then the other. The corridor was empty. There were no guards. If it *was* a cell and he *was* a prisoner, they weren't doing a great job of guarding him.

Carefully, slowly, silently he walked down the corridor, trying to keep as close to the right-hand side as possible. He had no real idea where he was within the building, which worried him. He'd had no chance to orient himself to the layout, and he was tired, possibly suffering the lingering effects of the drug they'd given him. Besides, the whole place looked the same.

He came to a junction. One way might lead to the outside. The other way might mean running smack dab into some of those guards.

"Hello."

Billy spun around, arms up, ready to fight, and . . . it was a girl, maybe a little younger, definitely a lot smaller than him.

"Are you planning to hit me?" the girl asked.

"No, of course not . . . sorry, you just surprised me." He lowered his hands.

"Do you normally react so violently when people surprise you?"

"I don't normally get surprised," he said. "But when I am surprised . . . yeah, that would be my reaction. Wouldn't it be yours?"

"No," she said casually. "I imagine I'd just introduce myself. I'm Christina," she said, extending her hand.

He shook hands, but he didn't let his guard down.

"And you're William Phillips," she said.

"Yeah, I am . . . but how do you know that?"

"I was sent here to be your guide, to show you around and answer all your questions."

Billy felt unnerved and uncomfortable. So this wasn't a random meeting; he was her assignment. Was she just another kind of guard?

"Not that I know everything," she said. "I was only brought to the complex three weeks ago myself. My area of specialization is languages."

"What does that mean, your area of specialization?" he asked.

"The areas in which I have received my training. I am highly proficient in Arabic, English, French, Spanish, and Italian," she answered, "and passable in German and Latvian."

"Latvian?"

"Yes, Latvian. It is spoken in Latvia, a small country on the Baltic Sea. What languages do you speak?"

"I'm hoping to learn English one day."

"English? But you're speaking English right . . . oh, that was a joke," she said.

"Apparently not a good one," he replied.

This was definitely one strange girl. She was close to his age, neat, clean clothes, no makeup on her freshly scrubbed face. She was pretty, with blonde hair in a short cut and blue eyes. She was slim but not skinny. But there was something strange about those eyes. It wasn't the colour. It was what was *behind* them . . . or really, what *wasn't*. There was no fear. Instead he saw calmness, peace. Ironically, that almost made him more nervous. Why wasn't she worried? Why wasn't she scared? Anybody who wasn't scared or worried was dead, or soon to be dead.

"So if it isn't languages, what is your area of specialization?" she asked.

"Umm . . . what sorts of special skills are we talking about?" Billy asked.

"Well, besides linguistics, there is computer science, agriculture, music, electronics, literature, medicine, aerospace, government, transportation, psychology, law, philo—"

"Sounds like a lot of things," he said, cutting her off.

"And of course, most of us have a secondary specialization. Mine is music. I can play the piano, organ, harpsichord, and synthesizer. Do you play any—?"

"None," Billy said, "unless you consider humming to be musical."

"Oh," she responded, "that's another joke, right?" She gave him a slight, confused smile.

"That was a joke. I'm glad that my new friend thinks I have a sense of humour," he said.

"Am I your friend?" She sounded both surprised and pleased.

"Around here, you're my *closest* friend. Matter of fact, you're my *only* friend," Billy answered.

The reality of what he had just said sank in, and he felt a wave of loneliness wash over him. He was no longer surrounded by the kids who had become his family. They were thousands of kilometres away, without him and his leadership and protection. And he was here, without them, and alone. He *did* need a friend. But more than that, he needed somebody to explain things to him, provide him with information . . . and maybe a way out, an escape.

"Since you were sent to be my guide, can you show me around?" Billy said. "And, you know, answer all my questions?"

"I'll respond to all questions for which I have answers. I can also find additional sources of information or the appropriate experts to answer questions that are beyond my specialty."

"And you'll take me wherever I want to go, too?"

"Of course."

"So . . . I want to go outside," he said

"Certainly, come this way."

She turned and started walking. He stood there, hesitating for a few seconds, surprised. He'd expected her to say no.

He hurried after her, walking in stride beside her as she

led him through the empty corridor until they came to a large metal doorway blocking their route. This was the end of the line.

"Do you have your identification card?" she asked.

"Not on me," he said, truthfully. "I must have left it in my room by accident," he added, the last part a lie. "Why don't we use yours?"

"Certainly."

She took a small plastic card from her pocket and inserted it in a slot beside the door. Suddenly and silently the door slid open to reveal bright light—sunlight. Once Billy's eyes had adjusted he could see grass and trees.

"Are you coming?" she asked.

She had stepped out. Billy hurried after her, afraid that the door might close before he could. Anxiously he looked over his shoulder, waiting for somebody to stop them or come running after him, but there was nobody. The door slid shut behind them.

Billy walked across the rocks and open ground toward the low fence that surrounded the complex. He knew it was electrified, but he was still confident he could clear it with a jump.

"It is a beautiful day," Christina said, "although I've heard that it gets very cold here in the winter. Not like where I'm from."

"Where are you from?" he asked.

"I was raised in Morocco."

"That's where your parents are?"

"I don't have parents," she replied.

131

He suddenly felt very awkward. "Sorry, me neither. Mine were killed."

"How old were you?" she asked.

"Ten."

"That's so sad, but at least you have memories of them, I suppose."

"Yeah, some. Don't you remember *your* parents?" Billy asked.

"I have no memories of them. I never had contact with my parents. I was raised in the collective from the time I was a baby."

"The collective?"

"You don't know about the collectives?" she asked, sounding genuinely surprised.

"I wouldn't be asking if I knew."

"I was part of a colony of young people who lived and were educated and trained in the same facility," she said.

"You mean like an orphanage?"

"We were all without parents, but it was hardly an orphanage. It was a facility designed to train us in our areas of specialization."

"And how many of you were there . . . *are* there?"

"There were twenty-five in my collective. I imagine that number stays fairly constant."

"And are there's more than one of these collective things?"

"The are others in different places around the world. There are already people here from collectives in France, Kenya, China, Australia, Canada, Japan, and India."

"So there are lots of kids like you?" Billy questioned.

"Not the same as me. We range in age from ten to sixteen, and as I said, each has his or her own area of specialization. We represent a diverse cross-section of—"

"I mean there are hundreds of kids raised the same way, right?" Billy said.

"Yes. And soon they will all be here," she said.

"Why here?"

"We are all being gathered as the time nears." She paused. "I was wondering, if you don't mind my asking, if you weren't raised in the collective, where were you raised?"

"In New York. I was on my own before they kidnapped me and brought me here."

"Kidnapped? What do you mean? Oh, that's another of your jokes . . . right?"

"No, I was put in handcuffs and brought here, and I don't know why. If they already have hundreds of kids like you, why do they need one kid like me?"

His question was sincere and heartfelt. Why was he here?

"They must have a good reason. They always have a good reason for everything. Have you asked?"

"I was told I was chosen," he admitted. What he didn't want to admit was that he was afraid to ask what he'd been chosen for.

"If you were chosen, then obviously you must possess some very important skills or abilities or knowledge," she said.

"I guess I'll just have to wait for them to tell me what they are."

They stopped at the fence.

"Do you know what's out there?" he asked.

"I've been told mainly coniferous trees, assorted flora and fauna associated with a temperate climatic zone."

She continued to offer technical information. Billy was both confused and fascinated—this was just one more strange part of an already very strange situation. It was like a bizarre dream. In a few short hours he'd been taken at gunpoint, then driven and flown, threatened and handcuffed and drugged, and now here he was listening to this girl explain trees to him.

"Yeah, thanks, that's all really interesting," he said, "but I wanted to know stuff more like is there a road close by?"

She shook her head. "This location was selected because of its distance from both population centres and transportation corridors."

"What?"

"It's far away from people and hard to get to," she explained.

"Oh, okay."

He wondered if she was telling the truth, or if she'd been sent to him and allowed to bring him outside just to reinforce the idea that he couldn't escape. She didn't strike him as the kind of person who *could* trick him, but maybe that just made her the best possible candidate for the job.

Billy looked over his shoulder. Nobody was visible. Nobody was coming for them. This was the best chance he'd had, maybe the best chance he was going to have.

"What if I want to go out there?" he said, pointing into the trees.

"Then you could go. I could bring you."

"But what about the fence, isn't it electric?" he asked.

"It is, but I could turn it off. You could too if you had your identity card. We can go, but I don't think it would be too wise to go too far."

"Why not?" Was it because if they went too far he'd see there was a road?

"We might get lost . . . or we could get found."

"What does that mean, *get found*?"

"As I mentioned, there is fauna typical of this region."

"You keep losing me with your words. You have to speak English," he said.

"I was speaking English, although technically the word "fauna" is Latin and means animals. There are animals in the forest."

"Like bunnies and deer?"

"And cougars and black bears and grizzly bears. I think it would be wise if we took along an escort or a guide if we plan to travel much beyond the fence."

Billy didn't want a guide—a *guard*—but he didn't want to meet a bear, either . . . if there really were bears. Was this just another strategy to keep him inside the fence?

"I'll try to arrange for an escort tomorrow, but right now we should probably go to the main hall. It's almost time for dinner and I'm hungry. Are you hungry?"

His initial response was to simply say no, but he *was* hungry. Things could wait until they'd eaten. He'd get farther on a full stomach anyway.

CHAPTER SEVENTEEN

"We have to get your identification before we go to eat," Christina told Billy as she used her card to get back into the building. "They use the identification to monitor and regulate our food intake, to provide us with the ideal diet for our optimal health."

"Again . . . this time in English."

"They make sure we eat the right things, and they can check through the identification card."

"What if I don't want to be checked?" Billy asked.

"Why *wouldn't* you? It *is* for your benefit."

"Maybe I don't like carrying the card around. There's probably something in there that lets them track exactly where we are."

"Yes, there is, but why wouldn't you want your location known? It is for your safety."

"And what do I need safety from in here?" Billy asked. "Bears and cougars?"

She laughed. Apparently she recognized that this one was a joke. "I guess you're right. We are safe here, but out there, there is always the potential for danger. Not that I ever saw anything, but I was told that it could be very dangerous outside the walls of our collective."

"But you don't know?" Billy asked.

"We really didn't go outside very often, and we were always under heavy guard when we did," she explained.

"It sounds like you were in a jail, not a home."

"We had to be protected. Was that what it was like for you, where you were raised?"

"It was dangerous, but there were no guards," he said without adding more. "Maybe that's why I don't want to carry around that card."

It was the best answer he could come up with, without saying that it was better his whereabouts remain unknown if he was going to try to escape.

She stopped, and he bumped into her.

"Sorry," she said, even though he had bumped into her, not the other way around. "This is your room."

He looked at the door. To him it looked like every other door along the corridor. He stood in front of it. The last time he'd approached it, the door had simply opened. He moved closer until he was practically up against it. It stayed shut. He probably needed his identification to get in—identification that was already in the room. He was locked out . . . or . . .

"Could you use your identification to open my door?"

"My identification card is programmed to open some of the doors in the complex but it won't open restricted or personal areas, such as your room. Your door can be opened only by *your* identification card or your biometrics."

"I don't have a biometric," he said.

Christina giggled. "I like your jokes."

"I'm not joking. I don't even know what a biometric is."

"Oh . . . I'm sorry . . . I can explain it. Biometrics refers to the use of physical characteristics to verify identification and can include DNA, retinal scanning, fingerprints, and both face and voice recognition."

"Nobody has done any of that with me."

"Some of it might have been done with only your passive agreement." She had lost him again. "It might have happened without you knowing. Talk to the door."

"What?"

"Ask the door to open," she suggested.

This felt really stupid, but what else could he do? "This is Billy. Could you . . . open?"

The door slid to the side. Now he felt even stupider. He walked in and grabbed his identification card from the top of the dresser and slipped it in his pocket. It probably wouldn't be a bad thing to have them think that he was co-operating. Besides, his card could probably open a door to the outside.

Christina stood in the hall waiting. He walked out and the door closed behind him.

"Other biometric measurements are needed for other, more restricted areas. You can either place your hand against the pad at the side of the door," she said, showing him the place, "or stand close enough to the optics reader to allow your retina to be scanned." Again she showed him that spot.

"That's good to know," he said. He was already thinking of the doors along his escape route.

He trailed after her down the corridor. "Do you ever get lost in here?" he asked. "All the halls and doors look the same to me."

"It can be a bit confusing at first," she admitted. "But if you're ever in doubt, simply ask and you will be offered guidance."

"What if nobody is around?"

"You're not asking a person. Ask the complex. Touch your identification with your hand and tell it where you want to go."

"I want to go to—"

"Put your hand on your card," she said.

Reluctantly he pulled out the ID. "I'm hungry. I want food."

Nothing happened.

"You have to give more specific parameters to facilitate a response. Tell it where you want to go," she said.

"Okay. Main dining hall."

Almost instantly a line of green lights appeared along the top of the wall, leading down the corridor and out of sight.

"Follow the lights and they will lead us to the main dining area," Christina explained.

Slowly, hesitantly, Billy walked along the corridor. As they walked, the trail of lights blinked off behind them. They moved through one curving corridor to a curving junction.

Billy would have been lost without the lights, but he was starting to get a sense of the overall structure. He tried to picture it in his mind.

It resembled a series of curving, circular main corridors that were linked by shorter, straighter sections. The closest image he could come up with was a series of wheels within wheels, with shorter connecting passages like spokes.

Billy stopped in front of a large metal door. In bold letters it read "Restricted Admission, Highest Security, Priority 3 Clearance."

"What's behind this door?" he asked.

"I was told that it leads down to the underground facility."

"And what's down there?" Billy asked.

"I have not been informed, and I don't have the level of clearance necessary to access either that level or the information concerning it," she said.

"And doesn't that make you curious?"

"Not really."

"Are there lots of places like that where we're not supposed to go?" Billy asked. "That are restricted?"

"There are some other areas with that same designation."

"I just can't believe that you aren't curious to see what's down there," he said.

"If I need to know, I'll be shown."

She started to walk away, but he grabbed her by the arm and spun her around. "Do you *always* accept what they tell you and do what you're told?"

"Yes . . . why wouldn't I?"

"Because maybe what you're being told is wrong."

"They are *never* wrong," she stated. There was no question or doubt in her voice.

"And just who are *they*?" he asked.

"Our teachers, our instructors, our guides. They are always right."

Billy laughed. "Nobody is always right. Besides, maybe it's okay to disagree with somebody just because."

"Just because what?"

"Because you're a person, and people get to make up their own minds about things sometimes," he replied.

"I make up my mind about many things. We have been taught to critically analyze literature, philosophy, mathematical equations, and many—"

"I'm talking about life. Don't you ever just do what you want to do?"

She looked genuinely confused. She tried to pull away but he held her firmly in his grip—and for the first time he saw a hint of fear behind those blue eyes.

"Please, could you release my—"

He let go of her arm.

"Thank you," she said.

He felt bad. He realized that he had been gripping her tightly—too tightly.

"I have one more question," he said. "What happens to people who do question, who do argue?"

She shook her head. That look of fear seemed to be growing. "It's important that we listen and learn. There isn't time for arguing, only for *becoming*."

"Becoming what?"

"Becoming skilled in our specialty. Becoming closer to perfection."

"And for those who can't master that specialty, who can't become perfect? Certainly not everybody in your collective thing became perfect like you."

"I'm not perfect," she said.

"Careful, you're almost arguing with me."

"But . . . but . . ."

"Another joke," he said. "But still, you were assigned to answer my questions, so answer that one. What happens to people who don't master their specialty?"

She looked hesitantly down the corridor. First one way and then the other. She leaned in close. "They are not here. They are sent away."

"Away where?"

"Outside. They are not chosen. Most from my collective were chosen . . . but not all . . . not all."

"And instead they went and found people like me. I'm not even close to perfect, and I don't have anything that I can do like you can do."

"They know," she said. "They don't make mistakes."

"I told you, everybody makes mistakes," he argued.

She shook her head. "Not them. You are here for a reason, and that reason will reveal itself."

"And that my purpose is unknown doesn't make you at least a little curious?" he asked.

She hesitated. "Maybe a little. Maybe I *should* be more curious. It's just that we've always been taken care of, so there's really only been a need for *intellectual* curiosity about things. It's just that I *trust* them."

Billy laughed. He didn't trust anyone or anything, except for trusting that if something bad could be done to him, it would. But then he thought about all the people who trusted him, depended on him, and he was here . . . letting them down. How would they survive without him? Kids could die—kids *would* die—without him there to take care of them.

"The dining hall isn't much farther," Christina offered. It was obvious that she desperately wanted to change the subject.

"Sure . . . good," he said. Maybe it was best not to push her any further—at least not yet.

They continued to follow the lights down the corridor. He looked back at the door. Whatever was down there—whatever he wasn't supposed to see—was what he wanted to see.

Another door opened at their approach. Billy walked in and stopped dead in his tracks. It was a large room filled with hundreds of people—a whole lot of them were kids, but most were teenagers. Maybe that should have been reassuring— he was used to being surrounded by hundreds of kids—but this was different . . . *unnervingly* different. These kids and teenagers were all sitting around long tables. And it was so quiet . . . deadly quiet. The conversations were muted, with no loud laughter or angry voices. They were eating, engaged in polite conversations, reading, and there were a few games of chess taking place. Were they quiet because they were afraid?

He looked at those sitting closest to him. They weren't just quiet, they were calm. There was no fear in their eyes.

He moved closer to Christina. "Why is it so quiet?" he whispered.

"It's not that quiet."

"Yes, it is!" he said, loudly, and he noticed that people looked up from their books or conversations to see who was making all the noise.

"This is how it always is," she replied. "I guess everybody is just focused."

Focused wasn't the word that Billy had thought of. Comatose, unconscious, asleep, bored, boring were all words that seemed to fit better.

Christina handed him a tray and took one for herself. They fell in line behind a few other kids waiting to be served. Billy could smell the food. He breathed in deeply. He was savouring a memory.

"Is that meat I smell?" he asked.

"It could be. They'll have almost everything you could want."

"I want a burger. Do you know how long it's been since I ate a hamburger?"

"I'm really not sure about the food availability where you were living, so I'm not able to make a . . . oh, that was a rhetorical question, wasn't it?"

"Yeah, sort of like a joke, but not funny."

They shuffled forward. The smell was stronger and he could hear the food sizzling on the grill. For the last year food had been harder to find, cooked food even harder to get, and the only meat came from one of three sources—rat, cat, or dog.

"Place your card against the reader," Christina said, "and your specially formulated diet will be provided."

"I don't want a specially formulated diet. I want a burger . . . no, *three* burgers."

"You can always order additional food, but you must also eat the diet that has been prepared for you," she said.

"And if I don't want to eat what they've prepared, what then?"

She shrugged. "I don't know. I've always eaten what is prepared."

He wanted to argue or ask more, but what was the point? He'd take what they offered, eat the burgers first, and then leave their food if he didn't like it. Then again, after eating so little over the past few months, he was hard-pressed to figure out what it was that he wouldn't eat. Beggars couldn't be choosers, and food was food. He knew that he could use a few good meals.

"Here, let me show you how to use the identification card."

He dug into his pocket and handed it to her. She looked at it, and a strange expression crossed her face.

"Is something wrong?" he asked.

"Your card is different from mine," she said. "The security level is different."

"Big surprise there. I just got here." And obviously they were wise enough not to trust him.

"No, you don't understand," she said. "Your security level is *higher* than mine—*much* higher."

"Higher? But that doesn't make any sense at all. There must be some sort of mistake."

He instantly regretted saying that. If there had been a mistake, he didn't want them to change it.

"No," Christina said. "I told you, they don't make mistakes. If you have a higher clearance, then there has to be a reason."

Billy was happy to leave it at that.

She inserted his identification card into a slot, and a panel in front of them opened to reveal food—lots of food. There was a steaming bowl of soup, and a big green salad, and a plate filled with cooked vegetables—carrots and peas and green beans and some things he didn't even recognize—and mashed potatoes. And was that a steak? And beside them were an orange and an apple and a banana and, wow, an avocado! He almost laughed out loud. It had been years since he'd seen any type of fruit.

He picked up the banana and held it in his hand, turning it around, examining it.

"It's a banana," Christina said.

"I know *what* it is. I just didn't expect I'd ever see one again."

"Really? Are they unusual where you come from?" she asked innocently.

"*All* food is unusual where I come from," he snapped. "I'm assuming it wasn't like that in the collective."

She shook her hand. "There was always all the food we could want. Food and water and books and everything that we asked for or needed."

Billy shook his head slowly. Of everything, that was perhaps the most impossible for him to believe . . . enough food . . . *everything that we asked for or needed.* But looking around he saw a group of well-dressed, clean, well-fed people sitting around tables with food on their plates— enough food to feed thousands. Here was the proof of what she was saying.

"You can have all the bananas you want," she said. "You can have all the fruit you want."

She gestured to a shelf that was piled high with apples and bananas and oranges and other fruits he didn't know the names of. And beside them were raw vegetables and crackers and cheese and buns and bread. It was almost more than he could comprehend, almost beyond his ability to understand. In some ways it was harder to believe that all the food was there than it was to believe the sequence of events that had led to him being here, from the arrest to the car ride to the airplane.

Christina started to move items onto his tray. He helped with one hand, the other holding on to the banana. He couldn't bear to let go of it.

"They seem to have provided you with a diet rich in proteins and fresh fruit and vegetables," she said. "Was your environment lacking in those food groups?"

"Like I told you, my environment was lacking in all food—"

There was a hand on Billy's back—someone reaching for his food?—and instinctively he spun around, grabbed it, pulled it up and back, and used his foot to sweep the legs out from under the person, who smashed to the ground!

Billy dropped his knee onto the person's chest and raised his hand to punch, but he held back. It was just some boy, his age, in a suit and tie, a look of absolute terror on his face.

"I . . . I . . . I'm sorry," the boy stammered.

"What were you doing?" Billy demanded.

"I was just . . . just going to ask if you could pass me an apple . . . I'm sorry . . . I'm so sorry."

Billy slowly lowered his cocked arm and his fingers relaxed from a fist. He looked around. The murmur of sound, the near silence, had been replaced by complete silence. Every eye seemed to be looking at him. The other kids all looked as surprised and horrified as the boy beneath his knee . . . his knee.

Billy slowly rose to his feet. Everybody was still staring. Christina looked as shocked as the rest. Billy didn't know what to say. He hadn't started it. He'd just reacted. That boy shouldn't have snuck up on him, and he sure shouldn't have reached for his food. Taking somebody's food was asking for a fight, asking to be hurt or worse.

Without saying a word, Billy stood up and grabbed his food and hurried away. The soup sloshed out of the bowl and onto the tray as he rushed out of the dining hall, trying not to meet any of the eyes staring at him.

CHAPTER EIGHTEEN

The special lighting system had led him back to his room with his food—he'd simply "asked" to be brought there. All the way he'd expected to be met by security forces, the police, somebody. After all, he'd knocked down one of these *special* children. He hadn't really hurt the guy, just knocked him down, but who knew? Maybe he was delicate.

He got inside his room and the door slid shut behind him. He let out a big sigh of relief and then greedily began to gobble down the food. If they were coming to get him they might be sending him away, and he wanted to have a good meal inside him in case it was a long time before he could eat again.

The seconds turned to minutes and nobody came to his door. Maybe they hadn't heard what had happened yet. Maybe he'd be better off getting out of there before they found out and came after him. Christina had told him that sometimes people were sent away. Surely assaulting one of these kids would be more than enough of a crime to warrant his expulsion.

Okay, so he needed to leave, but he definitely needed to eat first. He crammed in as much food as quickly as he could, then took the fruit and stuffed it in his pockets for later.

He walked toward the door and it opened. He took the identification card out of his pocket and went to throw it back into the room but stopped himself. He'd probably need it to get outside or to turn off the electric fence. He could leave it in the forest, or even toss it back over the fence so they would think he was still on the grounds of the compound.

Just before leaving he grabbed his knife and fork. The knife wasn't even very sharp, but he knew from experience that any piece of metal, ground and filed and sharpened to a point, could become an effective weapon. He'd find rocks to do that job once he got out into the forest.

Billy stopped and looked down the corridor in both directions. He couldn't remember the route that Christina had taken when she'd led him outside. What if he just asked?

"Umm . . . this is Billy and I want out."

There were no lights leading the way. "Out" was probably not specific enough.

"I want to leave the complex. Show me the quickest route to leave."

Green lights materialized on the wall. Stupid, but he thought he'd miss these lights. It was tiring to always have to figure out where to go and how to get there and have hundreds of kids looking at him to lead, while he pretended to be confident even when he had no idea what he was going to do next.

He heard some sounds, footsteps and voices, coming from behind him. He hurried off at a fast pace, trying to catch up with the lights, which dimmed instantly as he passed. He started running, racing down one corridor, through a connecting passage, and into another curving hallway. This route seemed very familiar. Wasn't this the way to the dining hall? That was the last place in the world he wanted to go.

The lights stopped. They led right up to the big security door, the one with restricted access and priority clearance. Was this some sort of mistake? How could this be a way out? Wait, maybe that *did* make sense. It was probably why it was marked that way, to stop people from leaving through that door. Maybe he could find where they parked their vehicles and take one to get away. Driving would definitely be better and faster than walking. There was no telling how far that road went. But of course he wouldn't know anything if he couldn't get through that door, and he had no way to get through.

Unless . . . Christina had said that she couldn't get in through that door, but she had also said that his card had a higher security clearance than hers. Could it be Priority 3 Clearance, whatever that was?

He dug into his pocket and brought his card up to look at. It didn't say anything about security clearance. It didn't say anything that he could understand, but obviously it had made sense to Christina. He took the card and went to insert it in the little slot.

"Do you want to go in there?"

Billy spun around, his arms raised, ready to strike or defend. It was Joshua Fitchett. He was alone.

"Do you want to go in there?" Fitchett asked again.

Billy didn't answer, but he didn't have to. He was still holding the identification card and he'd been caught in the act. Instinctively his other hand started to reach behind his back to where he had stuffed the knife. He stopped himself.

"You *are* allowed to go in there, if you wish," Fitchett said. "Just insert your card."

Billy remained frozen in place.

"You do want to see what's behind there, don't you?" Fitchett asked. "It is pretty interesting."

"Why are you letting me go in there when other people can't?" Billy asked.

"Because most people are not allowed entry. *You* are authorized."

"Why am I even here in the first place?"

"As I've told you, you're here because you've been chosen. You have been selected to survive."

"You said that, but *why* have I been selected?"

"Another excellent question. How about if I show you while I tell you? Please, insert your card and let's start the tour."

Hesitantly, keeping his head turned so he could still watch Fitchett, he slipped his identification card into the slot. The door slowly slid open. It was much thicker, stronger looking than the other doors in the complex. This was a door designed to keep people out . . . or in.

"Please go ahead," Fitchett said.

"You first," Billy offered. He wasn't being polite. He just didn't want to get trapped in there, didn't want to turn his back on Fitchett. Better to let the old man lead the way.

"As you wish."

He entered, and Billy followed, looking around him carefully. There wasn't much to see. It was a small area, like a cubicle, with shiny, curved metallic walls and roof, like the rest of the building, and another door on the other side.

"This is an elevator," Billy said. "I've been on one before . . . you know, a long time ago."

"There aren't many operating these days outside of secure facilities and priority government sites. This one is a little different from any elevator you've ever been in before. Down, please."

The door closed and there was a slight motion.

"There are only two floors," Fitchett said. "Top and bottom."

"How far is it between the two floors?" Billy asked. "How many storeys does this elevator go down?"

"It's not really divided into storeys, but it's slightly over six hundred metres, so at three metres per floor that would be around the equivalent of two hundred storeys."

"You're joking, right?"

"No," he said, shaking his head. "We're going down twice the depth that the Empire State Building goes up. Have you ever been to the top of the Empire State Building?"

"I've seen it . . . from a distance," Billy said.

"It was magnificent in its time. I owned it for a while."

"You owned it?" Billy exclaimed.

He shrugged. "Remember, I was the richest man in the world . . . thank goodness. Even after so much was taken from me, I still had the resources left to do all of this."

Billy could feel the elevator slowing down, and then it came to a stop. The door slid open and Billy followed Fitchett out and into bright light. They were outdoors. Somehow they'd gone *up*, not *down*, but why would Fitchett have lied about that?

"It really does look as though we're above ground," Fitchett said.

"We *are* above ground. Why did you tell me we were going down?" Billy demanded.

Fitchett laughed. "We did go down. We're six hundred metres *below* the surface of the Earth."

That was crazy; of course they were above the ground. They were standing in a canyon filled with trees and bushes, and there was a little stream running through, and the sky, the sky was bright and blue and . . . no, it wasn't the sky. It was a ceiling, soaring more than thirty metres above their heads, that *looked* like the sky.

"I . . . I . . . I don't understand," Billy sputtered.

"Don't feel bad. It fools most people," Fitchett said. "We call this the canyon or the outdoor room, for obvious reasons. It's a place where people can come, gather, toss a ball, have a picnic, even wade in the creek and feel as though they're outside. Pretty impressive, isn't it?"

Mouth open, astonished, Billy nodded in agreement.

"We feel that, psychologically, it will benefit our

residents to have the chance to escape the subterranean world, even if it is just an artificial escape. We can even simulate different weather conditions, make it brighter or windier or overcast, and of course, my favourite is the night sky. Nighttime, please!" he called out.

The entire sky slowly darkened, the bright sunlight fading away, and then, slowly, stars began to twinkle and a full moon appeared!

"This is the exact star pattern you would see from this location at this time of year. It is programmed to simulate the rotation of the Earth and the real phases of the moon. Each twenty-four-hour cycle will replicate what would be taking place at the surface, including the same beautiful sunrises and sunsets."

"This is just . . . just . . . I don't have words."

"This is nothing," Fitchett said. "Let's throw a little light on the scene." He raised his hands up to the sky. "Let there be light!" he called out.

The night sky quickly gave way to daytime once again.

"You'll have to excuse me for the God reference, but I *did* create this world. Except much of it was already constructed over a fifty-year period of mining, and then it took me another seventeen years instead of seven days, and I had a whole lot of help."

Billy walked behind Fitchett. He looked all around. It seemed so real—no, *better* than real. He couldn't remember ever seeing anything on the surface that was this perfect.

"The stream is from a spring that leads to the reservoir that provides fresh drinking water to our residents," Fitchett said. He bent down beside the little stream, cupped his hands, and sipped a little. "Ice cold, completely pure."

Billy dipped a hand into the water. It was cold.

They continued to walk and went through a little passage, leaving behind the "outdoors" and entering what looked like a gigantic mall. Again the ceiling soared above their heads, and the lighting, which seemed like sunlight, was bright.

Billy also noticed that they were no longer alone. There were men and women working on construction projects.

"We're down to the finishing touches," Fitchett said. "The electricity is provided by a small nuclear generator. There is a second electric generator that is available in the event of a fault developing with the nuclear power source, and in addition, once the weather on the surface is stable we'll be harvesting the winds to generate power."

"Why three sources of power?"

"It's an unwise man who does not provide a backup plan," Fitchett said.

"But two backups?" Billy asked.

"That's because I'm a *very* wise man. I build in a certain redundancy in everything. I always have a backup plan," he said. "But you'd know about that . . . always making sure you have an alternative."

Billy did understand. He had lived his life always looking for the alternate route, whether it was to escape, or to obtain something, or to defeat somebody.

"Within this facility are separate living accommodations for over twelve hundred people, with the potential to expand to sixteen hundred as time passes."

"I don't understand . . . where will the extra people come from?"

Fitchett laughed. "Births. You have to remember that the projections call for the surface to be uninhabitable for a minimum of twenty years."

That thought came as a sobering reality. So this was the old man's plan: to create a compound, a complete environment, that would house his "chosen" ones—and the generation to follow—after the asteroid hit. Billy knew that survivalists talked about going underground until the planet's surface stabilized; he just hadn't thought of it needing to be for that long. What would it be like to live underground for all that time? If he didn't leave, he realized, he might be finding out.

"I'm going to show you everything," Fitchett said. "There's a medical facility, as well as an entertainment complex with copies of every movie, television show, CD, and book ever made. We have a school that has databases of all known information and a record of all languages. In our museum we have accumulated artifacts of cultural and societal significance from around the world. In fact, we have some of the world's greatest pieces of art, including the *Mona Lisa* and—"

"Even I know the *Mona Lisa* is in Paris," Billy snorted.

"It *was* in Paris. Now in its place is a very good forgery. We have had, shall we say, *assistance* in moving treasures to our museum. Among the people who will be taking resi-dence underground when the asteroid strikes are the director of the Louvre, his wife, and their young daughter. We offered them sanctuary, and they offered the preservation of some of the greatest pieces of art the world has ever known. Those will be maintained for future generations of mankind." He paused. "There *will* be future generations."

Billy believed him. Billy wanted to believe him.

"There is a separate technological archive that contains schematic drawings and plans for every known mechanical device in the world, details of all patented items, and samples of the most significant inventions, from the chariot to the cement mixer, from the first cars and airplanes to hovercrafts and jets, computers, duplication machines, printing presses, and all the mechanisms needed to recreate a functioning society.

"There are full sports and exercise facilities for those who will live here, stores, facilities to repair and replace all components, and storage areas. And of course we had to plan for a significant agricultural capacity. We have over twenty-five acres of land under intense cultivation—enough capacity to feed the entire colony. Soil was brought from the surface, and the lighting is, of course, all artificial. But before we go on, I need to show you the very cornerstone of our project. This is one of *the* most impressive parts."

Billy could scarcely imagine what might be more impressive than what he'd already seen, but he'd started to learn not to doubt Fitchett. Wasn't that what Christina had said? *They never make mistakes.*

He hurried to catch up to Fitchett, who moved very quickly for an old man.

"Are you religious, Billy?"

"I used to go to church with my parents . . . you know . . . before."

"And do you remember any of the Bible stories? David and Goliath? Or Jonah and the whale? Adam and Eve?"

"I remember some of them."

"How about the story of Noah and the Ark?"

"Yeah, I know that one."

"Tell me what you remember," Fitchett said.

"Well, it's about a man named Noah, and God told him he was going to destroy the Earth by flooding it."

"Yes, a deluge from above," Fitchett said.

"Forty days and forty nights," Billy said. "And that's why Noah was asked to build an ark, to save himself and his family."

"And the animals, which were innocent?" Fitchett asked.

"Yeah, that's right. They came on board the ark, two by two, a pair of every type of animal."

"Exactly!" Fitchett agreed. "What an incredible story."

"But you don't actually believe it, do you?" Billy asked.

"Of course not. Do I look like a member of Judgment Day? The story lacks both science and logic. It would have been impossible with the technology of that period to build an ark sufficiently large to hold all those animals and the food they would require during a voyage of that length."

"Well, it is just a story," Billy said.

"But even stories have to be credible. And having only one pair of animals would not provide the genetic diversity necessary to reproduce a species. A pair would be nothing. In order to do that, you would need approximately *fifty* breeding pairs."

Billy laughed. "So you think it's not credible that he could build a boat big enough to hold a pair of every animal, but you think it should have been *fifty* pairs of everything, so the boat would have had to be that much bigger."

"Much bigger. Fifty *breeding* pairs, or one hundred individual samples, are necessary to repopulate. Noah could not have had the space. But we do. And it's all right behind these doors," he said as he patted the heavy wooden door.

Billy looked up at the doors before them. A sign read "The Ark" in large letters. He had a vision of hundreds of animals being contained there. Lions and tigers and elephants running around and . . . that made no sense. They at least had to be in cages. Separate cages.

Fitchett opened the door and Billy held his breath. There was no sound. No smell. They stepped inside. It looked much more like a library than a zoo. No, not like a library, like a room full of gigantic dressers, ten drawers high, lining the walls and stretching out into the distance as far as he could see.

"In these drawers are one hundred samples of the DNA of every living organism, every example of flora and fauna on the entire planet."

Billy touched one of the drawers. "In here are lions and tigers."

"And all other forms of life. Our goal is not simply to ensure the survival of human life. We aim to guarantee the survival of *all* forms of life on Earth. When the planet can once again support their existence on the surface, then we shall make the waters teem with living creatures, and let birds fly above the Earth, and let the land produce living creatures according to their kinds."

"I . . . I think I know those words," Billy said, but he didn't know from where or why.

"You said you know the Bible stories, so you might have heard them before. Genesis, chapter one, verses twenty through twenty-four . . . of course I'm paraphrasing God."

Then it hit Billy. He understood . . . at least a little part of it. "The kids—like Christina—they're just like those animals. That's why they're here . . . to repopulate the Earth."

Fitchett nodded.

"The children are amazing specimens. Not only are they brilliant, talented, and skilled, but they are unfailingly polite, quiet, respectful, and compliant—they will basically do whatever they're told to do. They were genetically screened—they have virtually no genetic weaknesses. They are as close to human perfection as can be developed. In essence, they are *very* different from you."

Billy's eyes widened in shock.

"Don't look so surprised. They have been raised, in most cases from birth, in our facilities, in the collectives. They have been screened, nurtured, schooled, and trained according to a very detailed schedule to develop their skills and, ultimately, to repopulate the planet with superior human beings."

"But like you said, I'm not like them," he said. "Why am I here? There's nothing special about me."

"Really?" Fitchett asked. "That boy you knocked down in the dining hall, do you know what his specialization is?"

"No."

"He is trained in mechanical engineering. There is very little that he doesn't know about mechanics, including how to repair and craft mechanical devices. He is fully trained, incredibly bright, highly skilled, and those skills could be invaluable. How long do you think he would survive in the world you came from?"

Billy laughed. "He wouldn't make it through the day."

"But *you* made it through the day, and through many days and years. Do you see what I'm getting at?"

Maybe he did. "Are you saying my skill, my specialization, is that I know how to survive? Is that why I'm here, to be one of them?"

Fitchett shook his head. "You are *not* here to be *one* of them."

Billy felt a rush of fear. Had he been shown all of this simply to be thrown out? Had he somehow failed, or somehow even convinced the old man that he had nothing special to offer?

"You are not going to be *one* of them because you are going to be their *leader*."

"What?" he exclaimed.

"They need leadership. In trying to give them the best of humanity we somehow failed to give them some essential parts of humanity. Somehow I was so occupied in the mechanics of the process that I failed to fully understand the fuel that drives those mechanics. We were so focused on giving them only the best that we separated them from those interconnected parts that drive the best. Whether we label it aggression or tenacity, or simply the stubborn determination to survive against all odds, they seem to be lacking those qualities. Once the asteroid hits, anything can happen, and we can't predict what will be needed to survive. That is your specialty, and none of them possesses that to a degree sufficient to ensure their survival."

"I'm in here because I survived being out there?"

"Yes, exactly."

"But lots of people survived . . . lots of people were out there. Why me?" Billy persisted.

"You not only survived, you created a little society in which kindness and caring were present. That's the kind of leadership they will need."

"I can't lead them."

"Yes, you can."

"But you're the leader . . . aren't you?" Billy asked.

"I will be among a group of over a thousand adults who will also be in the complex when the asteroid hits, but the time of my leadership will end. You have to remember that I'm eighty-four years old."

"Really?"

"Judging by your reaction you thought I was either much older or much younger."

"Younger. Like, I knew you were old. I just didn't know you were *that* old."

Fitchett laughed. "I'll take that as a compliment. I am here now. I won't be when humanity returns to the surface of the planet. That will be under your leadership." He placed his hand on Billy's shoulder. "And I know you'll be the leader they need."

CHAPTER NINETEEN

T MINUS 9 MONTHS

CAPE CANAVERAL, FLORIDA

Sheppard followed along at the end of the group, trying to be inconspicuous. As they made their way through the gigantic spaceship, the only sounds were the voice of the guide explaining its features and the click of their feet against the metal floor. The mood was solemn, as though they were attending a funeral, when in reality it was more like a birth, or at least a rebirth. Sheppard also got the feeling that the hushed words and careful steps were a reaction to what surrounded them, as though they were afraid that if they spoke too loudly the devices would somehow be activated and they would all be incinerated. There was no danger of that, of course, and they knew it—they had been told about all of the safeguards that were in place. But still, the mind played its tricks.

It was intimidating enough to be in close proximity to even *one* nuclear warhead, let alone this many. It was almost beyond comprehension to think that they were standing on one of the decks of a spaceship that held fifteen hundred thermonuclear devices. That was the entire payload of the ship, its entire cargo, with the exception of the mechanisms necessary to arm and activate them.

There had been a tremendous debate before it was finally decided that this ship, and the others like it, would fly unmanned. Many wanted the comfort, the familiarity of the human presence piloting the ships and then arming and activating the explosives. Others wanted the ships manned by their own countrymen—to have the glory of being the nation that saved the world. Countries had been battling for too many centuries to completely put aside their parochial positions and support a world movement.

Ultimately they'd had to confront the sobering reality that not only would these astronauts be sent on a suicide mission, but they would be more vulnerable, more frail, and more prone to error. In essence, they would be less able to execute the mission than the cold certainty of computers. Besides, the computers wouldn't need the life-support mechanisms and supplies necessary to keep humans alive for a three-month journey. All of that constituted weight that took away from the payload—hundreds of thousands of kilograms that could then be devoted to carrying warheads.

In the end, sentiment gave way to scientific reasoning. Humans were a detriment. Humans *weren't* necessary. How ironic—people in the ships weren't necessary to save humanity on the ground; they could only get in the way.

Sheppard recognized many of the other people in the tour group. Aside from the obvious, the president and vice-president of the United States and the leaders of the House, there were prime ministers and presidents and dictators from other countries in the western hemisphere. The United States was the only nuclear power in the hemisphere, but each of these countries had participated in making this mission a reality. All countries, with all the means at their disposal, had worked in concert to save the planet. They all had a right to be here to represent their people, to see the end result of their efforts. Well . . . not the end, but at least, hopefully, the beginning of the end.

Nobody in the group recognized Sheppard or paid him the slightest attention. He was a little man in a wrinkled suit whose image was lost among the stars that walked with him. He was actually grateful for and reassured by that. Grateful because it meant he didn't have to talk about the mission. Reassured because if the president of the United States didn't know what he looked like, then it was unlikely any potential assassin would either. He wouldn't be the first target of any maniac with a gun. And there were people with guns all around them.

The entire ship was lined with guards, as were the launch site and the perimeter of the facility. Sheppard had been told there were over twenty thousand agents, police, and soldiers providing the security. He wondered if that would be enough.

It was official policy that Sheppard never appeared publicly, and all of the pictures that could be found of him prior to entering the program had been destroyed. There were many posts and blogs that *claimed* to have images of him. Sheppard had seen some of them, and they were laughable. One of the pictures showed him weighing about 150 kilograms; in another he was black, and he looked very athletic . . . which was more fanciful still.

There was one site, though, that had come frighteningly close to the truth. Sheppard had seen the picture, faded and fuzzy but unmistakable. It was him, part of a group shot taken at a conference two decades earlier. He could only hope that that image, one among the thousands that seemed to populate the Internet, wouldn't be the one that was focused on.

Sheppard had originally been hesitant to join the tour. Of course he wanted to be on site for the launch, but being on the tour was as close to being "out in public" as he'd been in years. He just needed to be there. After years of theoretical discussions, debate, mathematical calculations, and planning, the abstract had at last become reality. He needed to see it all with his own eyes, not hear about it in reports or see it play out on a screen. He wanted it to be real. He needed it to be real—although he still had trouble believing it.

This rocket—*these* rockets armed with nuclear devices were the physical result of the last twenty-four years of his intellectual life . . . the lives of tens of thousands of scientists and technicians and theorists and engineers from around the world. This was the culmination of the thinking of the greatest minds on the planet, the result of combining the resources of the entire world, with the most skilled labour. And it was all dedicated to one goal—to destroy or deflect the asteroid, to save the planet and the lives of billions of people.

He chuckled quietly to himself. No wonder it didn't seem real. It was more like something that he might have imagined in a daydream when he was a boy. That little boy was still there inside him.

Of course, back then he wouldn't have been dreaming of designing the program. He'd have wanted to be an astronaut riding in that rocket. That dream had ultimately been defeated by bad eyesight and a heart murmur, but it had led him to his eventual career. Maybe he could never get to space, but he could learn everything there was to *know* about space.

Now everything depended upon these ships having a successful launch.

Outside the perimeter of the facility, beyond the outermost fence, there were millions and millions of people waiting, wanting, needing to be part of it, if only by witnessing it from a distance. Sheppard also knew that this launch, and the launch of all the other ships from space ports around the world, would be seen through live feed, by almost every single person on the planet.

Their best estimate was that there were over three million people outside the fence. Most were hoping and even praying for the success of the mission. A secondary group, supporters of Judgment Day, were, of course, holding silent vigils and praying for its failure. The police maintained a presence between the two groups. A large faction of the Judgment Day group advocated violent opposition to the launch, and they might attempt to sabotage the project, destroy the rockets, or kill those responsible for their creation. This was their last and best chance to bring about the Rapture, the End of Days. Once the ships left Earth, it truly would be in the hands of God, because nobody on the planet would be able to stop what had by then been put into motion.

Sheppard, along with most of the scientists, observers, and dignitaries, had been flown in by helicopter, its flight path coming in off the ocean. There was less chance of a helicopter being shot down over the open waters, and security reports indicated that Judgment Day did possess ground-to-air weapons that could take down a helicopter or plane. The real fear, though, was that they had weapons that could take down a rocket, and that was why the security zones had been made so large around the launch sites.

"Excuse me," somebody asked the guide. "Just how powerful are the bombs on this ship?"

"The fifteen hundred devices on this ship," the guide explained, "have over seventy-five thousand times the explosive power of the bomb that was dropped on Hiroshima."

"And do each of the fourteen ships to be launched have equal capacity?" someone asked.

"Yes, in total there are twenty-one thousand devices that will be sent into space today from all the launch facilities."

Sheppard smiled to himself when he heard the word "devices." That was one of the words they'd all been told to use, along with "tool." There were other words that were to be avoided. They included "bomb," "warheads," and "thermonuclear."

"The devices on the two ships at this facility constitute one-third of the entire explosive capacity of the United States."

"And the remaining two-thirds?" a man with a thick accent asked.

"They will be launched from the British site, along with the entire English arsenal. As you are all aware, fourteen ships, each carrying fifteen hundred devices, will be launched today. Two rockets at each of seven locations—the U.S., Russia, Britain, France, India, and Pakistan."

"And all at once," somebody noted.

"There will be two synchronized launches at all sites. The initial launch will have seven ships. The second launch from each site will take place exactly thirty minutes after the first. This level of synchronization is necessary to allow all the ships to travel in a coordinated manner toward their destination."

That was a lie—although the guide didn't know it. They could have launched the ships weeks apart and adjusted speeds to allow them all to arrive at the asteroid at the same time. The launches were being done simultaneously because the large powers wanted to see their traditional enemies send warheads up at the same time. No nuclear countries—least of all the United States and Russia—wanted other countries to possess warheads when their own capacity had been launched into space. They didn't want to have the asteroid destroyed and the planet saved if they couldn't dominate it once again. Any country with even a few nuclear bombs left, if others had none, could simply erase an old enemy from the face of the planet.

As the bombs had travelled to their launch sites, they had been accompanied by a verification team. This was a group made up of representatives of all the nuclear countries, the United Nations, and selected neutral countries. Their task was to ensure that the weapons were protected at all times and then positioned as agreed on the ships. Trust only went so far, even in the face of an apocalypse.

"I was wondering," a man said, "if something happens during liftoff, are we safe being this close to so many nuclear devices?"

"This has been the most technically precise operation in the history of the world. Every effort has been made to assure that nothing will go wrong," the guide said confidently.

He was either a complete believer or an incredible liar, because his words didn't even hint at the possibility of failure.

Failure . . . Sheppard couldn't even entertain that thought. Failure wasn't an option. Besides, he had strong evidence to support his belief that this would succeed. First, there was all the theory, all the mathematics, all the calculations studied, checked, and rechecked. Beyond that, they had run innumerable simulations. Sheppard's faith in science was as complete and absolute as the belief of the Judgment Day adherents in the tenets of their own faith.

"You will all be viewing the launch in blast-proof bunkers that have been placed at a sufficient distance to ensure your safety," the guide continued.

"Nuclear-proof bunkers?" the man asked skeptically.

"Even if there were a malfunction at liftoff—and that will *not* happen—there is absolutely no danger of a nuclear device being triggered. Each device has a fail-safe that precludes detonation prior to a direct order initiating a sequence of events to enable and arm the nuclear mechanism. These orders will be sent via radio when the ships have achieved the correct position with respect to the asteroid. Now, I must defer any more questions as it is almost time for us to leave the ship. Please follow me as we proceed to the bunkers."

Quietly the group started to shuffle forward, following the guide to the elevator that would take them to the ground and the vehicles waiting to ferry them to the bunkers. Sheppard held back to allow the group to move away. He wanted to be alone for a few seconds. This was a historic moment—one of the most important moments in the entire story of mankind—and he wanted to drink it in.

He waited for the noise of the crowd to fade away. He stood there in silence, surrounded by enough explosive power to bring about a fiery apocalypse on Earth. How ironic, how strange, how unforeseen all of this was. For decades, mankind had lived in fear that these nuclear weapons would end life on this planet. Now they were its only hope for survival.

He reached out and put his hand against the casing of one of the warheads—not a "device" or a "tool" but a thermonuclear bomb.

"Good luck," he said. "Be a good little bomb."

"How cute."

He turned around. It was, of course, Parker, his body-guard. In the rush of the events he'd somehow forgotten he was there in the background. Parker had been with him for seventeen years, his ever-present shadow, so perhaps it was unsurprising that Sheppard didn't register him as being there any longer. Of course, their involvement went even farther back. Parker's was the first face Sheppard had seen when his eyes popped open on the fateful night he was kidnapped from his house.

"Do you want to tuck it in? Or can we leave now so *we're* not launched into space?" Parker asked.

"I think we should leave. I'm just not looking forward to the elevator ride down to the ground."

Parker laughed, and his deep baritone echoed off the walls. "You're surrounded by enough firepower to blow up the planet, and you're afraid of the elevator?"

"I didn't have a say in the design of the elevator," Sheppard replied.

They walked down the corridor toward the elevator. Parker was, of course, much more than simply Sheppard's security chief. Over the years he'd become a confidant, a person who could synthesize information more quickly than almost anybody Sheppard knew, a trusted aide.

"They asked a lot of questions," Parker said, "but nobody asked the one question that's on everybody's mind." He paused. "Do you think this is going to work?"

"The launch?" Sheppard asked.

"You know what I mean."

Sheppard nodded his head. "I know what I'm supposed to say to anybody who asks that question," he answered. "Nothing but confidence. Total faith in the success of the project."

"And the truth?"

For a few seconds Sheppard thought about providing the technical answers, but he knew that wasn't what Parker wanted.

"Really, nobody knows for certain. That answer will have to wait for three months or longer."

"Why longer? Aren't the intercept and detonation scheduled for three months?" Parker asked.

"Yes, but we won't know for possibly weeks after the explosion if what we did was successful."

"And do you think it will be successful?" he asked again.

"As I said, nobody knows—"

"I'm not asking what you *know*. I'm asking what you *think*. Of the nine billion people on this planet, nobody's more knowledgeable about this than you. What do you think is going to happen?"

Sheppard hesitated for a few seconds, gathering his thoughts. If there was anybody in the world he could be completely honest with it was Parker. Seventeen years at his side had proven that.

"There are a number of very critical moments, all of which must be successful in their sequence for the entire operation to be successful."

"So if one of those steps falls through, the whole operation fails?"

"Not necessarily 'fails' but becomes more problematic. And we are here to witness the riskiest of those steps, the launch of these ships into space. In a mission this massively complex there is always risk of error or failure, and today we are multiplying that risk by a factor of fourteen. In this case, there is also the additional risk of somebody trying to sabotage or destroy the rockets."

"Okay," said Parker, "so just for the sake of discussion, what will happen if something goes wrong with *one* of those liftoffs?"

"One will not constitute failure, if everything else works along the way," Sheppard explained. "But there's enormous potential for complications over the course of three months travelling through space—a ship going off course, a collision with a small object, stellar dust fouling the equipment, a failure to respond to the radio signal, some of the devices responding prematurely and destroying other ships, to name just a few possibilities."

The elevator door opened and they stepped in. Parker looked at Sheppard. "Not to mention the possibility of the elevator crashing and killing one of the most important people in the project."

Sheppard smiled nervously at the joke. He didn't like to admit it, but over the past decade he had been *the* most important person. Their first leader, Dr. Hay, who had been in charge when he was "enlisted," had simply died. She hadn't looked well for years. She was replaced by Donahue, who was killed—most people thought in a car accident, but Sheppard was one of the few people to know it had been an assassination. Some of the guards assigned to provide for his safety had been moles for Judgment Day and they killed him before taking their own lives—and, if what they believed was true, finding their souls soaring to Heaven while Donahue's dropped to the depths of Hell. Donahue was replaced by Dr. Markell, who combined genius with a quirky sense of creativity. Ultimately that quirkiness was his undoing. He found himself in a strange position. He was the ultimate rebel, fighting against authority, and suddenly he had become the ultimate authority, telling everybody else what to do. He was forced to step down—too valuable to lose completely, but unable to lead, or even be fully trusted to make the right decisions independently.

And then there was Sheppard.

Of course Sheppard knew there was another level of leadership entirely—shadowy figures and world leaders who made decisions unrelated to the scientific purpose of the project. But really, he didn't need to know those people. All he knew was that they never interfered with the science, and they gave them the resources and security necessary to carry out their mission.

The door slid shut, they started to go down, and all Sheppard could think about was the impending crash of the elevator.

CHAPTER TWENTY

The massive room was filled with scientists and technicians, all monitoring and coordinating the launch of the first ship. They either sat at the desks and consoles that filled the room or were frantically buzzing about. Despite the level of what looked like chaos to Sheppard, everything was going as planned. Everybody knew their job. It was calm, controlled chaos, overseen by the best and the brightest.

Sheppard secured a corner of the room and tried to stay out of the way. Ironically, there was really nothing for him to do now. It was as if he had invented the internal combustion engine but had no idea how to drive the car . . . actually, he really didn't know how to drive.

The electronic voice over the PA announced, *"T minus seven minutes."* So far, everything was on schedule and going according to plan.

Sheppard sat quietly in his chair, watching, trying to make sense of what was going on around him. His eye was caught by the far wall of the control room, which was dominated by a bank of television screens. They were showing closed-circuit live feed from the other launch sites around the world. Cameras recorded the ships themselves, the facilities, the security, and the crowds outside the perimeter.

Parker was standing in front of one of the screens and staring intently. Sheppard knew that if that screen was significant enough for Parker to be interested in, it had to be important. In a blur of activity Parker could always sort out the wheat from the chaff. He'd once told Sheppard that his whole job—and Sheppard's life—depended on that skill.

Sheppard joined him. The screen showed images of riot policemen, shields up, batons swinging, charging into a crowd. There were clouds of tear gas in the air and people on the ground, some of them not moving.

"Where is that?" Sheppard asked.

"Just outside our gates. A large group tried to breach the security fence."

"Oh, my goodness!"

"They were repelled, but not without loss of life."

"People died?" Sheppard gasped.

"Not many. Estimates have it at fewer than three hundred."

"And you consider three hundred people 'not many'?" Sheppard couldn't believe his ears.

"It's all relative," Parker explained. He pointed to another screen. "In France, there have been over four thousand deaths already confirmed."

There was a scene of cars burning and people fleeing, others throwing rocks and bricks, and the ground was littered with the injured and dead.

"That many people tried to enter their launch site?" Sheppard questioned.

"Judgment Day followers tried to storm the facility. They were attacked by others, who were there to cheer on our efforts. The fighting between the two groups became a riot. Very few deaths were caused by our security forces."

"And what about the other launch sites?" Sheppard asked.

"Britain has been relatively quiet. Same for Russia, India, and China."

"And Pakistan?"

"The entire country has been the site of mass demonstrations and riots for the past week. Additional troops from the United Nations were airlifted to protect the launch site. Estimates are that over twenty-five thousand people have been killed."

"Why didn't I hear anything about this?" Sheppard asked.

"What value would there have been in telling you?" Parker asked. "There was nothing you could do, and it was felt that you needed to focus your time and energy on any last-minute changes that might need to take place."

Sheppard couldn't argue with the logic.

"*T minus one minute,*" came the announcement.

"Are you going to have a seat?" Parker asked.

Sheppard shook his head. "I think this is a good place to watch all seven of the launches."

The top bank of screens showed all seven rockets at their launch pads. The location of each was given at the bottom of the screen, and they were arranged alphabetically, from left to right: China, England, France, India, Pakistan, Russia, and the United States.

"*T minus thirty seconds.*"

The tension in the room jumped up a notch. Now nobody was rushing around. All attention was focused on the controls and consoles. A voice in the background began to count down.

"*T minus 25 . . . 24 . . . all systems are go . . . 22 . . . 21 . . . 20 . . . guidance system released . . . 18 . . . 17 . . .*"

The only other sounds in the room were radio transmissions relaying information or confirming that things were as they should be. Every eye was focused either on the control panels or on the visual of the rocket sitting at the tower.

"*We have commit . . . 9 . . . 8 . . . 7 . . . 6 . . . we have ignition . . . 4 . . . 3 . . . 2 . . . 1 . . . we have liftoff.*"

The whole control room started to shake slightly as flames erupted from the bottom of the rocket, oranges and reds that became brilliant white as a cloud of smoke shot out. The rocket, almost in slow motion, began to rise from the ground.

"*It has cleared the tower . . . 34.5 million newtons of thrust . . . it has cleared the tower.*"

Despite the calmness of the voice, Sheppard knew this

was significant. Most malfunctions happened in the first few metres from the ground.

The ship quickly gained speed and elevation. The camera followed it up into the sky.

"Altitude 0.8 kilometres. . . trajectory is good . . . launch is good."

There was a cheer from the room.

Sheppard turned to the screens above his head. He scanned from one image to the next to the next. All seven flights looked good, but what could he tell from a picture?

"China reports successful launch," the announcer said. *"Russia reports successful launch. India reports successful launch. Britain reports successful launch. France reports successful launch."*

That left only one site—Pakistan. Sheppard looked at that screen. The rocket was disappearing into the clouds. Was there a problem?

"Pakistan reports successful launch. All seven sites confirm successful launches."

There was another cheer, even louder than the first, and then almost instantly the technicians settled back into their tasks. There was another launch scheduled in less than thirty minutes, so there was no time for a more prolonged celebration, and really, there wasn't cause for celebration yet.

"Feeling better?" Parker asked.

"Halfway to feeling better. I was anxious when the Pakistan site didn't report in right away."

"I wasn't worried about that site," Parker said.

"Why not?"

"Dictatorships and military governments have the capacity to do whatever they need to do to make a launch successful. We had enough security on the ground to safeguard that site."

"Even though it meant the deaths of thousands of people," Sheppard pointed out.

"I'm more worried about the riots in France," Parker said. "Democracies, even in today's distorted reality, still have to try, or appear to try, to follow the general rules of law."

"Is that what we call it . . . the general rules of law?" Sheppard asked.

"It's the best that can be done, and I guess it's been good enough. We've managed to keep sufficient order in place to launch those rockets . . . although, quite frankly, there were many times when I thought the whole thing was going to break down into complete anarchy."

"Was it really that close?" Sheppard asked.

"It's been a long time since you've been outside one of our complexes. You'd hardly recognize life out there. Food and resources are scarce, safety and security and law and order are even rarer."

"I really have lived in a bubble," Sheppard admitted.

"Which is the only reason you have lived. Out there it's become the proverbial jungle, with survival of the fittest the only real law in many places. It's come to what Thomas Hobbes suggested life is: poor, nasty, brutish, and rather short."

Sheppard knew he was right, but he also knew he didn't want to think about any of that anymore. He had to stay focused on the task at hand. He turned back to the screens. They were still following the rockets, which were getting smaller and smaller as they gained elevation and jettisoned the spent stages of the booster rockets. Soon they would be in space, safe from any possible interference or sabotage, heading toward the asteroid with nuclear warheads as their cargo.

If none of the second set of launches was successful, there would still be enough firepower to create the second-strongest power source in the solar system—second only to the sun. In fact, when all the nuclear bombs were deployed and exploded at the same time, as planned, then the flash would be twenty or thirty times brighter than the sun, and anybody watching without eye protection would experience corneal damage, risking at least temporary blindness.

Other screens showed the next rockets at the second towers, waiting to launch. It was exciting and sobering. All the success of the first seven rockets was washed away in the possibility that something could happen to the next seven ships.

"I'm going to step outside for a while," Sheppard said.

Parker got up to accompany him.

"You don't have to go. I'll be fine."

"You will be fine and I *do* have to go," Parker replied.

There was no point in arguing. Sheppard knew the rules as well as Parker did. There was no choice. He had to be protected at all times.

They exited the bunker. It was brighter outside, but the residue of the rocket firing had created a haze that partially blocked the sun.

"Do you smell it?" Parker asked.

"Yes, very strong. Is that rocket fuel?"

"Tear gas," he said. "It's blowing back from the demonstrations."

"I just wish none of that was happening out there," Sheppard said. "I regret every life that has to be taken."

"Sometimes you have to break a few eggs to make an omelette."

"These aren't eggs, Parker. They're human lives."

"Which have to be sacrificed for the common good. We're trying to save over nine billion lives, so losing a few thousand, even a few hundred thousand—that has to be an acceptable trade-off, wouldn't you think?"

"I suppose it makes sense, if you think about it that way," Sheppard said.

"There is no *other* way to think about it. This is a war, and in times of war there will be casualties. We have to do whatever is necessary to ensure the victory for the *good* guys, and *we're* the good guys. Heck, if you think about it, we're even trying to save the lives of the bad guys, the guys trying to kill us!"

"I wish everybody thought of us that way. It's hard to be considered the Devil incarnate by so many people. There must be hundreds of thousands of people who want me dead."

"No," Parker said, shaking his head. "It's *much* more than that. I would say more like twenty or thirty million people think you're evil and would happily dance on your grave."

"That's *so* much more reassuring."

"Just stating a fact. And remember that even though

millions of people want you dead, there are *billions* of good people, even deeply religious people, who pray for our success. I'll take billions over millions any day."

"I guess you're right," Sheppard admitted.

"I *know* I'm right. And these people who hate you are hardly innocents. They would take your life, my life, and the lives of all of these scientists in a second. And in doing so they would not only cause the deaths of billions, but destroy untold billions of people still to be born. How much sympathy can you have for people who want to destroy mankind?"

Sheppard had never seen Parker speak so passionately. He was always so cool, calm, professional—unseen eyes behind dark sunglasses watching everything around him, never showing his emotions.

"I think it's time for us to get back inside for the next launches," Parker said.

Sheppard was happy to head back into the bunker. Suddenly he felt very exposed standing outside. He wondered if any of those millions of people who wanted him dead were close at hand, just outside the fence . . . or even closer.

It was like watching a replay of the first round of launches. Sheppard knew that the success or failure of each launch was an independent variable, but having seen seven successes already he felt more confident. The announcer again gave the countdown.

"*We have commit . . . 9 . . . 8 . . . 7 . . . 6 . . . we have ignition . . . 4 . . . 3 . . . 2 . . . 1 . . . we have liftoff.*"

The ground started to shake and the rockets on all screens began to lift off. The announcer gave more assurances as the rockets gained elevation. With these ships and the seven already in orbit, that meant that—

Sheppard's eyes widened in shock as the image on the middle screen exploded into a fireball in the sky!

CHAPTER TWENTY-ONE

IDAHO, THIRTY MINUTES EARLIER

The sound was deafening and the room seemed to shake. All around them, on screens that filled the room, Joshua Fitchett and Billy watched as the first rockets soared into the sky. Seven ships from seven launch sites, and all were perfect. The cameras on the ground continued to follow them until they got smaller and smaller and finally disappeared from view.

Fitchett muted the sound and they stood in silence.

"That was amazing," Billy said.

"It's even more amazing in person."

"You've been to a launch?"

"You have to remember that this facility was once used as a launch site for satellites. I've been here for more than twenty-five launches. As well, I've been party to another dozen launches at the Cape Canaveral site. My companies developed and manufactured many of the components in those ships. Aerospace technology has always been one of my areas of interest and expertise."

"Everything seems to be your area of interest and expertise," Billy noted.

"You have to find lots of things interesting when you're trying to build a new world."

"How much time is there until the next launches?"

"The plan is for a thirty-minute interval, so we won't have long to wait."

"They seem so confident that if they can get all those ships into space and explode all those bombs, they can save the planet. But you don't think it'll have any effect?"

"I'm sure it will have *some* effect," Fitchett said.

"But not the effect of stopping the asteroid from hitting Earth?" Billy asked.

"There's always a chance it might work. But it could have other, negative effects. Do you understand the law of unintended consequences?"

Billy shook his head. Joshua Fitchett was always trying to teach him things, and he was always trying to understand. Over the past months the two of them had spent large parts of each day together. Sure, Fitchett was teaching him about "leadership," but more than that, there was a genuine connection between the two. Fitchett had told Billy that he found the other children "unsettling" in many ways and boring in others—perfection *was* rather boring. In Billy, though, he saw not only the potential but the raw edges, the pieces of him that made him rough but real. He even saw a little bit of himself, he said. Fitchett knew what it meant to survive.

"In its simplest form, the law of unintended consequences states that when we attempt to seek one end, we can create results, either negative or positive, other than those we initially sought. In practical terms, it refers more to the negative consequences."

"So by trying to do something good, you could end up doing something bad instead," Billy said.

"Exactly."

Billy was glad he understood. Sometimes what Fitchett was saying was just too technical or complicated—at least at first. Billy wasn't shy about saying he didn't understand something. He always made sure to have Fitchett explain until he did understand. The older man never seemed to mind, never seemed frustrated. He had once told Billy that if you can't explain something in a way that a seven-year-old can understand, you really don't know it yourself. Through the months, through their time together, through their discussions, Billy had learned that Fitchett *did* seem to know everything. That was reassuring, because everybody's life depended on it.

It was also reassuring in a different way. For years Billy had had to rely on himself for his very survival. And on top of that, there had been hundreds of others depending on him. Here he just had to *be*, and he was taken care of. He could understand how this might lull you into complacency. He'd wondered if the mere fact of being here would take away the qualities that had led to them bringing him here in the first place. He kept those doubts to himself.

Billy also couldn't help but wonder about those he'd left behind. He knew that they had more food and water and resources—Fitchett had kept his word on that score. But still, in some ways that only made them a target for those who didn't have enough. In a flash, he understood in his gut the law of unintended consequences.

"But what they're doing, trying to destroy the asteroid . . . I don't see how any unintended consequence could be worse. How could anything else not be better than what's going to happen, the world being destroyed?"

"Ah, that's where you're having difficulty, because you're working with the wrong premise. It is a 100 percent certainty that the asteroid will *not* destroy the world."

"It won't?" Billy said. "But you just said that what they're doing probably won't be successful."

"I'm saying both. On its present course, the asteroid will hit the world, killing almost all its life forms, but it will not destroy the *world*. Simply the vast majority of all *life forms* on it."

"Including all of us."

"Probably not you and me or the people in this project specifically, but most certainly all higher forms of flora and fauna, including the remaining nine billion people on the planet."

"So how could what they're doing cause anything worse to happen?" Billy asked. "It isn't like everybody can be killed twice. Either it hits Earth and everybody dies, or it misses Earth and we all live."

"Again, a faulty premise. If they change the course of the asteroid, but only slightly, then it could result in a glancing blow to our planet, causing an alteration of Earth's orbit."

"What does that mean?"

"Most likely it would result in Earth being nudged closer to the sun, which would cause massive climatic changes, probably resulting in the planet becoming too hot to sustain life on the surface. We're equipping the subterranean world to survive a temporary change in Earth's atmosphere so that our people can eventually reclaim the surface. Under that scenario, the alteration of the orbit, those underground will never resurface, and all of our efforts will have been wasted."

Billy felt a shudder go through his entire body. It had taken three months for him to even entertain the thought that life—that *his* life—could go on below ground, and now even that prospect was in jeopardy.

"So we'd be better off if they just left the asteroid alone," he said.

"We'd be *best* off if they could cause it to miss Earth completely. After that, the possible consequences of their efforts, the unintended consequences, might not be in our best interests," Fitchett explained. "Let's just hope they're successful."

"So there is a chance, right?"

"There are so many variables that are beyond our control, it's hard to provide anything more than a guesstimate."

"And your guess?" Billy asked.

"They've already overcome tremendous odds to get this far. Personally, I never thought they'd be able to coordinate the work of countries around the world. Somehow they were able to convince governments—even traditional enemies, those with conflicting ideologies and values—to work for a common goal. Then, under the leadership of a remarkable team of scientists, they were able to devise a functional plan. Again, almost impossible. Finally, they built the ships and armed them with nuclear devices capable of generating a force sufficient to effect an orbit-altering change to a planetary body. And they have managed to do all of that despite the efforts of a worldwide movement, Judgment Day, that is dedicated to stopping them and thinks nothing of killing scientists or destroying the facilities they need to complete their job."

It wasn't just the Aerospace Institute program that Judgment Day was hindering, though. Without even knowing Fitchett's project existed, they were endangering its efforts as well. But Billy wasn't worried. Fitchett kept finding ways around what they were doing.

"And today," Fitchett continued, "they have already successfully launched half the fleet. With each step, the odds continue to tilt in the institute's favour."

"So you think the chances are increasing that Earth—I mean, *life* on Earth—can be saved?" Billy asked.

"I'm saying that they now have a much greater chance of initiating an *attempt*. Will that attempt be successful? I don't know. I would say they have increased the odds from virtually none to 1 or even 2 percent. Not the kind of odds I'd bank on for my survival."

"And that's why you've done all of this," Billy said, gesturing around him. "Everything you've worked for, planned, created is based on the assumption that all efforts will fail and that Earth will be hit." Billy paused. "Or is all of this . . . all of *us* . . . are we just a backup plan in case they fail?"

"Maybe *they're* my backup plan, in case all of this fails," Fitchett said.

"But if they *are* successful, if the asteroid is pushed off its collision course with Earth, then all of the things you've done, all this work, all the planning, will have been unnecessary. All of this will mean nothing," Billy said.

"It will mean far more than nothing. We have catalogued all life forms, provided a library able to reproduce the entire fauna and flora of the planet. Over the past two decades, as society has degenerated, we have catalogued and preserved the things necessary to help civilization return again from the anarchy into which it has descended. In any event, civilization will have to be recreated, and we will be at the forefront of what needs to be done."

"But what about all of the people . . . all of us?" Billy asked.

"You will all be free to live a long and normal life," Fitchett replied.

"Normal? Is anybody here normal?" Billy questioned.

"Is anybody anywhere normal?" Fitchett replied. "Even if this asteroid misses the planet, it has already altered humanity, caused a massive decline in civilization. There will be both a need and an opportunity for a redefinition of mankind. Why couldn't that spark for the rebirth take place right here? These young people will possess all of the skills and knowledge necessary to create a renaissance of mankind. And you will be the leader, helping to make that happen."

Billy didn't know what to say, but he knew that Fitchett probably didn't expect an answer. Besides, his attention was captured elsewhere. The screens that surrounded them had become, one by one, filled with scenes of the seven launch sites. Billy was tired from thinking about what *could* happen and instead needed to focus on what *was* happening.

"Could we . . . ?" Billy pointed at the screens. Fitchett nodded in agreement.

Fitchett again pushed a button and the room was filled with sounds and voices. Simultaneously, checks and countdowns were taking place at seven sites with different languages or accents. From the two English-speaking sites—in the United States and England—enough could be determined to know that the launch of the next rockets was about to happen.

Billy leaned in closer to Fitchett. "Could we just hear the U.S. launch so it isn't so confusing?"

Fitchett pushed another button and the sound dropped dramatically in volume. He'd cut out not just the announcer but the background chatter and the sounds of the rockets from six of the seven sites.

"Fifteen seconds to launch. T minus 13 . . . 12 . . . 11 . . . we have commit . . . 9 . . . 8 . . . 7 . . . 6 . . . we have ignition . . . 4 . . . 3 . . . 2 . . . 1 . . . we have liftoff."

Simultaneously the seven ships started off the ground. Billy felt a pressure in his chest, as if the rockets were pushing against him, or as if, somehow, his effort would help them make it.

"It has cleared the tower . . . 34.5 million newtons of thrust . . . it has cleared the tower."

Fitchett leaned in close so he could talk. "The first

thirty seconds are the most critical," he yelled in Billy's ear. "If anything is going to happen, it will happen then."

The ships gained speed and elevation. The camera followed them up into the sky, and Billy silently counted along in his head, thinking that once he reached thirty all would be good.

"Altitude 0.8 kilometres . . . trajectory is good . . . launch is good."

Sixteen . . . seventeen . . . eighteen . . . nineteen . . . he was almost two-thirds of the way to safety and—

"Oh, dear God!" Fitchett screamed out.

There was no need to ask what he was reacting to. One of the ships was now a brilliant ball of orange flames, and projectiles, large and small, flew out in different directions from the blaze.

The other six rockets continued to soar skyward, oblivious to the fate of their sister ship as she fell back to Earth in a million fiery pieces.

CHAPTER TWENTY-TWO

SWITZERLAND

The screen showed the rocket rising up into the sky. Everybody in the room knew what was going to happen next, having seen the images replayed dozens of times. Some had a bizarre belief that maybe this time it wouldn't explode, but delusion would soon give way to reality. Others just hoped, on a subconscious level, that they were watching one of the other thirteen rockets, those that had launched successfully, rather than the one that had been destroyed.

"Freeze the image, right there!" a man called out, and the rocket become static, just a few seconds before the explosion. "You will notice that up to this point it was a successful launch." He walked up to the screen. "There is a perfect trajectory, and not even a hint of a breach in the superstructure or integrity of the ship." He ran his fingers along one side and then the other of the rocket. "Roll forward at super-slow-motion speed, please."

The image seemed frozen in place, but then there was a slight flutter in the flames from the ignition.

"Stop!" The image froze just as a small orange dot appeared on the side of the rocket. "This is where the explosion erupted," he said as he touched it with his outstretched hand. "This is the midsection, an area that has no seals, rings, or joints. It is well clear of the booster rockets and should not be experiencing either internal or external forces to account for this reaction. Forward again, in super-slow-motion."

The dot turned into a thin line of orange, and then the whole side of the rocket blew out, leaving a gaping hole, and a micro-second later the entire ship was nothing more than a large orange fireball. Sheppard averted his gaze—even after twenty viewings, it was still unnerving for him to watch.

"We do not believe that this was the result of a malfunction within the ship itself," the engineer said.

"Then how do you account for it?" Sheppard asked.

"We believe that a foreign element was introduced to the ship."

"And what exactly does that mean?" Sheppard demanded.

"We have insufficient data to predict the exact nature of—"

"I think I have an explanation," Parker said, cutting him off. He stood up and walked to the front of the room. Behind him the fragments of the exploding ship were still firing into the sky.

"Can we turn that off?" he asked, gesturing to the screen. "None of us needs to see it any further to know the results."

The screen quickly went blank.

"We looked at all the available closed-circuit security camera tapes. It appears that one of our agents entered that ship during the final inspection and then failed to leave the ship prior to launch," Parker said. "It is believed that he had with him a quantity of plastic explosives, probably carried strapped to his person and sealed in such a way to avoid tripping monitors equipped to detect explosives. Once the ship was airborne this device was detonated, either by remote or by means of a timer, or perhaps he trigged the explosion prior to blacking out."

"Are you sure of this?" Sheppard asked.

"We're certain of some and surmise the rest. Does the nature of the explosion witnessed match that profile?"

"Yes . . . yes, it does," the engineer said. "An internal explosion is the most likely explanation. But how is it possible that one of our own security people could do this? How could it be allowed? Obviously somebody wasn't doing his job correctly."

"There's no need to point fingers at—"

"It's all right, Professor Sheppard," Parker said, cutting him off. "He's right. This shouldn't have happened, but the reality of multiple launches left us severely understaffed. We were able to intercept and neutralize similar attempts made at three other launch sites."

"Three others?" Sheppard gasped.

"Yes, and in all three incidents attempts were made by individuals to detonate explosives either in the ship or in its immediate vicinity. In one case, at the U.S. launch site, an agent was intercepted just prior to entering the control room."

"The control room?" Sheppard asked.

Parker nodded. "Where you and I were seated. He was captured alive before he could detonate his device. His plan was to destroy the control room and kill all those scientists, technicians, and specialists necessary to launch the rockets."

"How is it that some of the infiltrators were apprehended but others were not?" somebody asked.

"In the three cases where they were stopped, the person trying to infiltrate was either a technician or a scientist—people like those in this room," Parker explained.

Sheppard looked around slowly at the people sitting with him. He noticed that he wasn't the only one anxiously scanning the room.

"The successful operative was not a scientist but one of our agents. He was trained in security, so he knew exactly how to circumvent the system. Further, that same training kept him calm and able to execute his plan without detection. In the other cases, *civilians* were involved."

Parker pronounced the word "civilian" with the distaste he felt for them. He might have been working for them and he knew their value, but he still didn't understand or respect them.

"It is not reassuring, to say the least, that the very agents we count on to guarantee our security are the people in the best position to jeopardize our safety and our operations," Sheppard said.

"Not reassuring, but certainly not surprising," Parker noted. "The very nature of their training, their access to weapons, and the course of their work—it all makes them excellent candidates to successfully complete either an act of sabotage or an assassination." He paused and smiled. "But without us you'd all be dead anyway."

Sheppard shook his head slowly. He'd gotten to know Parker's dark sense of humour. He also knew that *his* life did depend on Parker and his men, and he couldn't think of one other person in the world he trusted more than Parker.

"And can I assume that Judgment Day has taken full responsibility for these attacks?" Sheppard said.

"Affirmative," Parker noted. "Capturing their other operatives alive has allowed us many insights into their techniques of infiltration. We have identified and isolated over a dozen other moles who were 'sleepers' in position to make the next wave of attempts."

"Were any of those operatives in *this* facility?" Sheppard asked.

Parker nodded. "Three. All have been *neutralized.*"

Sheppard felt a small shiver go up his spine. He knew full well what "neutralized" meant. He also knew that the more dangerous effect of these attacks and infiltrations was to deflect time and energy away from their goal. That was the only way they'd fail.

"Has the debris from the accident been secured?" Sheppard asked Parker.

"Fragments fell within a two-kilometre area downwind of the launch site. We have established a no-go zone around the crash areas. The whole area is hot. While no nuclear devices were activated, high-grade uranium is scattered through the site."

"Have any attempts been made to gather that uranium?" Sheppard asked.

"Efforts have been specifically made *not* to allow anybody to harvest it. We wouldn't want it to find its way into a nuclear device," Parker said. "Probably the safest place for it to be is in plain sight."

"Were there casualties on the ground?" Sheppard asked.

"Fewer than one hundred were killed initially. Contact with the radioactive material will potentially result in further deaths in the long term . . . assuming that there *is* a long term."

"This has all been terrible," Sheppard said. "But we must remember that the unfortunate destruction of one ship has not—I repeat, has *not*—impacted our plan. We deliberately sent more devices than we felt were necessary, to provide a backup for this or other incidents. This was done not only as a failsafe measure but also to provide a guarantee to superpowers that all nuclear devices would be sent from the planet. We have now established, for the first time since late 1944, a planet that is free of nuclear weapons."

The group broke into spontaneous applause.

This did give Sheppard a degree of satisfaction. He hoped that maybe, just maybe, once their mission was completed, there would be a permanent ban on all nuclear weapons, and that the people with power would dedicate themselves to a new order of co-operation after they'd seen the power they possessed when they worked together. He was, he acknowledged to himself, a dreamer.

What he feared, though, was the idea that in spite of all the speeches about goodwill and trust and all the efforts to police and ensure that all weapons had been gathered, almost all the nuclear countries had probably managed to secret away a few nuclear devices. The world was *almost* nuclear-weapons free, but if they were successful in saving the planet it might be only a matter of months, or even weeks, before the nuclear race was back at full gallop. If the external threat could be ended, it wouldn't take long for the old policies, practices, and hatreds to resurface.

Even now the old rivalries were festering just beneath the surface. Already world powers were planning how to thrive and eventually dominate in the new order, once the world had been saved. It would be a different world, but not necessarily a better one.

CHAPTER TWENTY-THREE

IDAHO

Billy stopped as he entered the dining hall. He took a deep breath, greedily inhaling the aromas. After so many years of so little food it was still exciting, intoxicating, almost unbelievable. He often found himself passing through the dining hall for no other reason than to confirm that it was still there, that it hadn't disappeared. There was food, food everywhere, and he could have anything, and as much of anything as he wanted.

Absently his hand went into his pocket to where his ID was—his key to getting food. He wasn't even hungry. He could hardly remember what hungry was like. That was reassuring and troubling all at once. It was important not to forget. Not to forget about the kids in the "family" he'd left, not to forget his real family . . . his mother and father and brother, who had been taken away from him and—

"Excuse me."

He jumped backwards, fists raised, ready to strike out. It was a girl. A small girl who had been smiling but now looked as startled as he was.

"I'm . . . I'm sorry," she stammered. "I didn't mean to disturb you."

Slowly he lowered his fists and a smile replaced his scowl. It brought a smile to her face as well.

"I was just deep in thought," he explained.

"I wanted to show you something," she said. "If you're not busy . . . if you have time."

"I am busy, but I do have time . . . Amanda."

"You know who I am?" she asked.

"Of course I know who you are."

Billy knew every one of the kids in the program by face, name, and specialty. He understood that to be a leader he had to know all about the people he was going to lead.

"You've been here about six weeks, were raised in the French collective, are a very fine artist, and will be twelve on your next birthday . . . which is in less than two weeks."

She beamed brightly.

Billy knew it was the wise thing to do, but it was also just his nature. He was good at remembering information about people . . . the same way he knew all about the people he'd been leading before coming here. He tried to push them out of his head.

"So what did you want to show me?" Billy asked.

"I've been working on an art piece and it's finished, and I want you to see it."

"In that case, lead the way," he said.

She reached out and took his hand. "Come with me."

She led him toward the study area, the place where the kids learned under the direction of their instructors. That was how they spent most of their time during the day—working, studying, learning. And they seemed to like it. They seemed to like everything. They never complained or protested. In the same way, none of them had ever protested about Billy being named their leader. They had just accepted that he was placed in that role because he was the best qualified. It was so different from where he'd come from. There he'd had to fight and scratch his way to the top, and then spend every day watching, waiting, wondering when he was going to be challenged again. Here there were no challenges.

As they walked they were offered smiles and greetings by everybody they passed. These kids were unfailingly friendly, polite, and encouraging. He'd come to realize how quickly this world could dull his senses. You became so relaxed, so un-threatened, that you stopped paying close attention. The way Amanda had snuck up on him. That would never have happened out there.

He caught sight of Christina through the glass of a soundproof booth. She was playing the piano.

"Can you hold on a minute, please?" Billy said.

He carefully opened up the door to the booth and the music flowed out. Beautiful music. He looked at her. She was as beautiful as the music. He stepped into the room— she was so engrossed, so lost in the music, that she didn't even notice him.

She finished the piece, and both Billy and Amanda clapped. Christina got to her feet and bowed graciously.

"That was really wonderful, Christina," Billy said. "Very impressive."

"Thank you. Who's your friend?" she asked.

"This is Amanda. She hasn't been here very long."

"Hello, Amanda. I'm pleased to meet you," Christina said.

"Pleased to meet you, too," Amanda said.

The two of them talked—about the centre, about their collectives, about their specialties—and Billy listened. The more he knew about their lives, the way they'd been raised, the better he understood them. They had never had to fight to survive, so they really didn't know much about fighting . . . or surviving.

He looked at Christina. He found himself doing that more and more. Other than Joshua Fitchett she was the person he spent the most time with. There was something a little different about her. Something a little more normal. He'd seen her frustrated with her playing, caught her giving another person a look of annoyance, and on more than one occasion she'd let him know—subtly—that he was saying something that she thought was wrong.

He also found himself wondering about what was going to come later. There were two hundred kids and teenagers in the project. Just like the samples of flora and other fauna, they were eventually supposed to breed and reproduce the human population. Was she going to be his partner? Was that why she had been sent to be his guide originally? Was that the ultimate—?

She looked up at him and he looked away, embarrassed, as though he'd been caught doing something bad.

She reached out and touched his hand and he felt a surge of tingles run up his arm. He looked back and she was smiling.

"Would it be all right with you if I came along to see Amanda's work?" she asked.

"Of course! That would be great!"

Amanda took one of his hands and Christina took the other and together they led him away. He felt happy. He wondered if it was obvious to anybody else how he was starting to feel about Christina, and he wondered, too . . . did she feel the same way?

He couldn't help but chuckle to himself. In the shadow of the disaster that would end the world, he was wondering if a girl liked him.

PART 5

CHAPTER TWENTY-FOUR

T MINUS 6 MONTHS

SWITZERLAND

Dr. Andrew Markell held up his identification but he was shaking so badly he couldn't put it into the slot. He brought up his other hand, and holding the tag in two hands, he was able to steady it sufficiently to enter the slot and trigger the door.

He looked around anxiously, trying not to look too obvious. The guards at the end of the passage were far away and surely couldn't have seen, and the closed-circuit cameras—which were everywhere in the complex—wouldn't have been able to pick up anything as subtle as a mild shaking.

He forced a smile onto his face but instantly thought better of it. Nobody had seen him smile for over a year—not since he'd been forced to abandon his section and step down from heading his department. He had been pushed aside once again, each new demotion moving him further and further away from significance, and . . . he tried to stop the thoughts. This was the obsessive thinking that had plagued him, forced him out of the picture, condemned him to *useless* make-work projects that were just a way of *pretending* he was still part of the important work!

He stopped smiling. He knew that even that slightest change in behaviour might be enough to set off somebody's silent alarms. They'd all been warned to watch for changes in somebody's behaviour or habits as a sign of possible danger and to report it immediately. Ironically, knowing those instructions simply allowed somebody like him to avoid being detected. Or at least that was what he hoped and prayed.

He prayed often these days, seeking both God's wisdom and His approval. He'd never thought of himself as a religious man, but sitting there at his desk, all alone with just his thoughts and staring at the numbers, he'd found God. Free of any real responsibility, he'd spent hours at his desk praying and thinking, which had given way finally to plotting and planning. He was always careful to keep his eyes open when he was praying. Was that disrespectful, to pray with your eyes open? Would that offend God? He worried about things that like, but he hoped that his actions today would guarantee him a place in Heaven. He'd find out soon enough.

Walking along the corridor he silently recited his favourite passage from the Bible—the Psalm 23. When he came to "*Yea, though I walk through the valley of the shadow of death, I will fear no evil,*" he smiled. The underground passages in the complex were like little valleys, and certainly evil was all around him, but he had no fear or doubts. He knew what he was doing was right. More than right, it was *sacred*.

Looking down at his watch, Markell was pleased to see that he still had plenty of time. There was enough time to get to his office, do a bit of work, and then make up an excuse to get close to the control room, where they'd all be working. Even though he had no real reason to be there, he knew that as long as his good friend, the *illustrious* Professor Daniel Sheppard, was there he wouldn't be stopped. Good old Sheppard, his buddy, his friend . . . or at least as close to a friend as anybody here could be anymore. A little part of him felt bad about what was going to happen, but really, he was doing Sheppard a favour. He was doing *all* of them a favour.

He knew that Daniel wasn't evil, just misguided, taken in by the false god of science. But in that way he was breaking the First Commandment—"*Thou shalt have no other gods before me*"—and the Second Commandment—"*Thou shalt not make unto thee any graven image, or any likeness of any thing that is in Heaven above, or that is in the Earth beneath, or that is in the water under the Earth.*" The spaceships had become objects of worship, as people looked up into the heavens and saw only them and not God.

They would have to be punished for violating two of the Ten Commandments . . . although he *himself* was breaking both the Eighth and the Sixth Commandments: he had stolen the materials to make his bomb—"*Thou shalt not steal*"—and he was going to use that bomb to take lives—"*Thou shalt not kill.*"

It perplexed him, the fact that in order to fulfill his destiny he would have to break Commandments, but he knew in his heart that he was right. He was allowed to break two Commandments because *they* had broken two Commandments . . . well, at least they had broken two Commandments according to the Orthodox Christian faith, while both Roman Catholics and Jews combined those two into the First Commandment, so really they'd broken only one Commandment. But that one was the *First* Commandment, which had to be more important than the two that he was breaking or they would have been listed first, because you always listed the most important first, and . . . his mind went into another crazy series of circles. He forced himself to stop.

He couldn't let the logic of it get in the way . . . that was how the Devil worked—getting inside your head and filling it with bad information, distorting your thoughts, allowing the false god of logic to overwhelm your heart and your soul. He wouldn't let that happen.

He'd worked through his plans so many times before that if he closed his eyes he would be able to see the entire scenario playing out. Of course he wouldn't close his eyes, for fear that somebody would think he was praying.

Dozens of times, almost every day over the last few months, he'd done exactly what he was going to be doing today. That wasn't just for practice—it was also establishing a pattern of behaviour. The security forces looked for people breaking patterns as one of the tipoffs to potential problems. He smiled. If he *didn't* go to the control room today they might think that was a break in his pattern. He was just going to do what he always did.

He generally brought Daniel a tea, and the two of them would make pleasant conversation for a few minutes before going their separate ways—Daniel to lead and Markell sent off to the wilderness . . . not unlike Moses wandering the wilderness . . . and they had both found the signs they were looking for. There would be only one small difference today: Markell was not just bringing his friend a tea. Today he had three kilograms of explosives strapped to his chest.

Markell had prayed for guidance to help him choose the right time to act. For the last two weeks he had woken up every morning wondering if today was the day. Each day he'd waited for a sign, but none had come. The members of his support group had urged him to take action before it was too late. In three days' time the ships would be positioned around the asteroid and the signal would be sent to trigger the detonation.

He could feel sweat dripping down his sides. His initial fear was that somehow the moisture would cause the device to malfunction or short out, but he knew he couldn't sweat that badly . . . could he? It didn't help that he was wearing an extra layer of clothing today to disguise the subtle outline of the explosive vest. At least the lining would also hide the sweat dripping down his sides . . . but not the sweat on his face.

He wiped his face with the sleeve of his jacket. His jacket . . . not only was he still wearing it but it was still done up. There was no reason why he'd be wearing a zipped-up jacket in the tunnel. Anxiously he started to take it off.

"Excuse me!" a loud voice called out from behind.

He turned around. There was a guard walking briskly toward him. Somebody else must have noticed the jacket and become suspicious. Would a stupid jacket prevent him from fulfilling his mission?

He reached into his pocket. Inside was a small gun made entirely of plastic so that it wouldn't trigger the metal detectors. The guard came closer and closer.

"Dr. Markell!" the guard called out.

The guard was now only a couple of metres away. Markell pulled out the gun. The guard's expression changed to shock and then to fear as Markell pulled the trigger and the hard plastic bullet slammed into and through the guard's chest.

He dropped the gun to the ground—there was only the one bullet—and started to run. The control room was just up ahead. He wouldn't be able to get through the last checkpoint to enter, but if he got close enough the power of the explosives might damage the room, or kill or incapacitate some of the people inside, and—

A bullet ripped into his shoulder with such force that he was spun around and thrown to the ground. He heard footsteps and raised voices. They were coming. There was only one more thing to do.

"*Thy will be done on Earth as it is in Heaven,*" he said softly. Then he pushed the button.

There was a bustle in the control room. Everybody had a job to do and each job was important. Most people in the room wondered how an operation this important, this critical, could so suddenly and secretly have been moved up by three days. In less than thirty minutes they would be sending the signals to arm the nuclear devices and trigger detonation.

Sheppard, and no more than a score of others, knew that this wasn't a sudden change; it had been the original schedule all along. They had strategically announced the later date to provide misinformation to possible saboteurs. They justifiably feared that Judgment Day would move full force over those last days to attempt to stop them—their last chance to stop those who were trying to stop the asteroid.

Over the past month, acts of sabotage and terrorism had become more common and intense. Judgment Day followers were no longer attacking only chemical and industrial complexes or power plants—they were now attacking libraries, universities, and individuals who appeared to possibly be scientists or technicians or intellectuals. There had been rumours of people being targeted for death simply because they'd been seen carrying books or wearing glasses. Knowledge was to be feared, and anything or anybody who might possess knowledge was a potential target.

There was a strange symmetry to these attacks. The extremists were taking their orders from religious documents that dated back close to three thousand years, and now, having attacked so many of the pillars of modern civilization, they had driven society back almost to that point in time.

Sheppard couldn't help but think how misguided these attacks had been. If they had launched a coordinated attack on the basic elements of civilization—chemicals, steel, production and power plants—in the very beginning, perhaps they could have stopped the ships from being produced and launched.

When it was almost too late, they had got smart and carried out a systematic attack on the industries responsible for the production of rocket fuel, destroying all the relevant facilities, but not before the agency had stockpiled enough to launch twenty or thirty ships. Now it was too late . . . well, too late to do anything except attack the people and places responsible for triggering the explosions. Sheppard and his colleagues sat at the epicentre of that possibility, and they weren't the only ones who knew that.

Outside their walls gigantic rallies were nearly constant now. Protesters surrounded the complexes and attempted to enter and disrupt the process. And in order to deal with those people the security forces had become even more ruthless. Sheppard didn't know—he didn't even *want* to know—how many tens of thousands of people had been killed to keep the complex, and him, safe.

Most troubling had been the internal acts of violence. People who had been trusted colleagues for years had turned and committed some of the most horrendous attacks. So far most attempts had been foiled, with only a minimal loss of life, but still . . . how close had they come?

A booming sound, loud but muffled, filled the control room. For a second or two everyone stopped working and turned, looking for the source. Then, with their work not completed and time running down, they went back to their tasks as if nothing had happened. But what was it?

Sheppard's work was now more symbolic than real. He was present more as a spectator than a participant, so he had more time to be curious. He looked for Parker, but he and four of the other security officers were huddled in a corner, talking into their cuffs, getting word from the outside. There was no way to read anything from their actions or expressions. They always acted calmly, always had a look of cold, quiet disinterest on their faces.

Slowly, deliberately, Sheppard got up from his seat and started to angle around the room. He knew that Parker wouldn't say anything while he was in the company of the other security officers, but Sheppard was in a position to *order* him to provide an update for him. Not that they worked that way. Besides, he didn't want to be too obvious.

He pretended he was watching the work being done around him, looking down at screens and control panels, but really he was just waiting for his moment to approach Parker. The four other men split off, going back to their observation spots, two at the main doors and the other two on opposite walls.

Sheppard moved to Parker's side.

"What was that sound?" he asked, not looking at Parker directly.

"It's under control."

"That wasn't my question. What happened?"

Parker stared straight ahead—at least that was what Sheppard assumed, as his eyes were hidden behind the dark glasses. "I don't have full details as yet."

"What do you have?" Sheppard insisted.

"One man . . . internal . . . we think working in isolation."

"Is he being questioned?"

"I think they're still trying to locate all his body parts right now," Parker said.

"Oh . . . I didn't know. Were there other deaths?"

"Six that we know of. Apparently he shot one of our security officers, and then two other officers and three civilians were killed by the blast."

"Do we know who he is . . . was?"

"No positive DNA ID as yet, but from the security steps he cleared and the videotapes we are fairly certain he was a scientist working with level-four clearance."

There were over ten thousand people working in the complex, but not many with a level of clearance that high. This was troubling in two ways—because somebody that high up had turned, but also because he was somebody Sheppard almost certainly would have known personally.

"Who was it?" Sheppard asked.

"We don't have DNA confirmation as—"

"I want to know who you *think* it was." He turned to look directly at Parker. "Right now."

Parker nodded. "Andrew Markell."

Sheppard felt as if somebody had punched him in the stomach. "It can't be . . . can it?"

"We're certain enough for me to tell you."

"But why . . . would he do it? Why?"

"He always operated outside of established patterns and organizations, and he felt alienated from the process. He would represent a potential for such behaviour. That's why he was under surveillance. At the time of his interception he was going to his office, but most certainly he would have gone on to the control room, as he did each morning."

Sheppard's shock suddenly morphed into fear. That muffled explosion was meant for here, meant for *him* and the men who surrounded him.

"Dr. Sheppard!"

He looked up. Every single person in the control room was looking at him.

"Dr. Sheppard," the dispatcher said, "do we have permission to send the signal, to arm and activate the devices?"

Sheppard's mind spun. He knew that they were waiting for him to give them permission to set the detonation sequence in motion. That's why he was in the control room. That's why he was right here in the room today and everybody was looking at him, waiting for him.

He took a deep breath and slowed down his racing pulse as best he could. He knew he could just say, "Yes, do it," but that wasn't what this occasion required, what was expected. Each of the people in this room was looking to him to say something that would mark this occasion, a defining moment in the history of the planet. He had thought of things, big and small, quotes and long-winded speeches. He wasn't going to offer any of those. Instead, he was going to rely on the words of a captain in an old TV show, a show about space.

He held up his hand and pointed a finger. "Make it so."

Most of the room burst into applause, and then the technicians set the sequence in motion by sending the signal.

Travelling at 300,000 kilometres per second, the speed of light, the signal raced across the solar system. Even at that speed it would take nine hours and thirty-six minutes to reach the ships. A further twenty minutes would pass to allow all the devices to be armed and readied. And then a synchronized explosion would take place. The light from that explosion would then travel the same distance, taking the same length of time to return to Earth. In slightly less than nineteen hours and thirty-two minutes they'd see the result of their actions. The world would see it.

CHAPTER TWENTY-FIVE

SWITZERLAND

Shortly after the signals were sent, a worldwide press release announced the impending explosion. This was done not just to celebrate the accomplishment—or to avert further attacks by announcing that the time for violent protest had passed—but to warn people. Staring at the explosion without protective goggles would result in temporary or, worse, permanent eye damage, possibly even blindness. What was known for sure was that for a flash lasting no longer than ten seconds, the sun would no longer be the brightest object in our solar system. For that brief period, the half of the planet turned away from the sun and facing the asteroid, the half of the planet in darkness, would experience a brightness stronger than any midday sun.

For some this was already the crowning achievement of human civilization. Not only did mankind possess the technology and knowledge to create this explosion, but it had also achieved the level of sophistication necessary for the international co-operation it took to realize this goal.

For others—for many outside the gates—this was just more confirmation of the power of evil. The fire in the sky would be a sign of the unholy alliance between mankind and the Devil, and science was the religion of that evil.

It would be, unquestionably, the most watched event in the history of the planet. Nine billion pairs of eyes— covered by protective shields, or watching through the filter of television or the Internet—would be looking upward, seeing this as either a signal of their potential rescue or the beginning of the end—the apocalypse, the End of Days, the Rapture being set into motion.

IDAHO

There were a million stars in the sky. Billy was amazed to see them. Many nights he came out alone just to stare and to think. Logically, he knew those same stars shone above New York, but in all the times he'd been on the roof of that apartment building he'd never seen them as clearly. Certainly, as civilization had retreated, as electricity had been lost, as the city had plunged into chaos, more and more of the night sky had become visible, but still, not the way it was here. He wondered if the others ever stood on the roof in New York, looking up, thinking of him the way he thought of them. Probably not. They'd be too busy trying to survive.

In those quiet moments when he sat by himself, then and now, he often thought about things. Not just what surrounded him but what had preceded him. The pictures of his family, which were in his room, framed and on the wall, brought back memories that he'd thought were lost forever. Or, more precisely, that he'd thought he'd never *allow* himself to have again.

And he'd started wondering a great deal about the afterlife, too. That was a luxury he could never have afforded in the days when death lurked around every corner. If there was something after death, he wondered what had become of his mother and his father and his brother. If they were anywhere, he thought it must be up there in the stars. When he was outside on a night like this maybe they could look down on him and feel happy for him. He couldn't help but think about how their deaths had put into motion the mechanism that would ultimately allow him to survive, and in his survival, a little part of them survived, too. Somehow all of this gave their deaths a purpose beyond anything he could even have imagined—the law of unintended consequences at work once more.

Tonight, he was far from alone. All around him were residents of the complex, well over a thousand people outside on the damp grass and among the rocks, sitting in the dark, looking up, waiting. They all were either already wearing or holding protective goggles.

Despite the size of the crowd it was eerily silent. There was a sense of occasion, a seriousness that was as present in the air as the cool mist of the forest.

Billy looked around at the kids. He knew them all. He liked them. He understood why they were the way they were. Still, sometimes he felt like shaking some of them just to get a reaction. Not that they were perfect. Being able to speak seven languages didn't stop somebody from being conceited. Being a specialist in biomechanics didn't guarantee confidence. Being able to play musical instruments didn't necessarily come with the soul to do anything more than robotically reproduce other people's creativity. But, all in all, they were nice, and they had an innocence about them that allowed him to let down his guard—at least a little. Nobody here meant him any harm.

Most of the people outside had been told just a few hours ago, just after the official announcement, that they would be assembling to watch the detonation. Billy had known for over a week, though, because Joshua Fitchett had known. It was more and more obvious now that Fitchett's power extended into the International Aerospace Research Institute. He obviously had agents, moles, informants, because he seemed to know everything that was going on. And more and more, he shared this information with Billy.

"It's a beautiful night."

Billy turned. It was Christina.

"Yes, it is nice," he replied.

"I heard that it's going to be brighter than day," she said.

"That's what I heard, too."

"Do you think it's going to work?" she asked. "Will it destroy the asteroid?"

"You'd be better off finding somebody who specializes in space and asking them," Billy joked.

"You'd know better."

"Me? Why would you think that?" he asked.

"Because you know lots of things you don't let on about," she explained. "I know how much time you spend with Mr. Fitchett, and how close the two of you are. He must tell you things he doesn't tell the rest of us," she said.

"We talk about lots of things," Billy admitted. Sometimes Billy was told specifically by Fitchett to keep things confidential. Other things Billy kept to himself almost instinctively, as if to tell anybody would break the bond between the two of them—a bond so strong that he hadn't felt anything like it since the death of his family. Although, more and more, he was beginning to feel a similar kind of connection with Christina.

"You knew about what was going to happen tonight a few days ago, didn't you?" she asked.

It would have been impossible to answer that question without either breaking a trust or telling her a lie. He wasn't going to break a trust, but he didn't want to lie to her.

"It's all right," she said. "You don't have to tell me. I know that Joshua trusts you and you don't want to betray that trust." She paused. "I just wanted you to know that I know."

She had read not only his thoughts but his emotions. Another sign of the growing bond between them.

"I've never lied to you about anything," Billy said. That was the truth, but the strangest part for him was how much it mattered. He'd spent years doing whatever was needed to survive, and lying was the least of the sins he'd committed.

"I understand." She reached out and took his hand.

For a few brief seconds he forgot all about what was going to happen in the sky and the crowd of people who surrounded them. All he could think of was her, and he hoped that his hand wasn't too sweaty.

That he and Christina would be a pair was a fact that they both seemed to understand in an unspoken way. Sometimes he thought he should make the unspoken *spoken*, but he was afraid that she'd tell him he was wrong, tell him she had chosen somebody else. When had her feelings become so important to him?

"You know," he began hesitantly, "I really don't like to keep anything from you."

She smiled. It was something she'd been doing more often these days. Not a polite smile, but a full, beautiful, happy smile. And somehow he knew that he was the reason for it.

"You're very important—"

"Please ensure that you are wearing your eye protection!" a mechanized voice called out over the speakers. "The light pulse is imminent. Put on your eye protection!"

Christina let go of his hand and they both put on their goggles. All around them people were doing the same. Billy looked at Christina.

"Here, let me help."

He reached over and adjusted her goggles, snugging them into place. She took his hand again, and all he wanted to do was take off those goggles and look into her eyes—but of course they couldn't do that. They both turned to look skyward. It was only going to be a few more—

The sky became brilliantly bright, so bright that people turned away slightly and recoiled, as if the weight of the light was slamming against them! Impossibly, it seemed, the glare got brighter and brighter, and then it quickly began to fade until it was gone and they were left in the dark once again.

In the sudden darkness after the brilliant light, eyes had trouble adjusting and some people panicked, assuming that they'd been blinded despite their protective goggles. Cries filled the air and goggles were tossed to the ground before eyes began to readjust and people realized they could see again.

They all stood, looking up at the night sky as the stars once again became visible. And then in some way it was as if it had never happened at all, as if it had been some sort of mass hallucination leaving no proof of its passage except that it had been shared.

All across the planet it wasn't just eyes but hearts and heads that tried to react. Was that it? Had it worked? Had they been saved? Collectively, nine billion people held their breath and waited for an answer.

CHAPTER TWENTY-SIX

T MINUS 4 MONTHS

SWITZERLAND

Sheppard shuffled the papers in front of him on the conference table. It was a nervous response, really. He was waiting for the meeting to start. Before him were reports from all the institute's departments. They contained the known, the unknown, and the best guesses about what was to come.

It had been almost two full months since the detonation. Those who had hoped for instant answers, instant salvation, had been frustrated.

They knew that the detonation itself had been perfect and complete and a scientific achievement unparalleled in human history. And some encouraging results had been apparent almost instantly. What had been one large asteroid mass had been blasted into tens of thousands of much smaller fragments. For the next two months scientists had tracked the path of this debris field. The force of the explosion had caused an ongoing momentum, and the field had continued to expand in size. From that data they were able to predict that the outer edges and the fragments they contained were most certain to pass wide of the Earth. So at least parts of the asteroid had been diverted.

Other answers, though, had doggedly defied definition. The core was still too obscured, hidden from electronic Earth eyes, for scientists to see what was at the centre of the cloud. How big were the fragments? How many were there? What danger did they still pose to life on Earth?

Their efforts to assess the situation had been limited by the continued deterioration and destruction in the outside world. Factions of Judgment Day had destroyed observatories, and repairing or replacing the optical equipment was problematic. Best guesses were more "guess" and less "best"— yet with each passing week the picture was getting clearer.

Many people had assumed that when answers weren't immediately forthcoming it meant the worst—that the explosions had been ineffective and the asteroid fragments were still going to doom the planet. More and more people had then abandoned even the last thin veneer of civilized behaviour, and chaos now reigned supreme. Others had embraced religion and were trying, in different ways, to "do the right thing," many of them repudiating the violent, fanatical stance adopted by the Judgment Day zealots in favour of a fatalistic acceptance of the end.

Others simply accepted the explanation that the scientists just didn't know—yet. They quietly went about their daily lives, hoping and praying and trying to survive in a world that continued to spiral downward with increased speed.

Today's meeting was to provide the most up-to-date assessment of the situation. Answers had been promised. There was only one question that mattered, though, only one answer that was needed. How big were the fragments that remained on a collision course with Earth?

The scientists and department heads filed into the room, taking their assigned seats. Sheppard might once have been tempted to allow the meeting to evolve as it naturally would, to not press or push the agenda as each department reported, to allow for hope, even if it was a false hope. But he had had enough of hope now, false or otherwise. Today he just wanted the answers. To him, it was preferable to know they were going to die than to continue living in limbo.

"I want to hear from one group only, just one report," he said to the assembled gathering. "I want to know about the fragments that still remain on an intercept course with Earth."

It felt as though the entire group collectively took a breath and then held it. This was the elephant in the room, and he'd tackled it head on.

A man cleared his throat. "I want to be clear that due to a number of constraints, some variables exist that—"

"We understand the limitations, and nobody is going to hold you personally accountable. We're not going to kill the messenger," Sheppard said. "Just tell us."

He cleared his throat again. "We can confirm that the fragments continue to disperse, and this increased dispersal will result in at least 40 percent of the original mass of the asteroid no longer being on an intercept course with Earth."

Sheppard knew that he wasn't saying anything that wasn't already widely known.

"And the remaining 60 percent?" Sheppard asked.

"A further 10 to 25 percent is believed to have been reduced to pieces small enough—from granular up to two metres in size—that they will burn up in the atmosphere on entry and won't reach the surface of the planet."

"That accounts for between 50 and 75 percent of the asteroid. And the remaining parts?"

"It is almost impossible to say with complete certainty."

"I don't expect complete certainty!" Sheppard snapped. "Just tell us what you think."

He took a deep breath. "We believe there are perhaps three hundred significant fragments that will impact the surface of the planet, and the biggest of these could be up to three hundred metres in diameter."

"That sounds encouraging," one of the scientists said.

Sheppard and half the people around the table looked at him incredulously. He was a rocket fuel specialist, and he did not have enough background to know how much devastation a fragment that size would create—information that seemed painfully obvious to everybody else.

"We're going to be okay . . . aren't we?" he persisted.

Sheppard looked at their chief climatologist. "Please, could you provide an answer?"

"That many fragments hitting the planet is unprecedented," he said. "We estimate that the asteroid that hit approximately sixty-five million years ago, the one that is believed to have led to the extinction of the dinosaurs and almost all land-based life forms along with over 95 percent of aquatic life, was only three times as large as that," he said.

"So this won't be so bad," the rocket scientist said. "Right?"

"That was only *one* asteroid strike," the climatology chief answered. "We estimate that the total energy released from all of the fragments that impact Earth will be up to two *hundred* times greater than the calamity that led to that mass extinction."

It was as if the air had been let out of the room, and people visibly sagged around the table. Sheppard slumped down and supported his head with his hands.

Finally he spoke. "Your degree of certainty for your report?"

"More than 98 percent that this is the result."

"And in that 2 percent margin of error, is there any question that you are *so* wrong that none of these fragments will hit, or that they will be so small that they will not significantly impact human life on the planet?" Sheppard asked.

He shook his head. "There is no chance that we have miscalculated to that extent. Earth will be hit by multiple fragments. It could be two hundred instead of three hundred, but it could just as easily be four hundred. They could be only two hundred metres in diameter, but they could also be larger, four or even five hundred metres across."

"I see. And are there any more efforts, any steps we can take to try to avert these impacts?" Sheppard asked of the people around the room.

Everybody looked down at the table and nobody answered—which was an answer in itself.

Sheppard suddenly laughed, catching everybody by surprise.

"Sorry, I was just thinking about a joke," he said. "A woman is waiting outside the operating room for the surgeon to emerge and tell her how the operation on her husband went. The doctor says to her that the surgery was successful. She is overjoyed, thanks him, and asks when her husband can come home. He says, 'You don't understand. Your husband is dead.' Confused, she says, 'But you told me the operation was a success,' and he replies, 'Yes, the operation was a success, but the patient still died.'"

Nobody else seemed to find Sheppard's joke funny, and he realized it really wasn't that funny after all.

"I'm going to ask that the information we have discussed today, these conclusions, not, at this time, be shared with anybody outside the room," Sheppard said. "There's no point in producing any internal mass panic . . . this information shall be kept from the general public . . . at least for now."

CHAPTER TWENTY-SEVEN

T MINUS 3 MONTHS

IDAHO

"Is he in his office?" Billy asked Joshua Fitchett's secretary.

"He's there but he's busy, and I don't think he can—"

The door to Fitchett's office opened and he came out in full flight and rushed away.

"Joshua!" Billy yelled. "Can we talk?"

"I was just coming to find you," he replied. "Come, we'll walk and talk and I'll show you something, all at the same time."

Fitchett hurried down the hall, not waiting for a response, and Billy ran after him, falling into step.

"I haven't seen you for almost two weeks," Billy said.

"I haven't been here for two weeks. I've been out there," he said with a wave of his hands, "taking care of problems and seeing to all the last-minute details."

"There must be lots to do."

"The most important elements seem to be falling into

place, finally. Today I've arranged a meeting—an important meeting—and I want you to be part of it."

"Me?"

"Yes, it's at the heart of our mission, and I believe you should be there."

Billy found himself struggling to keep up to Fitchett. His height and stride seemed to more than compensate for his age.

"What's it about?" Billy asked.

"It's all tied in to what I want to show you today. Always better to show."

"Could I ask you another question?" Billy asked.

"You can ask me anything, you know that."

"I was going over the information about the Ark, the DNA samples, and I noticed that with each animal, fish, or bird, each insect, each form of plant life, you provided either one hundred samples or fifty breeding pairs—fifty male and fifty female."

"That is the number that allows sufficient genetic diversity to more or less guarantee the viability of the species."

"But there aren't one hundred kids, there are *two* hundred . . . one hundred males and one hundred females . . . *one hundred* breeding pairs. Why would you think that there should be twice as many to create diversity among humans? Why should we be different from all the other life forms on the planet?"

"That's a very good question," Fitchett replied.

"And are you going to give me a good answer?" Billy asked.

"I certainly could, but it would be better if you gave *me* an answer. Why do you think that has been done?"

Billy had thought about this quite a bit over the past weeks, so he didn't have to struggle for an answer.

"You don't do anything without a backup plan," Billy said.

"I try not to."

"So if there are twice as many of us as is needed for genetic viability, then you have a backup plan that involves all of us as well."

Fitchett's face creased into a smile. "I'm not surprised you posed this question. None of the other young people have even asked. I'm not sure if that's because they haven't noticed or because they're too polite to ask."

"I think they're a little afraid of you . . . and a lot in awe of you," Billy said.

"I imagine that makes sense. After all, I *am* their father . . . not biologically, of course, but *psychologically*." He paused. "But you've never been afraid of me, have you?"

"You're not my father. So do you have a backup plan?"

"Of course I do. I haven't mentioned it because I was afraid that, due to circumstances, it might not be possible."

"And now it is?"

"Now there is a much stronger possibility. That's what this meeting is about. Your role as a leader makes your participation important."

"It's hard for me to lead when I don't even know what's happening or where I'm leading us to."

Fitchett skidded to a stop and spun around to face Billy. "You're right. You are definitely right. I *should* have told you everything sooner, including the difficulty. Will you please accept my sincere apology and 'forgive me?" He held out his hand.

Any annoyance or anger that Billy had been feeling faded away. He knew that Fitchett meant what he said. The two shook.

"Come."

Fitchett darted off then, and Billy hurried after him.

"As you deduced, there are going to be two groups, two plans. One you are very familiar with. Before the impact, two thousand people will be brought below ground and the outside blast doors will be sealed."

"And one hundred of those people will be kids."

"One hundred of the specialized children. There will also be the children of those who have worked on this project, so in total about two hundred and thirty children under the age of sixteen will be below ground."

"What about the rest? Where are they going?"

"They're going with you."

"I'm not going to be here at the complex?" Billy was stunned. "But where am I going? Is there another complex, another underground facility?"

Fitchett shook his head. "There's only one."

"But we can't survive on the surface . . . it's not possible . . . we'll all die."

"Of course you would die if you were on the surface. The surface will not support life for at least a decade, maybe two, possibly never."

"Then what's going to happen to us?" Billy demanded.

"You'll be completely safe. By the time the fragments hit you'll all be gone."

"Gone where?"

Fitchett pointed to the ceiling. "You'll all be in space."

Billy and Fitchett stood in an enormous launching bay, looking up at five rockets that towered hundreds of metres over their heads, tethered to several towers. The launching bay and the towers were alive with activity as technicians put the final touches on the ships, preparing them for their launches.

"I'm seeing it, but I still don't believe it," Billy said as he looked upward.

"I told you that I used to use this facility to launch private satellites," Fitchett said. "I made a great deal of money here. I just didn't realize that it would become so important one day."

"And you expect us—*me*—to get in those rockets?"

"There will be twenty of you in each ship."

"It will just be us . . . the kids?"

"Yes. It is prohibitively expensive to launch and maintain any individual in space for long. Only the most valuable among us can be offered those spots. We can always add a few people, or even a few *hundred*, o our deep-earth facilities, but spots in space are far too valuable to waste on adults who will never return to the surface. They are simply not necessary. Among the one hundred kids, you will have the specialization necessary not only to reproduce man's greatest skills and attributes but to live in space and maintain the space station."

"Wait . . . you're also going to launch a space station?" Billy asked.

"It was launched over three decades ago as a joint venture of a number of governments. It was used extensively and then ultimately abandoned as all scientific research was directed toward destroying the asteroid. I was able to get control of it. I have placed the space station into synchronistic orbit around Earth, in such a position that the planet will shield it from collision with any fragments," Fitchett explained. "It still has an atmosphere, and any modifications or repairs needed will be completed when you arrive."

"I'm not arriving anywhere," Billy said. "I'm not going into space."

"I know this is all very hard to digest," Fitchett said.

"It's hard to digest because it's crazy! Is that why you didn't tell me about this before now, because it's crazy?"

"My plan was to inform you immediately, but there was a problem. We didn't have the rocket fuel to send the ships into space."

"So you're telling me that you built five spaceships, did all the planning, but *forgot* to get fuel for them?" Billy said. "That's not the way you operate. I know that. You plan everything to the last detail."

"I didn't plan on all our fuel sources being destroyed by Judgment Day five months ago. I now have a plan to secure fuel."

"So you *still* don't have the fuel, but you have a plan to get some? Is that what you expect me to believe?"

"That is the focus of this meeting."

"And if you still can't get the fuel? What then?" Billy asked.

"Everybody will come below ground with us here."

"Then we could *still* do that, right?" Billy had dreaded the thought of spending years underground, but now that seemed like an inviting option compared to being stranded in space.

"There is room for everyone, but if we did that we would be risking everything."

"How would that risk everything?" Billy demanded. "The only thing you're risking with this plan is our lives— *my* life!"

Fitchett placed a hand on his shoulder and Billy had to fight the urge to brush it away.

"Do you trust me?" Fitchett asked.

"I *did* trust you, until you told me you want to blast me into space as some sort of stupid backup plan!"

"Billy, that's where you're completely wrong. You're not the *backup* plan. You *are* the plan. Everything else, everything that you've seen and been shown before this, has been done simply to allow this plan to take place. This always was *the* plan."

"I don't understand," Billy said. He felt as though his head was spinning.

"The underground facility was built so that I could offer a sanctuary for those who have been working on the plan to send you into space. I needed to offer them something to get them to work on the *real* plan. Everything we've constructed below—the living facilities for those workers and their families, all of the resources that have been assembled—will be for your use when you return from space. That is why all of this was done."

"I don't . . . I don't understand," Billy stammered. "You don't think the people below can survive? This was all just a lie?"

"Not a lie. I think they *can* survive . . . well, assuming that the facility is not hit directly by a large fragment."

"What?"

"If a large fragment hits this location directly, it won't matter how deeply we're buried beneath the surface. Everybody is going to die."

Billy couldn't believe his ears.

"Of course that's highly unlikely, statistically speaking. I assume they'll survive—I'm betting my life on it. Let me try to explain. When the fragments hit the planet we *know* that all life forms on the surface will be destroyed, either immediately or due to the effects of the cloud cover, which will block the sun for years and prevent all photosynthesis and thus plant life. The only life that will survive will be either deep below ground, possibly in the very depths of the ocean, and, in your case, in space."

"But why can't we all just go below ground, either here or someplace else?"

"It's not a true backup plan if you do the same thing twice," Fitchett said. "That way you are only leaving yourself vulnerable to the possibility of failing twice. We don't know exactly what is going to happen once those fragments hit. Have I ever talked to you about chaos theory?"

Billy shook his head in frustration. He wasn't in the mood to get a lesson or a lecture. He wanted answers.

"It's also known as 'the butterfly effect.' In its simplest form, it says that the fluttering of a butterfly's wings on one side of the planet can influence the weather half a continent away."

"That's just stupid!" Billy snapped.

"Not stupid, just simplistic. The idea is that a small difference or error can result in a chain of events leading to ends that are completely unknown and vastly different from those that could be predicted."

"Okay, so what are you saying?"

"We know the fragments will land. We know with a high degree of certainty when and where and how big they will be. Beyond that, the effects on Earth are just a guess."

"So life could go on?"

"Of course not. Extinction is certain. That is an immediate result of the fragments landing. What's not certain are the effects flowing out from there. All the scientific predictions are based on thousands of variables that we have never witnessed and cannot verify, and that are completely beyond our ability to know. What we predict will happen isn't so much scientific fact as it is a romantic, optimistic guess . . . a hope for the best."

"And the best is that all life forms become extinct?" Billy sneered.

"The best is that the planet will somehow rebound in a decade or two to allow life to return to the surface. But you have to understand that the entire world will not react or recover equally. It is possible that while the surface will remain uninhabitable in North America for two hundred years, it may recover in Australia in twenty years, or vice-versa. We just don't know, and buried deep in the ground here we won't be able to know what is happening on the rest of the planet."

"But we would know if we were orbiting in space," Billy said.

Fitchett nodded. "I knew you'd understand."

"And from up there we could tell the people in the underground facility what was happening."

"You could, but it wouldn't necessarily mean anything for those people at this complex. They—and I say 'they' because I will be long dead at that point—will not have the capacity to travel very far in an environment that is hostile to human life. You, however, already in space, will be able not just to identify where the new Eden will appear, but to board the re-entry vehicles and simply *land* at that location and recommence life."

What he was saying made sense—it was strange, dangerous, hard to believe, fantastic, almost unbelievable, but it did make sense.

"But potentially," Fitchett said, "the fragments might trigger a chain of events that will result in the entire surface of the Earth being completely inhospitable to human life for two *hundred* years, or two *thousand* years, or more. Human life, even with all that we've created below ground in our facility, cannot be sustained underground forever."

"It can't be sustained in space either, can it?" Billy asked. "We can't just keep circling up there forever."

"You're right, you can't. You will be equipped with the ability to sustain life for up to forty years."

"And if the planet still can't support life after forty years, what does it matter whether human life dies out below ground or in space, or in both places? It's still gone."

"Gone from this planet, but not gone," Fitchett said. "Those of us in the caverns will only have the choice of returning to the surface or facing extinction underground. Those of you in the ships above will have another option. You will have the capacity to take your ships and leave . . . to travel through space in search of a new home. There are planets on which human life can possibly survive. And you will carry with you the genetic material from tens of thousands of plant and animal species. Earth perhaps will perish, but the *seeds* of Earth will be sown in a new part of the galaxy. It will not be Genesis, but *re*-genesis." He paused and smiled. "In the beginning, man will use the heavens to find a new Earth. And he will make the new land to be filled with vegetation and living creatures of all kinds. And man will see that it is good."

CHAPTER TWENTY-EIGHT

There was a gentle knock on the door and Sheppard looked up from his notes. The door opened and Parker peeked in.

"Thought I'd check on you," he said. "You haven't left your office all day."

"Sorry . . . I just lost track of time."

Parker entered the room. He was carrying a tray that held just one thing—a large bowl of chocolate ice cream, Sheppard's favourite thing in the world.

"You missed dinner," Parker said. "Actually, you missed breakfast, lunch, and dinner, so I thought I'd bring you dessert." He shifted some papers and put the bowl down directly in front of Sheppard.

"I've just been going over the numbers," Sheppard said as he removed his glasses, picked up the spoon, and began to eat his ice cream.

"What's done is done, Daniel. You and everybody else did the best you could. There's no point in recalculating what you can't redo."

"No, that's not what I'm working on. I'm trying to plot the impact swath, the most likely points for asteroid fragments to hit."

Suddenly Parker was very interested. He pulled up a chair and sat down. "And?"

"It's a fairly complex computation that has to factor in the time of anticipated impact, the speed of the fragments, the rotation of the Earth, the gravitational influence of the moon, the interactive influence of the various pieces, while anticipating the potential—"

"Daniel, you know that none of this makes any sense to me. Just cut to the chase. Where will they land?"

"My figures have an error factor of up to five degrees latitude and perhaps up to ten degrees longitude, depending on the latitudinal errors."

"I get it. I promise not to sue you if you're wrong by a degree or two. Where are they going to hit?"

Sheppard put his glasses back on and picked up a sheet of paper filled with numbers.

"As you are aware, our efforts to distort or change the path of the asteroid resulted in it fragmenting into close to five thousand pieces, some small and others still very large. The nuclear explosions that caused the asteroid to fragment have resulted in those pieces being flung across a much larger area than originally occupied by the one mass."

"I know. It's about five thousand kilometres across the newly created asteroid field," Parker said.

"What you might not know concerns the ongoing transformation of these fragments. While those at the outside continue to move farther apart, still accelerated slightly by the lingering force of the explosion, those at the core are actually reconstituting as their combined gravity brings them back together again."

"So they're reforming into one asteroid?" Parker asked.

"Not reforming so much as *clustering*. And in doing so they are becoming potentially more dangerous."

"Are you saying that what we did, that explosion, accomplished nothing?" Parker asked.

"I'm not saying that. What I am saying is that I have many unanswered questions. I've been working on the simulation. Let me show you. Screen on, program simulation, Impact One," he said.

The wall behind Sheppard suddenly became a gigantic screen showing the Earth, all blue and white and innocent, slowly turning in the blackness of space.

"Please add political boundaries and place names," the professor said. The innocent blue sphere became tainted, the political boundaries marked, cities named, and different countries defined by different colours.

"The asteroid fragments will most certainly all hit in the northern hemisphere."

"Lucky us," Parker replied.

"Projected impact sites are between twenty-two degrees and fifty-seven degrees north latitude. Please show

247

those latitude lines," he said, and the computer responded.

Two lines showed up on the simulation of Earth. The bottom one cut across the top of Africa while the top was slightly below the northernmost tip of England. In between was most of Europe.

"Keeping in mind that these lines—"

"I know, could be wrong by five degrees," Parker said. "Where will the first asteroids hit?"

"I believe the leading edge of the asteroid belt will enter Earth's atmosphere directly above Italy and Libya."

"So they'll be hit first."

"Probably not."

"But you just said that—"

"That the leading edge of the belt will enter the atmosphere above those countries. The leading edge is composed of the smallest fragments, those that were tossed the farthest from the centre of the original asteroid. I believe that most of these will be burned up by the atmosphere upon entry, with the exception of a few smaller impacts—perhaps the size of cars or a truck."

"So not so big."

"Each of those will hit with the explosive power of a small atomic explosion, perhaps similar in power to the bomb that levelled Hiroshima."

The simulation showed the first bursts of colour in the atmosphere over Italy, and then, as the Earth rotated, the first impacts hitting Spain and Algeria and Morocco.

"The pieces will continue to fall as the Earth rotates."

Now the simulation showed impacts into the ocean.

Parker noticed that the results of these impacts, waves being thrown into the air and starting to radiate outward, were becoming consistently larger, a reflection of the continued increase in the size of the fragments.

"The largest fragments will hit in the middle of the Atlantic Ocean, clustered around forty-five degrees west."

"So North America will be spared?" Parker asked.

Sheppard laughed. "'Spared' is hardly how I would describe it. The initial waves—the tsunamis created by those larger impacts—will travel at a speed faster than Earth's rotation, hitting the East Coast prior to any actual asteroid impact."

"Not a good day to be at the beach."

"Or within hundreds of kilometres of the beach. Those waves could be in excess of three hundred metres high and obliterate every life form, every hint of a life form, within three hundred kilometres of the coast. Which means there will be virtually no life on the East Coast to witness the initial impacts of the asteroid fragments."

The simulated globe continued to spin, and impacts—similar to those that hit Spain—started to explode on the Eastern Seaboard of first Canada and then the United States. The planet continued to rotate, revealing the Midwest, and the impacts became smaller and smaller, finally resembling the burning of fragments in the atmosphere over Italy as the Rocky Mountains appeared on the simulation.

Parker got up from his seat and walked over to the screen. "So this area will not have any impacts," he said, as he touched an area just east of the mountains.

"Perhaps there will be a few smaller fragments but nothing of significance."

"That's good news."

Sheppard looked at him questioningly.

"I own a little property out that way. You know, just wanting to protect property values," Parker said with a shrug.

"You do realize, don't you, that the impacts will throw up a debris cloud that will obliterate the sun for decades, resulting in all life dying? At the same time, so much energy and heat will be released that the polar ice caps will melt, thus raising the water level to cover over one-third of the existing land mass."

"So you're saying that my land might even become beachfront property?" Parker asked. "Do you know how much beachfront property goes for?"

Sheppard finally realized that Parker was simply "joking around." Of all the theoretical things he understood, humour was one that seemed beyond his grasp.

"You're kidding . . . pulling my leg," he said.

"I don't see much alternative." Parker paused. "You're a mathematician. Let me ask you a question: What do you think the odds are that somebody in my line of work would live as long as I have?"

"I really would need much more data about your past to formulate an answer. I thought that perhaps, someday, you might share your past with me."

"It's not the sort of thing that I've ever wanted to share. There are things I've done that I am neither proud

of nor pleased with, but at the time, it seemed there was
no choice."

"I understand."

"Do you?" Parker asked.

Sheppard shrugged. "Probably not."

There was an uneasy silence. After so many years, the
silence between the two men had become comfortable. And
maybe it was all those years together that allowed Sheppard
to ask the next question.

"What is it like to take a life?"

There was no answer. Maybe he was wrong and he
didn't have that right.

"I'm sorry, that was uncalled for," Sheppard said.

"No," Parker said. "I'm surprised you haven't asked me
that before. I was just trying to think of what to say. You
know, each time can be very different, but in the end it's all
the same."

"How many times has it been?"

"Please, don't make me try to count."

"There have been *that*—? I'm sorry."

"That's all right. It's unbelievable, even to me, that I
don't know the exact answer. Don't get me wrong, I know
exactly how many people I've killed face to face." He paused,
his eyes closed. "I can still see their faces . . . each and every
one of them." He opened his eyes again. "It's the peripheral
casualties—people in the background, people killed by
others because of what I set in motion—that are unknown
to me. And that number far exceeds those lives taken with
my own hands."

"Do you ever regret what you did?"

"To not regret would mean not being human. I have regrets, but I believe what I did was necessary. Without that belief I don't think I could live with myself. I was simply completing my assignments."

"Doing your job."

"That's my excuse, just following orders." A sad smile came to his face. "I hope they know that I took no pleasure in what I did. I was simply performing my role . . . a role that made me a legalized serial killer, an assassin, a mass murderer."

Sheppard burst into laughter. Parker stopped talking and looked at him questioningly.

"I was just thinking about my own failures," Sheppard said. "Failures that will result in the deaths of over nine billion people, the death of our entire species. Certainly makes you seem like a small fish in the killing category."

"You're not responsible for those deaths," Parker said. "You did do something."

"Something?"

"You know as well as I do that the fragmentation will result in fewer pieces impacting. That will moderate the long-term effect on the planet, and ultimately will allow life to rebound sooner."

"That is a small blessing to the cockroaches that might be able to survive."

"Maybe it will be more than cockroaches," Parker said. "I was talking to some of the men in the biosphere division and they think that any life that can survive fifteen to thirty years will be able to re-emerge into a surface climate and atmosphere that can sustain life."

"If the dust cloud that will engulf the planet subsides to allow sunlight to penetrate to the surface, and volcanic activity dies down, and radiation levels decrease, then yes, life could start to return to the surface. Assuming there is life to return."

"I'm betting heavy on the cockroaches. I've had them in my apartment and, believe me, practically *nothing* can kill them," Parker joked.

"You are an optimist."

"I have to be. I'm human. I mean, who knows? Maybe some of those survivalists can dig down deep enough to withstand the impacts," Parker suggested

"The impacts, yes; the *results* of those impacts, no. I've done the calculations." Sheppard shifted papers on his desk, looking for the specific page on which those numbers were written. "And I do not believe that there is any mathematical—"

Parker reached out and grabbed the piece of paper from his hand. "Daniel, there's something your numbers can't tell you. I mean, think about the odds of mankind even being here in the first place. Think about the even higher odds against our being able to survive as a species this long. There's something about us humans that refuses to quit, that isn't smart enough to know we're not supposed to win. And somehow, maybe because of that ignorance, we survive. That's what I'm counting on."

"I wish I could be so confident."

"I'm not confident. I'm just saying, don't count us out. Do you believe in God?" Parker asked, suddenly steering the topic in an unexpected direction.

"My family always went to church," he answered.

"That wasn't my question. Do you believe in God?"

"The almighty, all-powerful, sitting-on-a-throne-in-Heaven God?" Sheppard asked.

"If that's how you see him, then sure. Do you believe?"

"I am a mathematician. I deal with probability, calculations, the pure truth of numbers."

"So you don't believe?"

"On the contrary. Because I know the odds against evolution, the mathematical improbability of it creating us, I think I do believe that we were given a push from above. I do believe in there being a God."

"And as he sits there on his throne and we pass before him, do you think we'll be judged?" Parker asked. There was a new anxiety in his voice.

"Muslims believe that a man is preceded to Heaven by his deeds, good and bad, and those deeds determine his future in the afterlife," Sheppard said.

"Good thing I'm not a Muslim," Parker replied, the calm tone back in his voice.

"Catholics believe that as long as you die having truly repented your sins, then you are forgiven."

"That's reassuring, but what do *you* think?" Parker asked.

"I'm far from a theologian, so I'm not sure I can give you any sort of—"

"No," Parker said, cutting him off. "I want to know *your* opinion. I *value* your opinion."

Sheppard didn't answer right away. He wasn't sure what to say, but he knew he had to say something.

"I think that God is gentle and kind," he finally said.

"You haven't spent much time thumbing through the Old Testament, have you?" Parker commented.

"I think he'll judge us not so much by what we did as by the motives behind those actions." He paused. "If there is a Heaven, I think we'll both get in."

"I hope you're right." Parker smiled. "All this talk about God and Heaven and the Bible makes me think about Judgment Day. Maybe those religious fanatics were right and we weren't supposed to stop that asteroid."

"I don't believe that for a second. We were given an opportunity. What failed was our technology and not the will of God," Sheppard said. "It is not God's will that we die."

"Now you're the one to sound overly confident," Parker noted.

"I guess in a few months we'll find out."

Parker had a strange look in his eyes. "It could be three months. You never can tell about things. Anyway, that wasn't the reason I came to see you. I want to take you for a drive."

Sheppard had never been taken for a drive. For the past few months he hadn't even been allowed outside of the compound. Why would Parker suggest . . . ? Sheppard's heart skipped a beat. He knew what this meant. He'd wondered if it would come to this.

Slowly he rose from his desk. There was no point in fighting or resisting in any way. He didn't even know if he would if he could. He had failed. Maybe he deserved what was going to happen.

"You've been a good friend," Sheppard said solemnly.

"So have you."

"I'm not just saying that," Sheppard said. "I know you've saved my life . . . at least twice that I know of."

"And some that you didn't," Parker said.

"Thank you for keeping me alive this long. I just want you to know that I understand, and more important, I forgive you."

"Forgive me for . . . " Parker suddenly understood and started to chuckle. "Daniel, I'm inviting you to go for a ride. I'm not *taking* you for a ride. I'm not going to kill you."

Sheppard let out a big sigh and his whole body flushed. Maybe he wasn't as ready to face death as he'd thought. He felt both relieved and embarrassed.

"Why would you ever think that there was reason for me to kill you?" Parker asked.

"I failed."

"We *all* failed."

"I know . . . it's just that I was in charge."

"And you led us well. Besides, if I was assigned to kill you I wouldn't drive you any place. I would simply do something that would look like an accident." He pointed at the empty bowl. "I would have poisoned your ice cream and made it look as though you'd died of a heart attack."

Sheppard's eyes widened in shock and surprise.

"But of course I didn't. Come on, you could *really* use a ride in the country. Get away from it all . . . relax . . . get some fresh air."

And then Parker did something he'd never done before. As he walked with Sheppard to the door, he put his arm around his friend's shoulders, and he finished with a hearty pat on the back as the two walked out together.

CHAPTER TWENTY-NINE

Sheppard climbed into the vehicle and its large metal door swung shut, sealing him and Parker inside. He settled into his seat feeling comfortable—and safe. Sitting behind the window's tinted bulletproof glass, he was invisible to outside eyes. And besides, it wasn't as if they were going outside in a minivan. This vehicle was clad with a combination of armour and a special polymer designed to withstand not only bullets but even rocket-launched grenades or land mines. They might be leaving the security of the compound behind, but they weren't leaving security behind.

Their vehicle rolled up to the main gate, one of only two entrances to the compound. Large steel doors were flanked by high concrete walls, which were in turn topped with electrified razor wire, cameras, and infrared sensors. The walls were punctuated at intervals by higher guard towers. Sheppard knew that all of this security was necessary—it was for his safety and the safety of every other person in the project—but they still looked like prison walls. In his mind, though, there was one wall but two prisons—one on the outside and one on the inside.

Sheppard had spent so many years indoors and underground that every time he saw the surface it was like seeing it for the first time. It was almost as if he'd forgotten this was all out here. Once, he'd been so occupied with his work that he'd missed two entire seasons. When he had finally journeyed outside after four or five months of concentration, he'd been astonished to find snow on the ground.

They stopped at the checkpoint.

"Request to leave the compound," Parker said to unseen guards through a com-link.

"Reason for permission to exit?" a voice replied.

"Beyond your level of clearance. Authorization code 787354."

There was silence as the authorization was checked and cleared.

"One to leave?" the voice asked.

"Yes, one," Parker replied.

Sheppard was about to say something but Parker quickly turned to him and gestured for silence. He complied, but he felt uncomfortable yet again. Why didn't Parker want anybody to know there was somebody else in the vehicle?

The steel gates slowly glided apart and Parker drove through toward a second gate, identical to the first. The first gate closed behind them, triggering the second to open in response. Beyond that second gate, behind a large fence, was a crowd of people. There was always a crowd outside, made up of the curious who just wanted to see, the religious who prayed for the souls of those evil-doers inside, and more ominously, those who might want to harm them. A squad of soldiers and security forces split the crowd open to allow them clear passage.

Parker slowed the vehicle slightly but kept moving. There were angry people violently shoving and straining against the security line, trying to get to the car. Sheppard could see more than hear that they were yelling something at him. One of the protesters looked familiar—he'd seen that face many times on video screens, standing before the altar in a mammoth cathedral. The Reverend Abraham Honey had spoken then of fear, of a lake of fire, of a Heavenly Kingdom that would not welcome men, like Sheppard, who worshipped the false god of science. Sheppard felt a shiver run up his spine at the thought.

As they drove past he saw, too, ordinary men and women and children. He saw the signs that some of them held—protests for or against their project—as well as glimpses of their faces. He tried not to look. They were all going to die, and he was responsible. It was hard enough to know that without having to look them in the eye.

"Sorry about the secrecy," Parker said as they cleared the edge of the crowd and accelerated down the now open road. "No telling who might be listening in to our radio exchanges. Or, for that matter, whether any of the guards are actually counter-agents working for Judgment Day."

"Do you think that's possible?"

"No telling. We've lost a lot of people over the past two weeks."

"What do you mean 'lost'?" Sheppard was suddenly feeling anxious again.

"They don't see the point in working on or even guarding a project that's come to an end," Parker explained. "Could be that some of them have just decided to go and spend their last days with their families. Or maybe some of them used to believe in science but now believe that their only salvation lies in accepting that this is God's will. So many people are flocking to churches these days that they can't even come close to fitting them all in. It's got to the point where you really can't trust anybody. You know that, right?"

Sheppard felt the hairs on the back of his neck stand up.

"Other than me, of course," Parker added. "Are you nervous?"

"A little."

"You're sweating. Do you want the air conditioning turned up?"

"Maybe a bit."

Parker spun a little dial and the cab was filled with a rush of cool air.

"This is quite the vehicle," Sheppard said.

"I like it, although it's no Ferrari. Have you ever driven a Ferrari?"

"I never learned to drive."

"Really?" Parker was clearly shocked. "That must have really hindered your dating life as a teenager."

"I'm afraid I didn't have a dating life," Sheppard said. "I was a little preoccupied."

"Come on, you couldn't have been so preoccupied that there wasn't some girl you had a crush on in high school."

"I was eight years old when I entered high school, and eleven when I was accepted at a university."

"Wow, that would explain the lack of dating," Parker said. "And you never married."

"I was married to my work." Sheppard paused. "You never married either."

"There have been women, but in my line of work it just never seemed right to get involved, to expose somebody else to risk."

"Do you ever regret that?" Sheppard asked.

"I used to," Parker admitted. "I used to wonder what it would have been like to have a couple of kids . . . you know, somebody to live on after I checked out of this world." He laughed, sadly. "Now I guess that isn't such a big deal, is it?"

"Theoretically, I'm sure I could have learned to drive," Sheppard said, changing the subject. "I just never got around to it. There never seemed to be time. And now . . . it hardly seems to matter."

"I guess not."

"I wonder how long it's been since I've been outside the compound," Sheppard mused absently.

"Fifteen months," Parker answered.

Of course Parker would know, because he would have been with him.

"We couldn't risk you being outside during the last critical period."

"And now you *can* risk it?" Sheppard asked.

"Now the risk level is much lower. Since our plan to destroy the asteroid failed, the number of attacks from Judgment Day have fallen dramatically. They may be fanatics but they are *religious* fanatics. 'Thou shalt not kill' has come into effect again, since they don't necessarily see a reason to kill anymore. It's back to letting God make that decision."

"So the religious and strategic value of killing me has significantly diminished," Sheppard said.

"Your whole status has changed. You've gone from the Devil's right-hand man to a failed false prophet."

"I'm not sure if that's a promotion or a demotion."

"At least you're not on the top of their official death list," Parker said.

"They had a death list?" Sheppard gasped.

"Yeah, sort of America's Most Unwanted. At one point there was a bounty of more than fifty million dollars on you."

Sheppard shook his head sadly. "How ironic is it that they had to offer money instead of just a place in Heaven."

"I think the place in Heaven was understood. The money would just make the wait for Heaven more enjoyable. Anyway, you spent most of the last seven years either at the top of the list or in second place."

"Did I fall or rise in value?"

"Rise. You and Dr. Markell usually occupied those spots."

Sheppard thought of his friend often. Hard to believe what had happened. He still sometimes expected the door to his office to pop open and Andrew to barge in with some strange theory or idea, or a bad joke, or a cup of tea. What had driven him to take his own life, to try to destroy the project?

"It's not your fault that he did what he did," Parker said.

Sheppard had long been accustomed to Parker reading his mind. He'd found it amusing at first, then confusing, troubling, and eventually reassuring. What Parker didn't know was that Sheppard could often read his thoughts, too. He supposed that made them something like an old married couple.

"It was unfortunate what happened to him," Parker said. "Not only the end, but the way he was being excluded from decisions."

"That's what led him to that insanity, I suppose. I should have been more supportive, insisted that he remain in the top position instead of me. I should never have agreed to become the head of the project."

"His demotion was going to happen, whether you agreed to it or not. He was incapable of heading the program, and his mental deterioration was dooming the whole enterprise to failure."

"As opposed to the success I made of it?" Sheppard asked.

"You did as well as anybody else. Ultimately, I knew you would become the head," Parker said. "And do you know why?"

"Because the cream always rises to the top?" Sheppard joked.

"You became the chief because everybody knew that you were the best man for the job. You weren't about politics, or ego, or ambition. You were about the truth, about the solution. You were trusted."

That was what Sheppard had always aimed for, but it was nice to actually hear somebody say it. It made him happy and uncomfortable all at once.

"It all seems so peaceful out here," Sheppard said as he looked out the window at the passing scenery.

"It *is* more peaceful in the country. People grow their own food, heat their houses with wood from the forest. Still, no matter how calm it seems, I wouldn't want to be stopping to change a flat tire out here."

"Could this thing *get* a flat tire?"

"It could, but it can also drive over a hundred kilometres an hour on six flat tires, and it's equipped with twin forty-calibre machine guns and a rocket-grenade launcher."

"Not standard equipment on that Ferrari of yours."

"Although the two of them get about the same mileage," Parker said.

"Try not to run out of gas," Sheppard joked.

"If I did, I could scramble a Black Hawk helicopter to be here in less than five minutes with a can of gas, so no worries there, either."

"Then what *are* the worries, if Judgment Day is now dormant?"

"Not dormant, just reduced. They'd still like to capture or kill you. Can you imagine the coverage of them executing you?"

"I think I'll try *not* to imagine that," Sheppard admitted.

"But that's not the greatest risk right now. People are more desperate than ever. They'd happily kill us just for the resources that this vehicle represents. And when they find out about the impact sites, things are going to get even more turbulent," Parker said.

"It hasn't been decided if we're going to make that information public. Making the sites known wouldn't save anybody. It would do nothing more than provoke mass migration and panic, as people flee the East Coast for the West, or the northern hemisphere for the south, in a false belief that they'll be spared."

"I understand," Parker said. "But sometimes false hope is better than no hope. Maybe I'll take a little trip to my place in the country. You did say it wasn't going to be hit."

"Not hit, but not spared."

"What if I hid in the basement?" Parker asked playfully.

"I don't know—is your basement over 250 metres deep?"

"I could bring a shovel, I suppose."

"Right, well, you start digging, and when you hit 600 metres, let me know," Sheppard said. "That's a basement I'd like to see."

The vehicle slowed down and came to a stop. "We're here."

Sheppard looked around. Aside from the trees and rocks there was nothing but a little dirt path running off to the side.

"Where is here? Why did we stop?" He suddenly felt anxious and exposed again.

"Don't worry, Daniel. I told you, I'm not going to

whack you. This isn't a gangster movie. We have an appointment." He looked at his watch. "It won't be long now."

Sheppard felt that perhaps he ought to have been worried, scared. But he wasn't. He trusted Parker with his life. And for the first time, Parker had called him "Daniel." He supposed, without having much experience in this area, that they had, somewhere over the years, become friends. And he supposed that friends didn't take one another into the woods to kill them.

Sheppard's eye was caught by movement. A car—small and simple and old—was bumping along the dirt road toward them. He simultaneously became more alert—who was it?—and more relaxed. Obviously they had nothing to fear when they were inside their armoured vehicle.

The little car slowed and stopped. Two people—an older man, tall, with flaming red hair, and a boy, maybe fifteen or sixteen—climbed out. The man offered a friendly wave and a big smile. The boy did neither.

There was something about the man. Sheppard was sure that he didn't know him . . . but somehow he looked familiar.

"Are those people our appointment?" Sheppard asked.

"I believe so. See this button?" Parker said, pointing at a large knob in the centre of the console.

Sheppard nodded.

"That's the emergency com-link. Hit that and you'll have help within five minutes. Stay inside the vehicle."

Before Sheppard could even think to react, Parker had climbed out and closed the door behind him, sealing

Sheppard inside. He was locked in, safe and separated, able to see but not hear what was going to happen next. Able to watch, but unable to do anything about what he might see.

CHAPTER THIRTY

Parker extended his hand, and he and the old man shook.

"It's good to meet you after all these years," Joshua Fitchett said. "Your reports have been very helpful in our project."

"I'm glad. It's an honour to finally meet you, sir," Parker replied. He looked at the boy questioningly.

"He's my bodyguard," Fitchett explained. "You wouldn't expect me to come all this way out here without security, would you?" He laughed. Neither Parker nor Billy did.

"Billy, this is Agent Parker."

Each eyed the other suspiciously.

"Is he in there?" Fitchett asked, gesturing toward Parker's vehicle.

"As promised."

"Does he know who he's meeting with?"

"I haven't said anything," Parker replied.

"Is he coming out?"

Parker slowly and carefully surveyed the scene. He couldn't see anybody or anything out of the ordinary. Maybe that was what troubled him the most. He should have seen some sort of security.

"If you're wondering about security, you have my word that we are in the very centre of a completely secure zone," Fitchett said. "I actually did bring along a full team of security on our flight. They are ringing the site."

Parker had no reason to doubt him. If he had had any real doubts, he wouldn't have been there in the first place. Even though they'd never met before, he was willing to trust that this really was Fitchett, and that the request for a meeting had been legitimate. He was going out on a limb, knowing how easy it would have been for someone to break through the com-link, to send false messages, to find somebody to impersonate Fitchett, who had been so long presumed dead.

Parker heard the car door open behind him. Before he even had time to react Sheppard was out of the car. Slowly, Parker slipped his right hand inside his jacket to place his fingers against the handle of his gun. If this was a trap, they weren't going to be the only two people who died today.

"You're Joshua Fitchett!" Sheppard exclaimed as he rushed toward them, hand outstretched. "It is such a pleasure to meet you!"

The two men shook hands enthusiastically.

"You recognize him?" Parker asked.

"We were at a conference together . . . well, not

together, really—I was in the audience and he gave the keynote speech—but I've certainly seen enough pictures to recognize the man."

Parker started to remove his hand but then hesitated. It was reassuring to have a weapon that close.

"You don't seem surprised to see me alive," Fitchett said.

"I've learned to read obituaries with a certain amount of healthy skepticism," Sheppard said. "Especially after having read my own."

"Ah, yes. You yourself were dead for a few years, as I recall."

"The fire that supposedly killed you . . . ?" Sheppard began.

"That was of my own doing," Fitchett told him.

"But why?"

"I needed to disappear, to be free of the involvement and influence of others. I had work to do, and I didn't want anybody, including the International Aerospace Research Institute, to interfere with that."

"But your help could have been so valuable," Sheppard said. "Who knows, with your contribution we could have—"

"Done no better," Fitchett said. "Your course of action was completely correct."

"Had it been correct, it would have succeeded."

Fitchett shook his head. "Success was never possible. Involving me in the failure would only have stopped me from doing what *I* needed to do, being where *I* needed to be."

"Where *have* you been all these years?"

"I think that's what this meeting is about," Fitchett said.

"Excuse me, gentlemen," Parker interjected. "I feel very exposed out here. Perhaps we could talk about this in the safety of our vehicle?"

"I'm afraid not," Fitchett said. "That would make *my* security team uneasy. Speaking of which, I've been asked to request that you remove your right hand from your weapon . . . slowly."

Parker complied, pulling his hand slowly from his jacket to show that his hand was empty.

Fitchett turned his head slightly and motioned to an earpiece. "I'm in constant communication with the head of my security team. As I've said, we are in the middle of a safe zone, surrounded on all sides. We are far from exposed."

In a way, that information made Parker feel *more* exposed. If those security forces were able to see him slipping his hand into his jacket, they were also in position to take him out with a single shot.

"No one is here to harm anybody else," Fitchett offered reassuringly. "In fact, the continued safety of you two gentlemen is of extreme importance to me."

"Is that why we're here?" Sheppard asked. "So you can see that we're safe?"

Fitchett laughed. "First, before we get to the reason for this meeting, I wanted to offer my congratulations on your efforts."

"Are you being facetious?" Sheppard asked.

"Certainly not, and my sincere apology if you thought I was. What you did was nothing short of miraculous. You managed to hold together the largest organization ever assembled in the history of the planet, wrestling with competing interests, ideologies, governments, policies, politics, and opinions, and somehow you were able to make a valiant assault on the greatest danger that the planet has ever faced."

"I would take the credit, if that effort had actually succeeded," Sheppard said.

"But, Dr. Sheppard," Fitchett replied, "you *saved* the planet."

"Sir, you are completely mistaken. All human life will be obliterated."

"I didn't say you saved *mankind*. I said you saved the *planet*. My calculations indicate that the original mass of that asteroid, hitting in one location, would have potentially changed both the orbit and the rotation of the planet, almost certainly rendering it incapable of supporting life."

"There is a body of proof to support that theory," Sheppard acknowledged.

"But the asteroid was destroyed, deflecting some pieces completely and creating an asteroid field of thousands of smaller fragments, so that the energy absorbed by the collisions with Earth will be spread across a much greater area. The rotation of the planet will absorb and disperse the direct energy, which will result in *no* significant change in Earth's flight through space," Fitchett explained. "Thus saving the planet."

"That will be small comfort to the billions of people who will perish, not to mention the hundreds of thousands of other species that will become instantly extinct."

"Perhaps more life will survive than you believe, but most important, you have ensured that the environment in which life will be able to exist has been safeguarded."

"Again, small comfort to imagine that in a few million years we might, potentially, re-evolve as people."

"I do not wish to insult a mathematician of your renown, but I think your projection of millions of years might, in fact, be off . . . by millions of years."

Sheppard looked at him questioningly.

"What would you think if I were to say to you that I believe human life can be re-established as soon as thirty years from the time of impact?" Fitchett asked.

"If it were anybody except you saying that, I would think that they were either unable to accept reality or completely insane."

"There have always been those who have questioned my sanity," Fitchett replied.

"There is a fine line between genius and madness," Sheppard acknowledged.

He thought about the various options that had flowed across his desk over the years. Everything from cryonics—freezing humans in suspended animation until conditions would allow them to be revived—to survivalist plans to burrow into the earth or under the ocean with enough supplies to exist until the surface could support life again.

"Am I to believe that you have created a circumstance in which human life might not only survive the initial impact, but also survive the results of that impact for a sufficient length of time to allow the planet to readjust and return to habitable conditions before life re-emerges? Is that correct?" Sheppard asked.

"Yes," Fitchett simply replied.

"And which option have you pursued?" Sheppard asked.

"A below-ground facility. But I'd much rather *show* you than tell *you*," Fitchett said.

Sheppard smiled. It was a sad smile. "I guess at this time at least a possibility of survival is better than anything I can offer. I have nothing except information about the end."

"The end," Fitchett said, "but not necessarily *your* end."

"What do you mean?"

"I am offering you the opportunity to join our project, to become one of those people who will survive."

Sheppard heard the words and understood what he was being offered—his life. He took a deep breath. He needed to think—or at least to appear to be considering the offer— before he spoke.

"If you are correct and you have constructed a facility that could survive the impact and the years that follow, there is still no possible way for a man of my age to either live long enough to journey back to the surface or repro- duce offspring that could repopulate the planet when that time arrives."

"*Neither* of us will live to see that day," Fitchett agreed.

"Then humanity would be better served by offering our two spots to younger people, such as this boy, wouldn't you say?"

"My dear professor, my offer to you is more than a misguided act of charity. You are a brilliant mathematician, one whose talents can be harnessed to increase the likelihood of our project's success. I want you to survive because your survival makes it more possible for *mankind* to survive."

"But for me to live even another day after the inevitable deaths of nine billion people . . . deaths that are on my hands," Sheppard said.

"Dr. Sheppard, your goal was to ensure the survival of mankind. I am offering you an important and ongoing role in that goal. Sacrificing yourself would be against the very principles and purpose to which you have dedicated your life."

"But I can't just walk away from the people I've worked with. It wouldn't be fair to them or to—" He stopped and looked at Parker. "This is what you were trying to tell me. You knew all about this. That little place in Idaho you were telling me about . . . is this it?"

"Agent Parker has been offered a place," Fitchett explained.

Parker nodded his head. "I'm sorry I couldn't tell you."

"How long has it been?" Sheppard asked. "How long have you been going behind my back?"

"Many years."

"I just . . . I just can't believe that you would betray the organization . . . that you would betray *me*."

"He betrayed nothing and nobody," Fitchett said. "He has been operating under a higher set of directives. My actions have taken place with the implicit but covert assistance of many of those in your organization. You'll be surprised by the number of your colleagues who have been part of this operation. It's a sign of overconfidence not to have a backup plan."

"I just can't believe that I knew nothing . . . nothing about any of this," Sheppard sputtered.

"You were not *meant* to know anything about it," Fitchett said. "It was best that your total focus be on the goal of destroying or deflecting that asteroid. And up to three months ago we all lived with that hope . . . no matter how faint. Even as I've worked the last seventeen years to create the plan if you *did* fail, I hoped that you would be successful."

"So what now?" Sheppard asked.

"You return to your position. When the time is near, you and Agent Parker and a few others will be flown to our location."

"I'm not sure I can accept this invitation," Sheppard said.

"I understand your reluctance and will obviously accept whatever decision you make." He paused. "Although there is one thing we *would* ask you to do."

Sheppard looked at him questioningly.

"You are in control of numerous stores of materials— things that are no longer vital for your operation but are essential for our success. We need you to provide authorization to allow these supplies to be released. We, too, suffered from sabotage. Judgment Day damaged your facilities and operations and ours as well."

"What materials do you require?"

"Agent Parker has all of the information and coordinates necessary. All we ask is that you sign off on the requests as they cross your desk. Will you do that?"

"I'll sign," he quickly replied.

"I'm very pleased, but I must admit I'm surprised that you aren't asking more questions about the nature of the supplies and materials we need," Fitchett said.

Sheppard shrugged. "Does it matter? Whatever it is that you need can't help or hinder our agenda because we have none. I just know that I have no moral right to stand in the way of your plans."

"Because you think we might be successful?"

"Because I do not know that you *won't* be successful," Sheppard said.

"Thank you." Fitchett extended his hand and the two men shook.

"We'd better get back," Parker said, "before anybody realizes you're gone."

"Then I guess this is goodbye, for now," Fitchett said. He paused. "But, I hope, not forever."

Sheppard turned and walked back to his vehicle. Parker slowly backed away, keeping an eye on his surroundings until he, too, got into the vehicle.

Billy and Fitchett walked back to their car, while Fitchett gave instructions to his security team to stand down.

As they drove away, Billy turned to Fitchett. "So does that mean we have the rocket fuel?"

"That means that he'll *release* the fuel. Getting it to our facility might be even more difficult. How difficult, we'll soon find out."

PART 6

CHAPTER THIRTY-ONE

T MINUS 20 DAYS

SWITZERLAND

"We're ready to go in fifteen seconds. Cue the lights."

The already bright lights became brighter, and Sheppard squinted slightly as his eyes adjusted. He could feel sweat dripping down the side of his face and quickly wiped it off with the sleeve of his jacket. He tried not to think about the fact that in a few seconds, he'd be live to an audience of billions of people. He tried especially not to think of the message he was about to deliver to them.

"And five . . . four . . . three." The director held up two fingers, one finger, and pointed to signal that the cameras were rolling.

Sheppard froze for just a second, and then started to speak.

"Good evening. My name is Dr. Daniel Sheppard and I am the director of the International Aerospace Research Institute, the organization that was entrusted with the responsibility for saving the planet from collision with an asteroid, a collision that would end human life." He paused and took a breath. It was important to breathe. "After almost two decades of planning by the greatest minds of our planet, we initiated a plan to detonate an explosion to destroy or divert this asteroid. As you are all aware, this explosion took place on April 23 of this year.

"While I'm sure that we all hoped for an immediate answer as to the success of this mission, that answer was not forthcoming. The unprecedented nature of the threat, the complexity of the attempted solution, and the technology necessary to provide definite answers made this assessment difficult. And while we have been gathering this information, the vacuum has been filled with speculation, rumours, fears, and a great deal of misinformation and half-truths."

Sheppard struggled over "half-truths" because much of what the world knew was actually correct—was, in fact, information leaked from the institute.

"I feel we now have enough data, and also a moral responsibility, to share our findings with you."

He reached down and lifted the paper in front of him. He was now going to read, word for word, what was written there. He knew it was unspeakably important, maybe the most important thing ever written in human history, and he wanted to get it absolutely right.

"While the mission to destroy the asteroid was technically a triumph and resulted in more than 60 percent of the mass of the asteroid being diverted or converted to a form that is no longer a threat to our planet, the remaining mass will hit the surface of the Earth in twenty days' time, on September 19. The remaining fragments—over three hundred pieces large enough to cause significant planetary effects—will land in a path that is projected to be over sixteen hundred kilometres in width and over six thousand kilometres in length."

He took a drink from the glass of water on the table beside him.

"Our best estimates are that this impact area will begin over southern Europe and northern Africa and extend westward across the Atlantic Ocean, continuing as far as the central part of the North American continent.

"I am aware that there have been rumours, and that hundreds of thousands of people have already relocated to what they believe are safe areas outside of the impact zone. We need you to know that there are *no* safe areas. The impact of these fragments will release more than twenty times the energy of all the nuclear devices used in the attempt to destroy the asteroid.

"This will result in a cloud of ash, dust, and smoke obstructing the sun and eliminating all plant life. A drastic rise in global temperature will result in the melting of the polar ice caps, and the subsequent rise in ocean levels is predicted to be over four metres. The effect of this will be the extinction of all life, with the possible exception of certain primitive deep-sea creatures that do not rely on photosynthesis for their survival.

"It is with great sadness that I make this announcement, but we felt strongly that we had a moral responsibility to inform you of the impending events. I want you to know that we worked to our utmost capacity, using all the resources available, to change this outcome. But in the end, we failed. I wish to formally apologize for that failure to avert this tragedy, and as the leader of the institute, I acknowledge my ultimate responsibility."

Sheppard looked up from his papers and directly into the camera.

"I leave you now to spend these last days with your friends and loved ones, and to seek peace. Although I am not a deeply religious man, I am a man of faith. I hope, in the time that remains, that we can treat one another as if there is a God, and He is watching us. Good night."

There was a slight pause. "And we're clear!" the director called out.

The bright lights shut off and the camera was wheeled away from Sheppard. He tried to get up but his legs wobbled and he slumped back into the seat.

"Are you all right?" Parker asked.

"I would imagine I'm as fine as I can be, considering that I've just announced a death sentence on the entire planet."

Parker offered him a hand and he rose to his feet.

"Remember, you didn't cause this—you just announced it," Parker said.

"But I didn't stop it, either, and that, ultimately, was my job."

"If you failed it's because we all failed. What wasn't your job was to go on a world-wide broadcast and personally tell everybody," Parker said.

"I felt I had no choice."

"Well, I'm convinced it would have been better for them to believe in their safety until the end. Do you think that the world knowing the facts is going to change anything for the better?"

"They still had the moral right to know," Sheppard said.

"And do you think they're now going to act in a *more* moral way?" Parker questioned. "Look around at what's already happening out there."

"I can only hope."

Parker shook his head. "You really are an idealist."

"I guess we'll see."

"What I don't have to guess about is the fact that you've made my job that much harder," Parker said. "For seventeen years we've worked to keep your identity and image unknown. Now everybody knows who you are and what you look like. You might as well have painted a target on your back."

"I can't believe that Judgment Day cares anymore whether I live or die."

"They care. There's still a bounty on your head. Besides, every religious nut hoping to get to Heaven or paradise or reincarnation, or whatever, might think that killing you is their ticket to ride. And that's not even the worst of it," Parker said. "You've just gone and told the rest of the world that it's because of you that we're all going to die. If I didn't know you personally, I might want to shoot you myself."

"I guess tomorrow or in twenty days . . . it's all the same," Sheppard said.

Parker leaned in closer. "It doesn't have to be twenty days," he whispered. "You know that . . . there *is* a choice."

CHAPTER THIRTY-TWO

The door slid open and Sheppard started slightly. When he realized it was Parker he felt relieved and grateful . . . but why was Parker carrying a rifle? Parker always carried a weapon, but he had never seen him with a rifle before.

"Is everything all right?" Sheppard asked nervously.

"As right as it can be."

"But the gun . . . the assault rifle . . ."

"It's because things are only as right as they can be *given the circumstances*. How is it going out there?" he asked, gesturing to the news report playing on the screen behind Sheppard.

"The trickle of migration has become a mass exodus," Sheppard reported. "Large parts of Europe and the Eastern Seaboard of North America—coastal areas around the world are all being completely deserted."

The television and Internet had been dominated by

images of the migration. Millions of people—families, small children, entire cities—in motion. And the exodus was jagged and cruel and desperate and deadly. The crowds travelled without shelter or food or water, and left in their wake destruction, debris, and thousands of bodies, lives cut short of the few days that remained. When times were so desperate and life so short, there was no shortage of savagery.

More than once Sheppard had thought that informing the public was perhaps his greatest mistake. He should have listened to those advisers—people like Parker—who had cautioned him to keep the truth secret. But he felt there had been too many secrets for too long. It was better for truth to live as long as it could.

"Strange, they believed you about the points of impact, but they didn't seem to pick up on the fact that they're going to die no matter what," Parker said.

"There are reports of large-scale violence as groups defend their territory against those attempting to move in," Sheppard said.

"I guess they didn't listen to that 'God is watching' part, either," Parker said.

"I imagine this is the point where you should say 'I told you so'?"

"Not me," Parker replied. "When you start looking to me for moral guidance you've reached a new level of desperation."

"You know that isn't true. What is true is that I just made things worse . . . far worse."

"That's not your fault either. You were just working with false information."

"What do you mean?" Sheppard asked.

"Your problem is that you believe people are basically good. Me, I always knew better. I believe that civilization is at best nothing more than a very thin veneer. People are full of manners and follow rules, and pretend they care for their fellow man, but when push comes to shove my own grandmother would put a knife in my back."

"Your grandmother?" Sheppard asked.

"You've never met my grandmother . . . she's a tough old bird. That's just how people are."

Sheppard shook his head. "Not all. I would never do that to you, or to anybody else."

"And that's one of the things I've always liked about you. But, really, look around."

He gestured to the images on the screen. It showed a large urban area, debris on the streets, smoke rising from buildings on fire, abandoned cars. Sheppard turned away.

"Organized suicides are taking place all over the world. Couples taking poison, parents taking the lives of their children, whole families dying together," Parker said.

"I can't believe it," Sheppard said.

"I think it makes perfect sense," Parker replied. "Better to control your death, plan it in a good way, than allow it to unfold in a bad way."

"You've never struck me as a candidate for suicide."

"I'm not. I'm planning on living. And you?"

Sheppard didn't answer.

"It's not just getting worse out there every day," Parker said. "It's getting worse in *here*. More and more staff, including security, are deserting."

"And that's why you have the rifle, right?"

Parker nodded. "A pistol isn't necessarily enough. I think it's just a matter of time until we're overrun. The crowds are getting bigger outside the walls, and at the same time our forces are getting smaller and less able to keep them at bay."

"They can't *all* want to kill me."

"No, most of them just want in. They believe that we've built an underground facility here that will withstand the impacts."

"Well, they'll be deeply disappointed," Sheppard said. "And how long before you leave?"

"I guess the question is how long before *you* leave?" Parker asked.

"I don't think I'm going anywhere."

"Funny, you never struck me as the suicidal type either," Parker said.

"I'm not going to commit suicide," Sheppard said.

"Call it what you want, but whether the asteroid gets you or somebody else before that, it's still suicide. You're making a choice to die when you have an option to live."

"I don't see how I can, in good conscience, exercise that option," Sheppard said.

"Because billions are going to die? Well, every one of those billions would kill you or almost anybody else in a second if it meant that they, or maybe their children, could have what you're turning down. If you think about it, your choice is almost insulting to those who don't want to die," Parker said.

"I don't want to die either."

"So what is this, then? Is it all about your misguided sense of guilt?" Parker asked. "You didn't perform the miracle, so you want to die to punish yourself?"

"It isn't that simple."

"Then explain it to me."

"A captain doesn't desert a sinking ship," Sheppard said.

"Sure, he does. He just gets off last, and we're basically at that stage. You know, I should just make you leave. I could tie you up or hit you on the head or put something in your tea to knock you out. You'd wake up out of here, safe and sound."

"You wouldn't do that," Sheppard said.

"I *could*, and you couldn't stop me. You'd even thank me . . . eventually."

"But you won't."

Parker looked disgusted. "No, I won't, and that's the part that's most annoying. It's too late for me to have these sudden bouts of conscience. That sort of soppy sentimentality could cost me my life."

"I'm not asking you to stay."

"No, you're practically *ordering* me to stay," Parker snapped.

"That isn't my intent. You're free to go," Sheppard said.

"You know, it would be kinder for me to put a bullet in your head before I go than to leave you unguarded."

"I just want you to come and say goodbye, so that I can thank you for all that you've done."

"Look, what I'm saying is that I'm not going to say goodbye . . . or put a bullet in your head. My job was—*is*— to protect you, and that job isn't over yet. I *always* finish my assignments. I'm here as long as you're here."

"You can't make me responsible for your death," Sheppard said.

"Why not? You already feel responsible for the impending deaths of nine billion people, so what's one extra life?" Parker asked. "Look, all I'm asking you to do is not close the door to this idea. There's still time."

"How much time?" Sheppard asked.

"A few days if we're lucky . . . maybe five . . . maybe seven, but that would be pushing it." Parker leaned over and turned off the screen. "You didn't cause what's happening out there and you can't control it. They're going to die, whether you and I live or not. Those are independent factors."

He reached inside his jacket and pulled out a pistol, and for a split second Sheppard had a flickering thought about that bullet in his head.

"I want you to keep this with you at all times," Parker said as he placed it on the desk in front of Sheppard.

"I've never even *held* a gun. I wouldn't know how to use it. If I tried I'd probably blow my own foot off."

"You're a pretty smart guy, so I think you can figure out how to use it. I'll give you a little lesson."

He picked up the gun and practically forced it into Sheppard's hand.

"Click off the safety, right there beside your thumb," Parker said. "Do it!"

Sheppard clicked it off.

"Now, just point at the target—aim for the chest, no trick shots—and pull the trigger. Pretty simple. I want you to promise me you'll keep this with you at all times from now on."

"I don't think I could actually shoot anybody."

"You'd be surprised what you can do if somebody is getting ready to kill you. I'll leave you to think," Parker said, and he left the room.

Sheppard sat alone, the gun in his hand. He held it firmly, hefting its weight. He'd never held a pistol before, never even wanted to hold one. But somehow . . . it felt good.

CHAPTER THIRTY-THREE

The building's alarm shrieked and Sheppard sat bolt upright in bed. It was probably nothing—it had been going off intermittently for days. But he still had to check. He reached over to turn on the bedside lamp, but nothing happened, no light. Of course. They'd taken to turning off the generator at night to save the precious little fuel they still had. With the generator off, the air-conditioning and the air-circulation systems weren't functioning either. It was hot and sticky and the air was stale and still.

He fumbled around the top of the night table and his fingers brushed against the pistol first and then the flashlight. He flicked it on, opening up a small patch of light in the darkness.

Sheppard looked at his watch. It was just after three in the morning. He threw his legs over the side of the bed and got to his feet. He was already wearing clothes and his shoes and his glasses—a habit that had come back to him over the past few weeks. It was as though he was subconsciously preparing to flee, even if there was no place to flee to.

He needed to know what was going on. He started for the door, then stopped, spun around, and grabbed the pistol. He clicked the safety on. At night it was always off, ready to fire. He started for the door and— There was a loud pounding and he froze in his tracks.

"Daniel! Open up!"

He recognized the voice instantly. It was Parker.

He rushed to the door and unlocked it. Parker was standing there, his hair wild, wearing only a T-shirt and pants, without shoes, an assault rifle in his hand. Behind him in the hall others were moving about, weapons in hand, flashlight beams bobbing along in front of them as they ran.

"The complex wall has been breached," Parker said.

"Who is it?"

"Does it matter? There are hundreds, and some of them have weapons. They've come in through the main gate and over the wall."

"Will we be able to repel them?" Sheppard asked.

"Nobody is even trying. Everybody is leaving. We have to leave."

"And go where?"

"You know where," Parker said.

"Is there still time for us to get there?" Suddenly, now, with the end in sight, he realized that he didn't want the end to come.

"There will be if we can get out of here. Do you want to live?"

"Yes," Sheppard instantly replied. His quick answer surprised him, but not Parker.

"Then follow me."

"I just have to grab some things and—"

Parker grabbed him and spun him around as he tried to go back into his room. "You already have your gun," he said. "There's nothing else you'll need."

He kept his hand on Sheppard's shoulder and started to drag him away. Sheppard was tired and scared and confused, but he didn't resist.

The corridor was crowded. People Sheppard knew or recognized were standing or moving, but there seemed to be no point or direction or purpose to their movement. In quick glimpses of flashlight-illuminated faces he could see their confusion and fear.

Parker moved quickly, pushing people aside and making space for Sheppard to follow. He was obviously moving with a purpose. He knew where they were going.

Suddenly the quiet murmur of movement and voices was overwhelmed by the sound of gunfire. Parker dropped to his knees and pulled Sheppard down with him. People all around were doing the same thing—no, they were falling . . . people had been shot! Bullets whizzed by their heads, ricocheting off the metal walls, and he could see flashes ahead—gun flashes.

Sheppard jumped at an explosion of sound beside him, and Parker fired his weapon into the corridor ahead— two long, loud rapid-fire bursts. And then there was silence.

Whoever had been firing at them was either gone or dead.

"Get up!" Parker yelled, and his strong hands pulled Sheppard to his feet.

He led them off in the opposite direction, and Sheppard realized that he was now tripping over bodies that littered the floor. He stopped himself from looking down. There was nothing he could do to help. He didn't know if he himself would be dead in seconds or minutes, and he couldn't bear to think that his last act might be trampling over a dead or dying colleague.

In the dark and the confusion Sheppard couldn't tell where they were going, but Parker seemed certain. They took a turn down a small secondary corridor and left behind the people and the panic. But where were they going? It was almost pitch-black and Parker was moving without a flashlight, but fast enough that he would have left Sheppard behind in his dust if he hadn't been dragging him along by—

The lights flickered on and then off and on again, getting bright, filling the corridor with bright light. The two men froze in place.

"That's better. At least we can see where we're going now," Sheppard said.

"And everybody else can see us. We have to move quickly or he'll leave without us."

"Who will leave?"

Before Parker could answer, a group of men flooded into the passage ahead, blocking the way!

"Stop!" one of the men yelled. He was carrying a large

club, and the other men with him had pieces of pipe. One of them had a rifle!

In the blink of an eye Parker raised his gun and fired a volley at the men, cutting them down so they fell like kindling to the floor!

Parker didn't even break stride, and his grip on Sheppard propelled him along as well. The bloodied bodies of the men formed a partial barrier that they stepped over and around. In the now brightly lit corridor, Sheppard had no choice but to see their stricken faces. He was relieved to realize that they weren't people he knew.

"Who were they?" he gasped as they passed.

"I don't know. They were in our way and that's all that matters."

"But you just killed them."

"If I hadn't killed them they would have killed us," Parker said. His voice was calm, very matter-of-fact.

"Maybe we could have talked to them or—"

"Do you think they came here to talk?" Parker asked. "Why do you think they had weapons if they didn't mean to use them? Our only hope to live is to act, not react, and certainly not to talk."

Behind them they heard voices—yelling, screaming—and then came the unmistakable sound of gunfire. It was hard to tell in the confines of the corridor, but it sounded as though it was coming from in front of *and* behind them. Were they trapped?

Coming to a door, Parker pushed it open and pulled Sheppard through. They were in a small stairwell now. Parker slammed the door closed behind them.

"Climb," he ordered. "Go up until you reach the top, the door that leads to the roof. But whatever you do, do *not* go through that door. Do you understand?"

"Yes."

"Repeat it to me," Parker said.

"Climb the stairs and stop at the door."

"Good. Don't even *touch* the door. Understand?"

Sheppard didn't know why, but he understood what he was supposed to do. He nodded. The sounds of voices and footsteps from the corridor were getting louder.

"Now get going!" Parker barked.

"What about you?" Sheppard asked.

"I'll catch you. Just get going, now!"

He didn't need to be told again. He ran up the first steps, hitting the landing in a few bounds, and after making the turn he could no longer see Parker. He followed the concrete stairs up, flight after flight. They were blocked in at each landing, no doors or windows, just concrete walls and floors. He started to count—he knew he had already climbed six flights, or three floors. He had no way of knowing how far much farther he had to go, but it couldn't have been more than four or five floors.

He tried to hurry but his legs were getting tired and his breathing was becoming more laboured. He stopped, bent over, and tried to catch his breath. He was sweating and his heart was racing from both the climb and the terror that he was feeling. He wondered why he couldn't open or even touch the door at the top, and why Parker hadn't just come up with him. And where was Parker now?

And what would he do if something happened to him?

His silent thoughts were shattered by explosions of gunfire and the chilling screams—voices raised in anger and terror and pain—that echoed up the stairwell.

He was shocked, stunned, and terrified. His instinct was to run away, up the last few flights to the top to do what he was told. But what about Parker? What was going to happen to him? Sheppard looked down at the pistol he was still clutching in his hand. He couldn't just leave his friend below by himself. Maybe he could help. Maybe he would only die with him, but still, he had to try.

Sheppard moved back down the stairs, gravity pulling him faster than either his legs or his fears should have allowed him to move. From below he heard long blasts from an automatic weapon interspersed with single shots. He could hear voices getting louder and louder. He turned at the landing and froze in place—it was Parker, struggling against three, no, four men, blood flowing from his head. They were striking him with their fists, and one raised a club above his head, drawing it back to strike Parker!

Sheppard raised his pistol and fired. The club dropped from the man's hand and he started to spin and fall. As he fell, he looked up, and his eyes locked for a split second with Sheppard's before he crumpled to the ground. Sheppard fired again at a second man and he fell backwards down the stairs.

Parker punched a third, who tumbled over, and the fourth jumped backwards down the steps so that the wall of the stairwell provided protection.

In a few bounds Parker was by Sheppard's side. "Get climbing! Quickly, climb!"

Side by side the two men raced up the steps. Any hint of tiredness in Sheppard's legs was gone, overwhelmed by the adrenaline pumping through his veins and the sounds of feet rushing up behind them!

Flight after flight they raced until they reached the top and the closed door. Parker pounded on the door.

"It's me, it's Parker, and I have Sheppard!" he screamed through the door.

Without waiting for a reply he threw open the door. Instantly they were enveloped in the noise and wind of a waiting helicopter. There was another security officer and he was standing, assault rifle in hand, aiming it straight at them!

Parker practically tossed Sheppard into the open side door of the chopper, and then he and the other security agent jumped in. With the door still open, them barely inside, the engine of the helicopter raced as it lifted off, veered to the side, and raced away into the night sky.

Slowly and carefully the men started to disentangle themselves. Parker got free and slammed the door of the chopper shut, and some of the sound and all of the rushing wind died away.

"I started to think we were going to have to leave without you," the man said to Parker.

"And where were you going to go?" Parker questioned.

"That's what kept us on the ground. But we made it out just in time," he said, gesturing out of the window as the chopper again pitched to the side.

Below in the darkness there were patches of brilliant light—fires were blazing throughout the complex, smoke and flames reaching up into the sky. It was frightening and awe-inspiring all at once.

"This is what you were waiting for. Give this to the pilot," Parker said as he produced a small piece of paper from his pocket. "These are the coordinates of the jet that's going to take us the rest of the way."

He took them and went to the cabin of the craft, leaving Parker and Sheppard alone in the back.

"Are you okay?" Parker asked.

Sheppard shook his head. "I killed a man . . . two men, maybe. I took their lives."

"No, you didn't," Parker said firmly. "Everybody down there is going to be dead in five days, with or without your help. You *saved* a life—mine—as well as your own, and the lives of the other two men in this helicopter. If you hadn't completely disregarded my direction and done what you did, none of us would have got to our destination, none of us would have had a future. So don't even think about it anymore."

"It's not that easy," Sheppard said. Maybe it would have been easier, he thought, if he hadn't looked the man in the eyes.

Sheppard looked down and was shocked to see that he was still clutching the pistol. He felt a sense of revulsion and his stomach did a full flip, and he wondered if he was about to throw up. Maybe he needed some air. He pushed open a small window in the side of the helicopter and a breeze

299

rushed in. The cool night air felt good, and his stomach started to settle.

There was still one thing that would make him feel better. He reached over and dropped the pistol out the open window and into the night sky below.

CHAPTER THIRTY-FOUR

T MINUS 3 DAYS

IDAHO

Sheppard sat at a table at the edge of the dining hall. He was ravenous—they'd eaten very little over the two days it had taken them to reach the facility. The helicopter had taken them the first two hundred kilometres, then they'd had a ten-hour jet flight, finally landing in an isolated location where an all-terrain vehicle awaited them. They'd then travelled the remaining eight hundred kilometres. It had been slow, travelling cross-country and along nearly deserted back roads.

The people they had occasionally passed were most often on foot or horseback or in a carriage. Their vehicle—high-tech, highly defended, and heavily armed—was one of the few things on the road that still had fuel to power it. Everybody was moving westbound, away from the impact sites, just as they were. The only difference was that those people would all die, and the six of them in the vehicle—Sheppard, Parker, the other security agent, the helicopter pilot, and the two pilots of the jet—would live.

That was hard for Sheppard to accept. Some of the people he saw were just children, who waved and smiled as they drove by. He kept wondering if they couldn't perhaps take one or two along with them. He would happily have traded places with a child, but of course that wasn't possible. Even if he'd chosen not to go, they wouldn't have allowed a replacement.

Now Sheppard kept looking up from his food to the people who surrounded him. Here, too, many were children, a fact that made him happy. He did a quick headcount— there had to be more than two hundred children and young people sitting around, eating, talking, and dozens of them seemed to be playing chess or were occupied with their computers. He sat there thinking that he could be in a school cafeteria, watching the students have their lunch before they headed back to their studies.

But they weren't heading back to class. Soon they'd be heading down into the depths below, sealed in, safe from the events that were to unfold on the surface. He knew that once those doors were sealed *he* would never see the surface again, but those children would. At least he hoped they would. It made him feel good to think that they would survive, and that from their survival would come their children and the future of the human race. These were the sparks, and from those sparks, he hoped, would grow a flame that would fan out across the planet once again.

Somehow that made it all seem better . . . no, not better, just not as terrible.

"Dr. Sheppard, it's good to see you!"

He looked up. It was Joshua Fitchett and the boy. What was his name? Billy . . . that was it, wasn't it? He had never been good with names—or faces, for that matter.

"Believe me, it's good to be here. And please, call me Daniel."

"And you can call me Joshua, although hopefully we'll have a good few years to become better acquainted. You remember Billy, of course."

"Of course. Good to see you both again."

"I was beginning to think that you weren't going to accept my offer of sanctuary here at our facility," Fitchett said.

"I wasn't sure if I could, in all good conscience. And in truth we barely made it," Sheppard said. "If it hadn't been for Parker . . . Have you seen him this morning?"

"Actually, I've already put him to work. He's reviewing perimeter defences with my chief of security. As soon as he's through I'll arrange for the two of you to be given a tour of your new home, our underground facilities."

"That would be wonderful. I'm looking forward to it."

"But first, I must formally thank you for honouring my request and providing us with the rocket fuel."

"I'm just happy that I was able to help, although I did wonder—I *do* wonder—what you're planning to do with it."

"And what did you imagine we needed it for?" Fitchett asked.

"Initially, I wondered if somehow the rocket fuel could be used to provide power for the complex," he said. "But then I realized that many things could be used as fuel, and you specifically wanted rocket fuel. Therefore I assumed you were going to launch a rocket."

"A sensible assumption. And the reasons for us to launch a rocket would be . . . ?" Fitchett questioned.

"Being underground, you would be potentially safe but blind. By launching a rocket that contained a satellite you would be provided with an eye in the sky. It would let you know when the planet had recovered enough for life to return safely to the surface."

Sheppard believed that was the reason he had been invited. They wanted to have his help with the launch, to establish the orbital path, to interpret the data as it began to stream in.

"We will have eyes in the sky, orbiting the planet," Fitchett confirmed.

Sheppard leaned forward in his seat. "That is nothing short of brilliant," he said.

"Thank you. But we aren't simply launching *a* satellite," Fitchett said.

"More than one?"

Both Fitchett and Billy laughed.

"I'm going to ask young Billy to explain things to you. After all, he is soon going to be in charge. Now, if you'll excuse me, I have a few hundred things to do and less than three days to do them."

Fitchett rushed off, in full stride and at full speed, as always.

"I think I'd better show you," Billy said, "because if I just tell you, you probably won't believe me."

———

Billy was right. But for Sheppard, even seeing wasn't making the believing a whole lot easier. The technology that Billy was showing him at the launch site belonged more to the realm of science fiction than realistic expectation.

"I can't conceive of how *one* of these ships could have been constructed without my knowledge . . . but *five* . . . that's beyond the realm of possibility," Sheppard muttered. "It's amazing that enough materials and resources could have been marshalled to allow this to happen."

"It's more than amazing," Billy said. "But in the last few months I've learned never to doubt anything that Joshua puts his mind to. Besides, I think he had lots of help from the outside. You're not the first person from the International Aerospace Research Institute to arrive here over the past few weeks."

"Yes," Sheppard said, "I've discovered that there were many things going on that I was entirely unaware of. I guess I should simply be grateful that we have an alternative . . . really, I guess, two alternatives. How many people will be going into space?"

"Twenty in each rocket."

Sheppard looked confused. "You mean twenty in *total*—four astronauts on each ship—correct?"

"No, in total there are one hundred of us who will be launched into space."

"That's . . . that's unprecedented. The orbiting space station, at its peak, held only fifty people."

"I know all about the space station. We're going to be docking with it."

Billy explained the situation to Sheppard, as Fitchett had explained it to him. How the space station was still functional and responding to commands to move it into a protected orbit around Earth, away from collision with any of the fragments. How the children chosen for the mission had the knowledge and training to fix any problems and create a fully functional living space.

"It is fairly roomy," Sheppard agreed. "Although for a hundred people, for years to come, I suspect it will become rather claustrophobic."

It was becoming increasingly clear to Sheppard why, in fact, he was here.

"I don't know if you know, Billy, but I was instrumental in the design, launch, and assembly of the space station."

"I know . . . Joshua told me."

"I'll be able to provide information and direction, trouble-shoot, and generally help with any questions about the station, or how to repair or modify it." He sighed. "In a few days, you're going to be living my dream, going into space."

"You wanted to be an astronaut?" Billy asked.

"Like most little boys."

"Joshua told me you know more about space travel than almost anybody in the world."

"It's been my lifelong study. But this is as close as I've ever come," Sheppard replied. "Standing beside a rocket."

"What stopped you?"

"Bad eyes and a heart murmur." His gaze went up the

rockets to the very top. "But enough of my sad story. I think it would be excellent for me to meet with the head of the orbital team."

"You are," Billy said.

"No, I mean the adult who's in charge . . . no offence . . . I hope you understand."

"I'm not offended," Billy said, "and I do understand why you'd think that. But I *am* the one in charge. I'm the closest thing to an adult who'll be going into space."

"But that's impossible! They can't just send children into space and hope they'll survive, let alone have the skills to do what needs to be done!"

"We've been training, and remember, these aren't ordinary children. Besides, we'll have Joshua and you here on the ground to help us."

"Yes, but you'll need somebody up there, with you, to help make all the difficult decisions. I couldn't possibly be able to give you that level of direction from the ground. If only I could . . . " Sheppard stopped talking. He took a deep breath. "Please bring me to see Joshua. I have something I need to talk to him about."

"Daniel, what you are offering is generous and kind and—"

"And incredibly stupid," Parker said, cutting Fitchett off.

"I wouldn't use that word," Fitchett said, "but it is foolhardy and heroic."

"No, I'm sticking with 'stupid,'" Parker said. "Do you think I spent the last seventeen years of my life stopping people from killing you so that you could kill yourself?"

"I'm not trying to kill myself."

"You're talking about being blasted into space, and you don't see the dangers involved?" Parker questioned.

"He is right. It will be dangerous for somebody of your age and health, especially since you've received no training," Fitchett said.

"Who do you think helped write the training manuals?" Sheppard asked. "I know the procedures and routines better than anybody on the planet, and certainly better than anybody who'll be going up on this mission. Who could you possibly have who knows more about the space station?"

"I'm not arguing about any of that—you are the expert—and that's why we brought you here, to offer advice . . . from *down here*," Fitchett said.

"And what if they can't hear that advice?" Sheppard asked. "You know as well as I do that the impacts are going to produce electromagnetic disturbances that might make radio communication problematic. And what if your surface communications towers are damaged or destroyed? It could be months before you'd be able to venture to the surface to repair them. What then?"

"Even if we could never communicate with them—and that will not be the case—they could survive," Fitchett argued.

"Their chances of survival would be greatly enhanced by the information I can provide. You went to a lot of trouble to involve me—you must have understood how essential my input could be."

"The children have been trained and equipped to do

whatever needs to be done, even without communication from the ground," Fitchett reiterated.

"But if anything did become a problem I could be right there to help. How could that be anything but good?"

"You know the reasons why we chose to send only young people."

"Yes, I understand that I'd be consuming valuable space and limited resources. I know that there are dangers. But I also know that having me up there could be critical to the mission's success. I think I should be part of it."

"I fully appreciate your offer, Daniel, but—"

"I want him to come with us," Billy said quietly. He got up and walked over to Fitchett's side. "I'm the leader, and leaders get to make decisions. I think having him come would produce benefits greatly outweighing the negatives."

He put his hand on Sheppard's shoulder.

"Besides, sometimes it's just important to make somebody's dreams come true."

CHAPTER THIRTY-FIVE

T MINUS 2 HOURS

The door closed and the elevator started up. Sheppard felt a familiar queasy feeling in the pit of his stomach, but he worked hard not to show it, especially since he was aware that Parker not only knew his fear of elevators but was there watching. The elevator shook and shimmied as it rose. Billy and Fitchett were watching him, too, and they were the last people he wanted knowing about any weakness. It wasn't too late for them to change their minds—and maybe it would be better if they did. Was he crazy to do this?

The elevator came to a stop and the door opened to reveal the technicians on the platform, waiting to help strap them in and then seal the hatch. Soon there would be no going back.

Inside the ship the other nineteen crew members were already in position. And already launched, already in space, were the other four ships. They had all watched on the monitors from the control room as the rockets had, one after the other, lifted off, one hour between the launches.

Parker moved over to Sheppard's side and stood facing him. "Nice suit. Lucky they had one in your size."

"Lucky I'm small enough to fit into kid-sized suits."

"You know, it isn't too late. You don't have to go up," Parker said.

"I don't see that I have much choice. I'm certainly not riding in that *elevator* again."

Parker laughed. "I'm going to miss you."

"After seventeen years of being my babysitter, I thought you might be glad to finally be done with me."

"You have a point there. It's just hard when the little birdie grows up and leaves the nest." He paused. "It's been an honour to know you and to serve under you." Parker stepped back and offered Sheppard a salute.

"It's been *my* honour. And thank *you* . . . for everything."

Sheppard was trying hard not to cry, and then he noticed tears welling up in Parker's eyes as well. Sheppard threw his arms around his friend and the two men hugged.

"We'll talk . . . you know that," Sheppard said.

"Sure. And who knows, Daniel, maybe things will settle down earlier, and I'll still be around in ten years or so to help you out of the descent shuttle."

"That would be nice."

"In the meantime, don't take any unnecessary chances, and do what the kid tells you to do. Remember, you're not in charge anymore. *He* is."

ERIC WALTERS

"I'll remember. I've certainly had my chance to make the decisions. I . . . I'd better get inside now."

Sheppard turned and walked away, helmet tucked under his arm. He stopped at the door, turned, and waved goodbye. Parker had already slipped on his dark glasses and gave just the slightest nod of his head in response. No more emotions. He was back in control again.

Sheppard ducked down ever so slightly and entered the ship. He was scared but he wasn't afraid.

Joshua Fitchett and Billy stood side by side.

"You have the people you need to do whatever you need done," Fitchett told Billy.

"I have faith in them."

"Just remember, you're the leader, and they expect you to lead. Even Dr. Sheppard will be with you only as an adviser, not to be in charge."

"I know. I'm glad he's coming with us."

"I think you made the right decision . . . that's why you're the leader. I have complete faith in you . . . you know that."

"I know," Billy said. "Do you know I'm going to miss you?"

"We'll be communicating so much that you're going to be sick of hearing my voice and seeing my face."

"I don't know if I've said this before, but thank you for everything," Billy said.

"No need for thanks. Just fulfill your destiny."

"I'll try," Billy said.

"No, don't try. *Succeed.* Have no doubts, because I have none."

He held out his hand and the two men shook. Then Fitchett turned and walked away, at full speed, as always. Billy watched as he entered the elevator and the door slid shut, leaving him alone on the platform. It was time.

Billy squirmed restlessly in his seat. He was strapped in place, more lying down than sitting. Sheppard was directly beside him. On the other side was Christina. Her calm confidence was contagious. They all listened in on their headphones as the control booth continued to give orders, making checks and cross-checks.

Sheppard reached out a gloved hand and tapped Billy on the leg.

"I guess it's too late for either of us to change our minds," he said.

"Do you want to?" Billy asked.

"No. This is where I want to be. I need to thank you."

"Thank you for volunteering to come. We're going to need you."

"I'll be there . . . assuming I don't die of a heart attack during liftoff."

"I understand being afraid."

"I think 'terrified' might be a better word. Are you?"

Billy shook his head. "I *know* we'll be fine. I had to personally promise Parker that I'd take care of—"

A voice came over the speaker. *"This is the command centre. Do you read me?"*

"We read you," Billy replied.

"We are about to commence launch sequence."

"Everything's good here," Billy said. "We're ready."

Almost immediately he could feel an increase in vibrations as the rocket was fed more fuel. This was the moment of truth. There was no time for a mistake or a repair or a repeat. They had one shot, one chance to leave before the fragments hit.

"All systems are go . . . guidance system released . . . we have commit to launch . . . 9 . . . 8 . . . 7 . . . 6 . . ."

With each number of the countdown the vibrations and the noise increased, growing stronger and louder and more powerful.

"We have ignition . . . 4 . . . 3 . . . 2 . . . 1 . . . we have liftoff!"

Billy felt a growing pressure on his chest, but had they lifted off? He was vibrating, shaking so strongly that he felt sure he would have been tossed out of his chair if he hadn't been strapped in . . . but were they rising?

"The rocket has cleared the tower . . . I repeat, it has cleared the tower!"

The pressure on his chest pushed him into his seat with incredible force. He tried to lift his hand, but he couldn't. With great effort he turned his head so that he could see the others strapped in around him. They were motionless, trapped by the same forces that were holding him in place.

Unable to move, unable to see beyond the confines of the cabin, Billy closed his eyes and tried to imagine the flight of their ship. He saw in his mind the first four ships lifting off before them. He pictured them already out of the atmosphere, free of Earth's gravity, sailing through open space toward the moon and the protection it offered against the fragments.

There was a loud thud and his eyes popped open as the whole ship seemed to jump. He knew what it was—the booster rockets, fuel spent, had dropped away.

"Altitude three kilometres . . . trajectory is perfect."

The vibrations continued to get stronger, and the whole ship seemed to rattle and shake. If it went on like this, the whole ship would disintegrate and—no, it was lessening . . . the noise, the vibration, the pressure on his chest . . . everything.

Billy lifted his hand and reached out and touched Sheppard. He turned to face Billy, a small smile visible through the screen of his helmet, and he gave a thumbs-up. He had survived the launch—they'd all survived the launch.

"This is mission control . . . you are free of Earth's upper atmosphere . . . you are officially in space."

Billy undid the straps on his harness and felt his body begin to rise from the seat, weightlessly. He pulled himself from seat to seat, checking on everybody, making sure that they were all fine. At each seat he was greeted with a smile and a nod.

"Billy, this is Joshua. Can you hear me?"

"Loud and clear."

"We're going to be locking down communications in just a few minutes," he said. "It could be a while before we talk again, and I was wondering if you could do me a favour."

"Just tell me what," Billy replied.

"Can you confirm the first impacts? Can you go to your port-side window and describe what you see?"

ERIC WALTERS

Billy pushed off, directing himself toward the small window, swimming weightlessly across the capsule. Looking out, he saw the curving outline of Earth, all blues and greens and browns, white mist, clouds obscuring parts of the planet below. He could make out the oceans and the continents . . . there was the coast of North America, the British Isles, the Mediterranean Sea surrounded by Europe on the top and Africa on the bottom. It was all so unreal, like looking at a big map. It seemed so calm, so peaceful, so quiet. He could see before his eyes the slow but unmistakable rotation of the ground beneath the cloud cover. It was . . . it was . . . *so* beautiful.

He looked up from the Earth, up above the horizon and into the blackness, and he saw it, a thick cloud staining space. And then the leading edge of that cloud started to glow. It became red and then orange and then bright white as the first fragments entered the atmosphere, which was desperately trying to protect the planet below. It became brighter and brighter as more fragments plunged through, and then a large plume of red shot up from the Earth as the first chunk crashed into the ground below. It was followed by another, and another, and another, and a whole swath of the planet disappeared. And as he watched, the swath became larger, browns and reds replacing greens and blues.

"Billy, what do you see?" Fitchett asked.

"I see it happening . . . the fragments hitting."

"Can you describe it?"

"It's almost beyond words. I'm watching the end."

"No," Fitchett said. "Not the end . . . it's the beginning."

316